From the author of *Code Name Walter*

BLINK-OUT

A NOVEL

BY

ROGER B. ANDERSON

the Peppertree Press
Sarasota, Florida

This is a work of fiction. Names, characters and incidents portrayed are either products of the author's imagination or are used fictitiously. Any resemblance to actual events or persons, living or dead, is entirely coincidental. However, the setting of the story is the northwest coastal area of Florida. The author portrays the locations, communities, environmental conditions and listed species as realistically as possible.

Copyright © Roger B. Anderson, 2012

All rights reserved. Published by the Peppertree Press, LLC.
the Peppertree Press and associated logos are trademarks of
the Peppertree Press, LLC.

No part of this publication may be reproduced, stored in a retrieval system, transmitted in any form or by any means, electronic, mechanical, photocopying, recording, or otherwise, without prior written permission of the publisher and author/illustrator.
Graphic design by Rebecca Barbier.

For information regarding permission,
call 941-922-2662 or contact us at our website:
www.peppertreepublishing.com or write to:
the Peppertree Press, LLC.
Attention: Publisher
1269 First Street, Suite 7
Sarasota, Florida 34236

ISBN: 978-1-61493-136-2

Library of Congress Number: 2012

Printed in the U.S.A.

Printed November 2012

DEDICATION

Dedicated to Callie, we will miss your smiles. Also dedicated to Roger, Linda, Coleman and Caitlin for keeping her memory alive.

ACKNOWLEDGMENT

I would like to thank my wife, Rachel, and daughter, Joy Blinn, for their encouragement, recommendations and editorial assistance during the writing of this story. Also, I would like to thank Dr. Thomas St. Clair and Col. Carl Wells, USAF, Ret. for their reviews and comments on the early draft. Thanks also go to my mother Evelyn Anderson for her enthusiastic support during the writing of this novel.

TABLE OF CONTENTS

Chapter 1	On the Beach	1
Chapter 2	The Florida Gulf Coast	7
Chapter 3	Fauna	9
Chapter 4	The Endangered Species Act	13
Chapter 5	The Conference Room	16
Chapter 6	The Green Desk Lamp	22
Chapter 7	The Ultimatum	28
Chapter 8	Sea Turtles	31
Chapter 9	The Inspection	34
Chapter 10	Compliance	41
Chapter 11	Salamanders and Butterflies	45
Chapter 12	Salamander Survey	53
Chapter 13	The In-Basket	58
Chapter 14	On the Dunes	60
Chapter 15	The Arrest	63
Chapter 16	The Call Home	79
Chapter 17	FBI	81
Chapter 18	The Funeral	92
Chapter 19	Blue Funk	93
Chapter 20	Sea Turtles	94
Chapter 21	The Arrangement	105
Chapter 22	Turtle Crawl	106
Chapter 23	The Escape	114
Chapter 24	The Rescue	116

CHAPTER 25	Panic	131
CHAPTER 26	Reflections	132
CHAPTER 27	Exoneration	141
CHAPTER 28	The Conspiracy Theory	147
CHAPTER 29	The Interviews	154
CHAPTER 30	Scorched Earth	156
CHAPTER 31	The Contract	160
CHAPTER 32	The Accident	161
CHAPTER 33	The Hit	163
CHAPTER 34	Damage Control	165
CHAPTER 35	Duck for Cover	168
CHAPTER 36	Revenge	171
CHAPTER 37	The Morning Run	172
CHAPTER 38	Trial Prep	175
CHAPTER 39	The Interviews	180
CHAPTER 40	The Stairs to the Beach	192
CHAPTER 41	Ten Stitches	199
CHAPTER 42	The Cat Lady	202
CHAPTER 43	The Perpetrator	208
CHAPTER 44	The Arrest	210
CHAPTER 45	The Pretrial Case Management Conference	213
CHAPTER 46	Return to Court	235
CHAPTER 47	The Aftermath	243

CHAPTER 1

ON THE BEACH

Two men walked hurriedly along the shoreline. It was 2:00 a.m. in January and the recent winter storm front had brought a blanket of cold still air to the Florida Gulf Coast. The men each wore small LED headlamps that provided a meager illumination to their pathway. To their left the light surf of the Gulf of Mexico splashed gently on the shore. The stars in the clear night sky shone brightly and continued to be visible down to the horizon over the Gulf, since there was no glow from urban lights. It was the new moon phase in early January and pitch-black except for the pinpoints of light along the shoreline suggesting that this section of the Florida coastline supported only a small human population. To their right was the ghostly outline of sand dunes rising gently from the edge of the beach and growing larger inland.

The lead man came to a stop, his face illuminated by a GPS that he held in his gloved hand. His bare fingers protruding from the threadbare gloves manipulated the GPS until he appeared satisfied with the display. He was a large man with wide athletic shoulders and at 6'6" he stood a half-head taller than his companion. His bearded face was framed by a woolen watch cap pulled down over his ears. His otherwise rough face was softened by a pair of wireless bifocals, which he wore low on his nose, giving him an intellectual look. Without acknowledging his companion, he turned inland and started walking towards the dunes with a purposely long stride. His name was George

Mott, a PhD wildlife ecologist. This clandestine mission along the Florida northwest coastline was both a passion and obsession for George. He was a graduate of Auburn University in wildlife biology and had done his PhD thesis on beach mice, an endangered species that inhabit the dunes of this section of the Florida Gulf Coast. Dr. Mott was considered an international specialist on these small and very much imperiled mammals.

Their progress slowed as they reached the interior dunes. Here the white sand seemed to collect starlight and provide its own illumination as they followed an unmarked path to a valley among the 30-foot-high dunes. George held up his hand signaling his partner to stop, then he moved slowly forward and fell to his knees with his headlamp centered on a small metal box, the size of a carton of cigarettes, about six feet way. George searched the area around the box for any sign of activity. Small footprints in the sand and the closed trap door on the cage suggested activity. George's light now focused on the trap itself. He panned his headlight along the holes on the side of the trap until he saw a slight movement and heard a small squeak of panic emanating from the trap. They had a successful capture.

Without looking back, George raised his hand and motioned with two fingers for his companion to come closer. Quinn Wilson took a few steps forward and dropped to one knee beside George. He targeted his headlamp on the trap as he removed a small yellow field book from his jacket. He nodded slightly, causing the beam from his headlamp to move within George's line of vision, to acknowledge that he was in position.

Quinn was a consultant who had a long-term working relationship with George's firm, the largest landowner in Florida, with over one million acres in the Florida Panhandle. He had prepared the Habitat Conservation Plan (Habitat Conservation Plan) for the beach mice that required these quarterly trapping events. The purpose was to monitor the population and welfare of the colony in one of the last remaining enclaves of the Choctawhatchee beach mice (Choctawahatchee beach mouse), a federally endangered species that enjoyed protection under the federal Endangered Species Act (ESA). George's firm had agreed to conserve this 1.5 mile section of coastal habitat and had relocated twelve breeding pairs of mice into the protected dunes as mitigation for impact to 1.4 acres of dune habitat in the WaterColor project that was located seven miles to the west of the preserve. The commitment was done freely; however, it was reluctantly recorded on the company books as an $85 million loss of very valuable developable coastal lands.

As was his practice, Quinn liked to join George on these trapping events when time allowed in his busy schedule. He admired George's expertise with the mice and enjoyed assisting him in conducting a scientifically correct trapping event. They had worked together for a number of years now and were a well-organized team, both in the field and while dealing with the politics of the federal ESA.

George moved forward and picked up the trap and held it close to examine the specimen. A flash of light brown and white fur told him that the capture was indeed a Choctawahatchee beach mouse. This was the first capture of the night out of the 45 traps that had been set along the 1.5 mile section of dunes. Since the night was cold, George had opened the traps at 6:00 p.m. and inspected them every two hours to avoid a captured mouse from suffering exposure. He had placed a handful of cotton balls in each trap, to keep the mice warm until he had a chance to monitor the traps and record their data. So far there had been no other captures and both George and Quinn were notably concerned.

George opened the trap and expertly extracted the small mouse who was notably upset to find itself in the hands of a giant. He caressed the mouse with his fingertips to calm it down and assess its general condition. He noted its sex, approximate age and spoke for the first time to Quinn, who was already making notes of the time and location of the trap. "Virgin capture," he said in a hushed tone while examining the mouse's feet. "Young female," he relayed, with a hint of excitement in his voice, as he continued his examination. Both of these parameters were very good news for the beach mice population. George continued with weighing and measuring the little mouse, calling out the data to Quinn as he went. When he had finished, he took a small pair of clippers and after a verbal apology to his captive, he snipped off a toe from its left hind foot and passed it on to Quinn who had a small plastic jar open and ready to receive the specimen. Once back at the office, he would send the collected specimens from the trapping event to the Auburn University to confirm the DNA was indeed Choctawahatchee beach mouse. The mouse's worst fear had been realized with the snip and it squealed in pain and protest. George sympathized with the mouse, placed a drop of antibiotics on the stump and released it onto the sand. Both he and Quinn followed its rapid retreat with their headlamps until it was out of sight. George worked quickly to place a fresh roll of sea oats in the trap and repositioned it on the dune. Both he and Quinn smoothed out the disturbed sand as they retreated from the trap. A check of the other six traps that were deployed in the immediate area showed no other signs of activity.

As they walked back across the dunes towards the beach, George stopped abruptly causing Quinn to run into his back.

"What is it, George?" Quinn whispered.

"I do not recall seeing these tracks on our way into the traps. Look at these," he said as he knelt down to pan the light over a series of tracks. Beach mice were on the bottom of the food chain and were predated by any number of species that occupied habitat along the coast, including seabirds, fox, coyote, raccoon, and bobcat.

"Shit," George said as he closely examined the tracks. "It's a

Blink-Out

damn feral cat. I swear they are worse predators than any of the native species. People leave them outside at night and before long you have a colony of wild cats roaming the dunes. I have got to get some traps out here and get them out of the beach mice habitat. If they are on the dunes in any numbers, they can wipe out a colony of Choctawahatchee beach mouses in short order."

They began the final trap monitoring at 6:00 a.m., as the first glow of morning light began to show on the horizon. George closed all the traps after this final inspection. He would open them again at 6:00 p.m. in the evening and hope for better results. So far only five mice had been captured and recorded during this mid-January trapping, a notable reduction in the number from previous trapping events. Once charted, the projection of mice within this colony would continue to show a steady decline. Three years ago the trapping produced over 30 mice and subsequent modeling of the Choctawahatchee beach mouse population showed a reasonable 125 individuals occupied the habitat. If the final third night of trapping did not yield better response, George knew that a population range between 50 and 75 individuals would be predicted by the model, a perilously low number for the safe management of the population. Any lower than that and the population might not recover.

"No," he said as if to himself, "there will be no blink-out of this species on my watch. It's not going to happen."

Blink-out is a term used by wildlife biologist who dealt with endangered species. It referred to that point in time when the last individual of a species died. This sad event meant that an entire species of animals that had occupied a habitat niche on this planet for thousands, sometimes millions, of years was now gone forever. Biologists who have presided over a species blink-out talked of the overwhelming sadness and could not help but to look over their shoulder and wonder if somewhere in the distant future, it might be *Homo sapiens*' turn to experience this cataclysmic event. After all, no other species, other than man, had made such an impact on the planet in as relatively short time of dominance. The industrial revolution of the past 100 years had placed an enormous strain on the world's resources. Fossil fuels and mineral resources were being depleted at alarming rates. The demand for food from a burgeoning world population was causing rapid reductions in the ocean fisheries and increasing pressures on agricultural lands. The potential of a worldwide pandemic was increasing, due to the speed and opportunity of air travel. Wars and threats of wars continue to plague the governments of the world, while technological advances in weaponry increase the effectiveness and scale of warfare, death and destruction. No other species has ever developed such a program of self-destruction. Yes, blink-out of the human race either by natural or anthropogenic causes was a possibility.

Quinn had watched the rapid development of Florida and noted that humans exhibited many of the same traits as exotic species that had found their way into Florida's diverse ecosystems. Like humans, these species would displace native plants and animals, becoming mono-cultures with little or no value to native species. Humans were altering the landscape and Quinn was happy to be associated with a developer that took pride in protecting resources.

They parted at about 9:00 a.m. George headed home to get some rest and Quinn headed to WaterColor to meet with Brad Garner, President of St. Joe and George's boss.

CHAPTER 2

THE FLORIDA GULF COAST

The landscape of the Florida Gulf Coast is the byproduct of a long and arduous geological process. The coastal features owe their very existence to the Appalachian Mountains several hundred miles inland from the coast. The towering peaks have remained a dominant geological feature on the eastern portion of the North American continent throughout the eons. As dominant as they seemed, the relentless forces of nature continued to wear them down. The ice of winters long past, followed by the rains of countless summers, eroded the mountains and sent the sediments to streams and great rivers of the southeastern portion of the continent. The Chattahoochee River drained the southern foothills of the Appalachian Mountains. Further to the west, the rivers that would later bare the names, Alabama and Black Warrior, extended deep into the valleys of the Appalachians. These deep fast-moving rivers carried huge volumes of sand and silt south through what would become Georgia, Alabama and Florida. As these rivers left the higher elevations and the currents slowed, heavier sediments dropped from suspension and formed floodplains along the river's course and deltas along the Gulf Coast. During its transient rush down the rivers, sediments were washed, filtered and screened, so that the smallest grains of quartz sand remained in the current and reached the coast. These pure-white quartz sand grains were distributed along the Gulf coast shoreline by longshore drift, where they were subjected to the prevailing wind and waves and repeated storms, to slowly build the deep sand dune ridges of the Pamlico epoch along the coast. This geological building process would continue for millions more years before humans were to gain prominence and begin to alter the landscape.

CHAPTER 3

FAUNA

Animal life evolved separately on each of the continental plates. Each species was influenced by the climate and habitats of the geological epic. These species left evidence of their existence in fossil remains. There was the "Great Dying" 250 million years ago, when the CO_2 levels in the atmosphere increased rapidly, causing global warming and the extinction of almost all living species. The 160 million-year reign of the dinosaur began and lasted almost 100 million years before ending abruptly with an asteroid impact 65 million years ago. The impact point is believed to be in the Gulf of Mexico near Mexico's Yucatan Peninsula. While this catastrophe had a profound impact on the entire planet, the effects on the Gulf Coast were almost unimaginable. The tsunami that followed sent hot gases and a wall of water far inland along the coast of Florida. Antidote modeling of the event suggested that the tsunami passed over the entire Florida peninsula, killing every living plant and animal in its path. Life would be slow to return as the fallout from the impact sent clouds of debris into the atmosphere, blocking out the sun and sending the planet into an ice age.

As the planet recovered from this cataclysmic event, the door was opened for the era of mammals. The climate was much dryer and the majority of the peninsula was dominated by savanna grasslands. This was the era of mega-fauna with mammoth, camel, giant ground sloth and saber-toothed tiger roaming the Florida landscape.

Roger B. Anderson

One inconsequential species of mammal that will play a role in the future of the Gulf Coast was the lowly field mice. These were any number of species, today all bearing the Genus name of *Permyscus*. From the beginning, mice were at the bottom of the food chain and were pursued by predatory birds, reptiles and larger mammals alike. However, the genus was destined to survive, because it was robust in nature and adaptable to a number of habitats and food types. In addition, a female of these species might have three or even four litters of pups within her short lifespan of only four to six months in the wild, so that in a four-month period, a mated pair of mice would produce between 7 and 15 pups. Each of the pups would become sexually mature within one month of birth and produce litters of their own. The survivors of each generation were resourceful creatures who sharpened their survival skills generation after generation as they passed through prehistoric habitats. They overcame obstacles in their path, crossing streams and rivers, circling lakes and bays that they found in the way of their progress.

When man (*Homo sapiens*) first arrived in the ecosystem much later, the mice found a species whose habits supported their survival, so generations of mice lived alongside humans who unwittingly provided for their protection. The first Paleo-Indians arrived in the Florida Panhandle approximately ten to twelve thousand years ago. At this time the world was at the end of the last ice age and a slow and steady sea level rise brought the coastline to its current location, so a map of the Florida peninsula would be more recognizable to modern man. Food was plentiful, so these early humans prospered and the mice continued living within their shadow. These early inhabitants provided shelter to the mice in the haphazard structures in which they lived and they stored food in areas that were very accessible to the mice. Consequently, mice thrived in the presence of these early humans. In essence, mice developed a one-sided symbiosis with humans and followed their settlements to benefit from the protection and food provided by these generous benefactors.

No one knows whether the field mice arrived on the Gulf Coast before these early Paleo-Indians or accompanied the tribes among their first forays to the Gulf. On arrival, these early mice encountered a harsh, almost sterile environment of sand dunes and open beaches. The Gulf of Mexico stretched out in front of them barring their continued migration to the south. Generations that followed fanned out along the coast and again overcame obstacles until they populated entire coastal area of what would be known as the Florida and Alabama Gulf Coast. Having no farther to travel, the mice stayed in the sand dunes and began to adapt to the sparse environment. They became smaller in size, with larger ears and eyes. They would evolve to become a nocturnal species to avoid the seabirds and other predators that were common along the coast during the day. More importantly, they begin to lose much of their adaptive nature and become habitat specialist, living exclusively on the grains of sea oats, and other sparse coastal vegetation. They burrowed into the dunes and lived their lives within these shallow hideaways. Their choice of habitat was precarious at best. Periodic storms occurring along the coastline could send storm surges across the dunes, wiping out an entire colony. However, these were not the only hazards they encountered.

While beach mice continued to benefit from the presence of humans, development activities along the coast would have a profound and permanent impact on the species. These early humans were first drawn to the coastal embayments and sheltered bayous, where fish and oysters were found in abundance. Hundreds of years later they sought access to the Gulf for transportation of people and goods. Though the century's ships increased in size and towns grow up around the ports, as the population and economy of the nation increased and land transportation access became better established, more and more people accessed the coastline for recreation and relaxation. The attraction of the warm climate and beaches stirred a longing in the landlocked population of the interior and they came to the coast in increasing numbers to swim in the surf and bake in the sun. This increasingly affluent society paid no attention to the mice and, in many instances, was not even aware of their existence. To support these newcomers, the coastal development fragmented the beach habitat, thus separating colonies of beach mice from one another. With decreasing opportunity to intermate, each colony continued to adapt and began to show unique characteristics, so by the mid-20th century, when scientists discovered these colonies, the mice had evolved into subspecies of the parent Alabama field mouse. Each colony was named after the section of coastline where the beach mice were found: Alabama, Perdido Key, Choctawhatchee, and St. Andrew. Of these colonies, the Choctawhatchee beach mice were the most stressed, with less than 200 individual mice believed to occupy the colony at the time of discovery.

The stage was set for the life and death struggle for survival that was to be played out in the political arena, as well as within the dune habitats of Florida's northwest coastline.

CHAPTER 4

THE ENDANGERED SPECIES ACT

In 1973 the United State Congress passed the Endangered Species Act (ESA) and it was signed into law by President Nixon. The stated purpose of the ESA was "*to provide a means whereby the ecosystems upon which endangered species and threatened species depend may be conserved, to provide a program for the conservation of such endangered species and threatened species, and take such steps as may be appropriate to achieve the purposes...*" Embodied in the ESA were the bureaucracy of the U.S. government and the power of enforcement, which was delegated to the U.S. Fish and Wildlife Service (FWS) and the National Marine Fisheries Service. The Choctawhatchee beach mouse was subsequently listed as an endangered species under the Endangered Species Act and afforded the full measure of protection. Section 7 of the ESA required that any action taken by a federal agency that had a potential impact on a listed species be subject to review. This provision stated, "*Each Federal agency shall, in consultation, insure that any action authorized, funded or carried out by such Agency is not likely to jeopardize the continued existence of any endangered or threatened species...*" Since a federal permit is usually required from the U.S. Army Corps of Engineers Regulatory Division, under the provisions of the Clean Water Act, for any new development activity along the coastline; a consultation was required with the Fish and Wildlife Service to ensure that any listed species were adequately protected. The applications were transmitted to the resource agencies for review under the Endangered Species Act. The Fish and Wildlife Service conducted these consultations for land-based mammals. The knowledgeable and dedicated staff of the Service has had a profound effect in protecting these species and their habitat against impact. However, wherever there is power, greed and corruption cannot be far behind.

The Fish and Wildlife Service field office in Panama City was responsible for conducting the review. Beach mice were not the only threatened or endangered species that occupied habitat along this section of the Florida coastline. However, it was the beach mouse that got most of the Service's attention, since these subspecies of mice only occurred along this northwest section of Florida coastline and the coastal habitat was highly coveted for Gulf-front development. Plus, beach mice were also one of the endangered species that caught the attention of the public. These were cute with big eyes and ears, so the environmental advocacy groups adopted the mouse and used its plight to raise funds for a wide range of conservation initiatives.

Troy Pinkham was the Fish and Wildlife Service officer responsible for the beach mice consultations, a job he took very seriously. Officer Pinkham was a native of Troy, Alabama, and a graduate of Troy State University with a bachelor's degree in biology. His accent continued to reflect his Alabama upbringing, but he compensated for his slow southern drawl by wearing his uniform highly starched and crisp. He had been with the Service for 15 years. During this time he had developed a reputation as a strict enforcer of the Endangered Species Act. He had earned a number of commendations from the regional FWS headquarters and condemnations from the development community for his avid pursuit of unrealistic goals under the guise of the ESA. He wheeled his consultation authority like a sword. Any developer wanting a permit from the Army Corps of Engineers in northwest Florida had to deal with Officer Pinkham. He enjoyed the power and reflected a certain measure of pride—even arrogance—in his exalted position. He also hated developers who submitted applications to develop lands that included habitat occupied by listed species. He hated them and their consultants with a passion—he particularly hated George Mott. Not only was George a formable physical individual who towered above Officer Pinkham and outweighed him by 100 pounds, but he was smart as hell. His knowledge of beach mice far exceeded Officer Pinkham's and George had a habit of correcting Troy's misinterpretation of the species' life cycle at every opportunity. Troy hated to be corrected.

CHAPTER 5

THE CONFERENCE ROOM

After the all-night trapping effort, Quinn drove west on County Road 30A to WaterColor, the St. Joe Company's flagship project outside of San Destin. The project bore the name WaterColor because of its unique setting between the sand dunes of the Gulf Coast and Western Lake, a rare and picturesque coastal dune lake. Only about one dozen of these lakes existed along the Florida Gulf Coast—the only other place on the planet that had similar coastal lakes was the west coast of Africa. These Florida lakes were formed in back of the coastal sand dunes. Periodically a storm event would bring heavy rains and the resulting high lake levels would breach the dunes and the lakes would discharge directly into the Gulf until the longshore drift again closed the breach and then the freshwater lakes would reestablish themselves. The combination of high dunes, pine flatwoods and freshwater lakes created a mosaic of landscapes that could only be described as watercolor. The St. Joe Company had developed the project to protect these two assets. Development was moved off the coastline to protect the dunes and a 300-foot-wide preservation area was maintained around Western Lake. Interior development was planned by Jacque Robertson, a renowned "new urbanist" landscape architect, who took great pains to maintain the character and physical setting of the project. The preservation intent and design resulted in WaterColor becoming a showcase for environmentally sensitive development.

Quinn had a 10:00 a.m. meeting with Brad Garner, the president and chief executive officer of St. Joe. Since he had a few minutes before the meeting, he walked along Cerulean Park and enjoyed the ambiance of this tastefully designed project. He had worked closely with the team of landscape architects during the design of the project and obtained all of the project entitlements and environmental permits needed for development. These included an Habitat Conservation Plan, under Section 10 of the Endangered Species Act, to provide for the protection and management of the Choctawhatchee beach mice and the other listed species that occupied various habitats within the project. He and George Mott had worked hard to overcome the objections of Officer Pinkham regarding development along the coastal areas. WaterColor was located adjacent to the Grayton Beach State Park, whose coastal dunes provided habitat suitable for the mice. The Florida Department of Environmental Protection, who managed the park, was perfectly willing to preserve the dune, but had no funds for monitoring or maintaining the habitat. Therefore, little was known about the possible presence of beach mice on the dunes within the park. No historical trapping data or population estimates had been maintained by the Park. In fact, there was no record that the mice still occupied the beach dunes after the series of storms that had raked the Gulf Coast during the early 2000s. Increased recreational use within the park had also strained the habitat.

Despite the habitat's deteriorated condition, Officer Pinkham had treated the park as an irreplaceable beach mice asset that must be respected and encroachment of any kind would be a desecration. His view of WaterColor was that it would produce catastrophic and irreversible damage to one of the last remaining colonies of the Choctawhatchee beach mice. He chose to ignore the fact that WaterColor was on the fringe of the park and that quarterly monitoring on the WaterColor dunes showed no signs of beach mice. Officer Pinkham had held the line and caused over a year's delay in the project, while no requests were made to the state park system to monitor and maintain the primary portion of their habitat within the park. St. Joe's offer to preserve 1.5 miles of coastal dunes, relocate mice to the area and provide long-term monitoring and management of the habitat had broken the deadlock with the regional director of Fish and Wildlife Service and won Officer Pinkham accolades from the Service and from environmental advocacy groups, even though he fought both the issuance of the Army Corps permit and the approval of the Habitat Conservation Plan bitterly. He was their hero.

Quinn realized that he had been staring out across the dunes remembering the battles of the past. He looked at his watch as he headed towards the St. Joe offices on the third floor overlooking Cerulean Park.

Brad Garner was a young project manager a few short years ago when he and Quinn had worked together on WaterColor. His vision and attention to details had resulted in a series of promotions until he preceded the venerable Peter Rummell as president of the company. Brad was an affable young man, who looked almost out of place in the executive corridors of the company. He always wore an open-collar shirt, Dockers pants and boat shoes to work. He looked ready for a fishing trip or a round of golf rather than the high-pressure business of running the development firm that was the largest landowner in Florida. Brad had an uncanny ability to gauge the market and balance the land uses with the type of development that would attract people to the project. WaterColor was a tribute to his management style and now the last phase of development was underway. The WaterColor Inn would occupy the coastal parcel that had been the bone of contention with Troy Pinkham. The four-story, 60-room inn had been reduced in size from the originally envisioned 250 rooms, in part because of the beach mice issue and in part because of Brad's sense of style. "It would fit better into the environment and convey a sense of exclusiveness that would be in demand and attract more people than the Holiday Inn-style hotel," he had said when he announced the change.

"Good morning, Quinn! It looks like you have been up all night," Brad offered as Quinn came out of the elevator. "Can I get you a cup of coffee?"

"Thank you very much and, yes, I have been up all night out on the trap line with George."

"I'm interested in what you've found. Come on into the conference room and tell me all about it," Brad said.

The WaterColor conference room was an austere, unpretentious room with a large picture window looking out on the project's main entrance off CR 30A. To the north were Cerulean Park and a panoramic view of Western Lake and the BoatHouse. To the south were the coastal dunes and beaches with the inn taking shape and form adjacent to the dunes. Brad pointed out that the dune walkovers were finally underway. He laughed and said, "George Mott had scared the construction team so badly, they were afraid to set foot in the area for fear of stepping on a mouse. It took them six weeks to figure out how to do the top-down construction, while George watched their every move."

They moved to the conference table as they talked and reminisced some more about the project and the regulatory battles that had cemented their relationship. Finally the conversation turned to the trapping event.

Quinn gave the rundown. "George and I have completed the second night's trapping. He will reopen the traps and begin the final night starting at about 6:00 p.m. We have only captured five Choctawahatchee beach mice in the last two nights, which is substantially lower than this quarter last year. While it is not uncommon for the winter quarter to have lower trap counts, both

George and I are concerned about these very low counts. Last week George trapped the dunes here at WaterColor and again there were no captures at all. We checked with Grayton Beach and there were no additional trapping events last year and none are planned, due to a lack of funding. If George's trap counts are low again tonight, the population forecast model will reflect a substantial decrease in the resident population and that will get Troy Pinkham's attention."

"We have followed through with all of our commitments in the Habitat Conservation Plan, so how will Troy interpret the low counts?" Brad asked with concern.

"My guess is that he will interpret it as a failure on our part and want proof that we have followed through with both the intent and purpose of the Habitat Conservation Plan. While in theory the Plan provides us protection from further government action, the question can still be raised about our compliance with its provisions. So expect something from Troy and once we receive the notice, we'll deal with it," Quinn added.

"You and I have talked through this before, but I just need to say it again, it is not about the Habitat Conservation Plan and our compliance with the best management commitments. It's about the resources and our ability to protect them. We have both a company position and the understanding that people come to this coastal area for the resources. If we stomp on the resources, we are destroying the reason that people will want to come here. We'll do anything and everything in our power to protect those resources with or without Troy Pinkham's mandates. We can let him take credit for our actions if he wants to, but we are committed to protection of the resources. I know, I am preaching to the choir and I am saying this for my own admonishment, but it is the truth that we need to revisit on occasion.

"It's always good to hear you state your position on the environmental resources. However, you know that neither of us can hold a candle to George's concern for the mice. Did I tell you that he put cotton balls into each of the traps, so any trapped mice would not suffer exposure before he could release them?"

"No, you did not tell me that, but I am not surprised. We and the mice are both lucky to have George on our side," Brad said with a laugh.

"I agree one hundred percent. But just so you know, we have not heard the last of Troy Pinkham."

"I know, and I think you're right."

Brad and Quinn shook hands and traded a few barbs about the Jaguar football team as Quinn was leaving. He headed for the hotel to get some sleep before heading home to St. Petersburg. It had been a long night.

CHAPTER 6

THE GREEN DESK LAMP

One week after George Mott submitted the quarterly trapping report, Troy sat at his desk reviewing the results and laughing out loud. It was late at night and the Fish and Wildlife Service office was closed and dark, with the exception of light from the green desk lamp on his desk. Seated across from Troy was Cal Summerford, chief litigator for the International Natural Resource Council. A bottle of Jim Beam Kentucky bourbon sat at the edge of the pool of light and both men were drinking from coffee mugs and periodically refilling their cups from the bottle. It was a party to celebrate their success.

Cal Summerford had spent much of his early law career as an accident and injury attorney or ambulance chaser, as it was called in the profession. He had honed his courtroom skills arguing cases against insurance companies and had done very well. At the request of a friend, he had taken a small case on behalf of the Sierra Club regarding a developer's perceived impact on a minor salmon stream in northwest Oregon. While he took the case pro bono, he was surprised to see the amount of money that was available for legal cases from the national Sierra organizations. In addition, a number of other environmental organizations would volunteer to support even the most obscure cases in the name of environmental preservation. From that point on, Cal had reinvented himself as an environmentalist and built the International Natural Resource Council to serve as the legal arm for these environmental organizations. His creed was to bleed the organizations and sue the developers for fat settlements, for which he got 40 percent. Business was very good.

"Troy, you're doing a great job painting those bastards into a corner. Let's keep the pressure on. At this rate, it won't be long before we can start filing the law suits. They won't know what hit them," Cal said with an insidious laugh as he took another slug of bourbon from his Green Peace coffee cup. "We have enough information now to make their lives uncomfortable without tipping our hand, so keep those cats roaming the dunes!"

Troy Pinkham had been hellbent to compel the Army Corps of Engineers to deny the Section 404 permit for the WaterColor project. He had forced the issue about the beach mice consultation, demanded the Habitat Conservation Plan and used every trick in the book to further delay and derail the project. Then the St. Joe Company had gone above him to the FWS regional administrator and offered to preserve and repopulate that section of coastal dunes. It was an offer they could not refuse. Troy received positive responses from administrator in Atlanta and was forced to accept the offer. Of course, he also received commendations and a promotion for the successful negotiations. However, he hated the St. Joe Company for beating him at his own game and vowed to get even. He had worked with Cal Summerford on Endangered Species Act ligation in the past and knew that Cal had been following his "consultation" on the WaterColor project. Sure enough, Cal had given him a call after the Habitat Conservation Plan was noticed in the Federal Register and suggested they meet.

Cal was better at putting their plan into words. "I don't give a shit about beach mice. They are mice for God's sake. Ten miles from here, the feed stores are full of rodent poisons to kill them off by the number. Let them blink-out. I do not give a damn. What we have here is a fat developer that is poised for fleecing. If we play our cards right, we can sue them for every penny they have, make a fortune and close the project down. I can get all our supporters riled up about these cute little mice and they will send hundreds of thousands of dollars to us, while we are suing this developer for millions. That will be like killing two mice with one stone! I'm telling you it is a gold mine!"

The plan was simple. Troy would arrange for feral cats to be released on the dunes and keep the pressure on the population until he could officially say that the developer's plan was failing and the mouse was in jeopardy of extinction. Then Cal would file a suit on behalf of every environmental advocacy group in existence and the money would come rolling in by the bails. It was foolproof and Troy would probably get another commendation from the Fish and Wildlife Service, along with 25 percent of the proceeds from the donations and lawsuits. It was the perfect application of the Endangered Species Act and they both toasted their plan with their Green Peace and Audubon coffee mugs.

When George Mott had completed the relocation of 12 mated pair of mice to the new coastal habitat, the quarterly trapping events had been very encouraging. The population projections increased steadily every quarter and Troy became concerned that population would become so large that even feral cats would not be able to subdue it. So he sought a partner to help with the cats, someone he would keep at arm's length from the effort. While making a presentation to the Seaside citizens group, he met an enthusiastic woman who was looking for a cause. She was a socialite who was staying alone at the family vacation home in Seaside during the winter, while her husband continued to work in Detroit. Like most of the part-time residents of the Gulf Coast, she was enamored with the beach, water and sun and wanted a mission to help protect her newfound home. Troy had suggested they have a drink and talk about the environmental needs. With his southern charm and starched uniform, he was able to seduce her in more ways than one. While they lay in each other's arms in her bedroom overlooking the beach, Troy got down to business.

"You know, one of the environmental needs in this area is to do something about the wild housecats. They roam the woods trying to survive and often die of starvation."

"Oh, I love cats. What can I do?"

"You could feed them. There are just a few areas along the coast with a population of cats. If you could put out food and water in these areas, they would have a better chance of survival. However, you would have to do it every few days in out-of-the-way areas. I could provide you a map of the known population, if you are interested. Also on occasion, people bring wild cats into the office. I could drop them off and you could release them in the area. With food and water available, they would survive very well."

"That is a great idea. I have always owned a cat and know how to take care of them. This way I can use my experience and take care of the environment at the same time," she said with enthusiasm. "So, we are partners?"

"Yes, we are partners, but due to my position with the Service, I need to stay anonymous. Don't tell anyone that we are working together on this project, okay? I want you to take all the credit. Also, this will give us a chance to see each other more often, if you know what I mean."

"I know what you mean. This is so exciting."

Virginia Stratford was an overachiever and social climber from Detroit, Michigan. She had married below her family's social position and had driven her husband to maintain the standard of living to which she was accustomed. She pushed him to return to school and instructed him on how to move up the ranks of the automobile industry by criticizing management and backstabbing his immediate supervisor. Her goal had been partially reached with the purchase of a vacation home in Seaside. With their children in boarding school in upstate New York, she was free to spend the winters on the Gulf Coast, while her husband worked two jobs back in Detroit. While at Seaside, she attended all the social events and sought every opportunity to improve her social position within the community. She had attended the lecture series offered by the community association and had been very impressed with Officer Pinkham. After his talk she had used her physical good looks and cunning to lure him into her bed. "It was so easy," she said smiling to herself.

It had been a good night's work for Troy. He had secured a silent partner to help maintain a feral cat population in the beach mice preserve. He knew that these cats were some of the most ferocious predators in the wild and they would forage on the dunes day and night. The beach mice would become their primary prey and given sufficient time, the feral cats would wipe out the entire population. "Blink-out," he laughed to himself. "It is only a matter of time and that son-of-a-bitch Dr. Mott won't figure it out until it's too late. Those bastard developers are going to pay for this!"

Cal had laughed outrageously at Troy's conquest. "Perfect, just perfect," he said, once he was able to subdue his jocular mood. "Okay, now we start putting pressure on the bastards. You send them an official letter accusing them of failing to comply with the letter and intent of the Habitat Conservation Plan. Find a way to make them bleed money. I think the WaterColor Inn is your best bet. If they are one inch further into beach mice habitat than the permit allowed, make them tear the f…ing thing down. If the dune walkovers are too close to a burrow, fine them to the maximum allowed under the Endangered Species Act. Bleed them! Make them hemorrhage money! Stop work at the site! Delay them in any way possible. The ESA gives you plenty of leverage and you have the authority to push the issue. In the meantime, I will call out the crazies! They are every bit as gullible as your mistress at Seaside and they will rant and rave, picket the site, write letters, threaten lawsuits and best of all, send money. It will be good background noise to cover our mission." Once again the coffee cups were filled and clanked together in celebration of their flawless plan.

The next week Brad Garner received an official letter from the U.S. Fish and Wildlife Service stating:

> You are hereby informed that the U.S. Fish and Wildlife Service has found the St. Joe Company in violation of the terms and conditions of the Habitat Conservation Plan for the protection of the Choctawhatchee beach mice, an endangered species under the Federal Endangered Species Act. Your failure to comply with the provisions of this plan has resulted in a severe reduction in the population of beach mice in the WaterSound Preserve. Any further reductions will result in a jeopardy finding by the Service. Once this occurs, all work on the WaterColor project that is in or associated with the beach mice critical habitat is to cease immediately. Failure to comply with this notice will subject those responsible to fines or imprisonment.
>
> You are further ordered to contact Officer Troy Pinkham at the U.S. Fish and Wildlife Service Field office in Panama City, Florida, within three days of this notice to show means of compliance and discuss a remedial action plan.

Brad took a deep breath after reading the letter and picked up the phone to call Quinn Wilson. "Quinn, this is Brad! You were right. We just got a letter from Troy Pinkham. I'll fax it over to you and then we need to talk."

CHAPTER 7

THE ULTIMATUM

Two days later, Quinn and George sat in the lobby of the Panama City Fish and Wildlife Service field office and waited for Troy. George was still furious over the letter and ready to do battle. Quinn had attempted to calm him down and told him that they were there to listen and learn more about the Service's position. There would be time for action in the future, but an adversarial attitude would not help the situation. Their marching orders from Brad were clear, "We will do whatever it takes to resolve the issue. Remember, it is environmental protection more than regulatory compliance, so take the high road in solving the issues."

Troy keep them waiting over 30 minutes while he sat in his office and read the latest *Audubon* magazine. "No use rushing to talk to the trash," he told himself. Once he thought they had stewed long enough, he asked them, with a certain distain in attitude, to join him in the conference room.

"To begin with, I want you to know how serious this is. The Service has put you on notice that your development activities may have placed an endangered species in jeopardy of extinction and they intend to press this issue to the fullest extent. If we do not see substantial improvement in the population numbers by next quarter, we will move to have the Army Corps of Engineers revoke your 404 permit and officially stop your project. Am I clear on that or do you need me to give you a simpler explanation?"

Quinn was aware that George was getting ready to jump across the table, so he intervened. "I think you were quite clear in your statement. Tell me, has this position received the approval of the regional administrator in Atlanta? I noticed that he was not cc'ed on the letter."

"We have discretion to issue a violation notice of this nature from this field office without the consent of the administrator. What is your point?"

"I'm sure you will have no objections to my contacting him regarding this letter. As you said, this is serious and, as the holder of an approved Habitat Conservation Plan, which we have entered into in good faith, we have certain rights, along with the obligations you referenced. As you recall, St. Joe also has a federal court order that was part of the conveyance of the Topsail tract to the state, authorizing the development of the WaterColor tract. Senator Nelson was party to that district court decision and I have forwarded a copy of your letter to him. I also will be meeting with him on Thursday to discuss these issues in more detail. You may be receiving a call from his office prior to that meeting," Quinn offered in a mild manner.

It was now Troy's turn to boil with anger, "The court order has nothing to do with your violation of the conditions of the Habitat Conservation Plan. Senator Nelson knows nothing about the Endangered Species Act or our mandate to enforce its provisions. Our position will not be swayed by political pressure."

"Let's talk for a minute about those things we have in common," said Quinn. "I think we both want to see the beach mice survive and prosper. Agreed? We have also fulfilled our obligation of placing a conservation easement on the coastal tract and followed through with the translocation of 12 mated pair of mice. You're not taking issue with these commitments, are you?"

"I'm taking issue with the successes that were promised in the Habitat Conservation Plan. It was implied that the mice would prosper and survive in the conserved habitat and we can see from the quarterly reports that the population is diminishing—not prospering. Do you agree with that?"

"George and I both have been concerned with the population trends and have taken steps to determine the cause and remediate the situation. Yes, we share your concern, but keep in mind that historically the winter quarter captures have always been lower, so while we share your concern, we do not think the situation is as hopeless as referenced in your letter."

"We are getting nowhere here. You are not offering me anything. Let me tell you what I want, just to make it simple and easy to understand. I want to see a set of construction plans for the WaterColor Inn by tomorrow. We are going to inspect the construction that is currently in place to make sure you have not violated any other provisions of the 404 Permit or the Habitat Conservation Plan. I want to do that inspection on Thursday… oh, yes, that was the day you were meeting with Senator Nelson, wasn't it? You're just going to have to be in two places at once, because I want you and George both present at that inspection. Do I make myself clear?"

Quinn saw out of the corner of his eye that George was turning blue with rage, so he thought it best to end the meeting before there was an altercation. "You will have the plans tomorrow and George and I will be there to conduct the inspection on Thursday starting at 9:00 a.m."

CHAPTER 8

SEA TURTLES

While the beach mice were the primary concern of the U.S. Fish and Wildlife Service, there are other threatened and endangered species that occupied the Gulf Coast habitats during their life cycles. Primary among these are the five species of sea turtles that nest along the beaches. These include the loggerhead, hawksbill, green, leatherback, and the Atlantic ridley sea turtles. These free-swimming or pelagic sea turtles spend their lives in the open waters of the Gulf and Atlantic Ocean. There they roam, forage and mate at sea. Scientists remain impressed by both the range of travel and the navigational skills of all the turtle species. Geographic Positioning Systems (GPS) placed on individual turtles reveal that they log thousands of miles every year. Beginning in the spring of each year, the turtles return to the beaches of their birth to lay their eggs. They crawl out of the water in the dead of night to dig a burrow at the base of sand dunes along the beaches and deposit their eggs. Unlike the beach mice that spend their entire life within the dune habitat, the sea turtles only return to deposit their eggs. Once females have performed that duty, they return to the Gulf and provide no support for the young turtles that emerge from the burrows and race to the water 90 days after the eggs are deposited. The young turtles' attraction to the water after only minutes of hatching has been a mystery to scientists. However, in more urban areas with artificial lights creating either direct lighting on the beach or a background glow in the sky, young turtles sometimes get confused and crawl away from the water. The results are usually fatal. Consequently, artificial illumination on coastal buildings has become a regulatory issue that is enforced by the Fish and Wildlife Service. Turtle lighting is required on all newly constructed building along nesting beaches and the illumination of buildings inland from the coastline are watched carefully to ensure the glow in the sky is kept to a minimum.

Clara Fullerton was the local turtle watch volunteer. At a young 58 years of age, Clara had retired from teaching middle school science. She had risen to principal of one of the largest middle schools in Dayton, Ohio, and had retired to the Gulf Coast of Florida with her husband of 35 years. Unlike many transplants to Florida, she was well-grounded in the sciences and had immediately volunteered with the local dedicated group of turtle watchers. Every morning beginning in early spring, Clara was up before dawn riding her all-terrain vehicle (ATV) along the shoreline looking for crawl lines and nesting sites. She patrolled a 15-mile section of beach between Topsail and St. Andrews Pass. When she located a crawl, she would follow it to the nest, record the GPS coordinates and report them to the Florida Fish and Wildlife Conservation Commission, who maintained the statewide records of sea turtle nesting activities. Often Clara would encounter a female turtle returning to the Gulf in the predawn hours. She always looked forward to these events and marveled at the beauty of these giant turtles. She was one of those dedicated natural resource volunteers who could be counted on to be on the job rain or shine.

From time to time she would find George Mott completing a night's work trapping the dunes for beach mice. She had overcome her fear of finding this large man on the deserted beach and they had become fast friends. She talked to George often and took advantage of his vast knowledge of coastal wildlife. She also looked forward to seeing him on the beach and kept an eye on his trapping schedule so that she would know when he was on the dunes.

She was delighted to receive a call from George one evening after supper. "What's up, George?" she asked.

"Clara, I wanted to ask if you have noticed an increase in the number of feral cats on the beach. Something is impacting our colony of beach mice and I am trying to figure out why."

"As a matter of fact, I have. The last three nests I surveyed had a cat hanging around waiting for the mother to finish laying her eggs. The last one had two cats sitting next to the mother. It did seem unusual. I should have given you a call."

"Well, let me know if you see any more. Our Choctawahatchee beach mouse trap counts are down and I'm going to start trapping the cats, in case they are the problem. Bring some extra coffee next week when you are out my way."

"I'll do that. Take care of those cute little mice and I'll see you at WaterSound Beach."

CHAPTER 9

THE INSPECTION

On Thursday morning at 9:00 a.m. Quinn and George stood in front of the WaterColor Inn and waited for Troy Pinkham's arrival.

"It does not make sense that Troy would want to inspect the inn, when the beach mice colony is seven miles away. The Department of Environmental Protection has mismanaged the Grayton Beach population so much that there are probably no mice left on the dunes. If Troy wants to do something to help the species, he should go talk to them. We are only on a narrow fringe of the habitat. There is only so much we can do!" George said with a certain amount of frustration.

"You're right, George, but we are the ones with the Habitat Conservation Plan and the Fish and Wildlife Service has authority to monitor the plan for compliance," Quinn said.

"I hate these damn politics of the Endangered Species Act. Why can't we work together to save the mice, instead of playing these power and authority games?" George queried.

"You're preaching to the choir, George." Quinn was well aware of George's lack of tolerance for the politics of environmental protection and had often sought to conduct this portion of the business and let George do what he does better than anyone in managing the species and their habitat. Together they made a good team.

At 9:15 a.m. Brad Garner joined them at the construction site. "Hey, guys, has Officer Pinkham shown up yet?"

"Not yet, Brad, I'll give the Fish and Wildlife Service office a call and made sure he is on the way and bringing his supervisor with him. Quinn called while George and Brad talked.

"George, how is that new baby girl?"

"Oh, she is just great. She is over her early problems and growing by leaps and bounds."

"How old is she?"

"She's 18 months now and up to a strapping 20 pounds."

"That's good to hear. How are you reading this situation with Troy?"

"I'm really pissed about it, to tell you the truth. It is bad enough that the population counts are down, but to have Officer Pinkham inspect the construction here at WaterColor, when the colony of mice is seven miles way, sounds punitive to me."

"It does sound that way, but we will play their game and see what they want."

Quinn got off the phone and said, "Troy has not left the office yet and Jan, the assistant supervisor, was unaware of the letter or the meeting. The earliest he will be here is 10:00 a.m."

"Well, I am going to leave it with you two. I was hoping to set the tone for the meeting, but I will have to leave that in your capable hands. Quinn, look me up before you go and let me know how it went."

"I can't believe he is an hour late for this meeting, especially since you had to cancel your meeting with Senator Nelson. That is disrespectful, even for Troy."

"I'm hoping it was a coincidence, rather than a power play on Troy's part. We will just have to wait and hear his reasons. Let's take a walk around and look at the construction."

They were joined by the construction superintendent while they walked the site. George was particularly proud of the work done on the dune walkovers. "The guys have done a good job of constructing the walkovers from the top down. Look, not one footprint in the sand below the installation. Also, look at the turtle lighting package—shielded lights on the buildings and low bollards along the paths. Interior lighting will be reduced by tinted glass and the drapes will be drawn at sunset in every room to prevent light from reaching the beach. While they have not been installed yet, there will be a series of information signs informing the guest about the beach habitat, sea turtles, and mice," George said. "Guests at the inn will love the details."

Troy arrived in a huff and offered no explanation for his delay nor did he explain why Jan did not accompany him. "I have reviewed your plans in detail and I am very concerned with what I see. First, you have cabbage palms planted in the landscape areas. Those palms are not native to Walton County and I want them all taken out."

"Wait a minute, what do you mean they are not native. You are talking about the state tree. They are all over the place. I've got hundreds of them along the beach at WindMark in Gulf County and they are common in Bay County." George said with consternation.

"You are not listening to me. I said I want them taken out! Also, your exterior lighting plan is inferior and causes light pollution on the dunes. It's dangerous for the beach mice to be exposed to that much illumination."

"Troy, these are certified turtle lights and we have met with you and Jan to discuss these at least twice. To my knowledge, there are no specifications for beach mice lights," Quinn offered.

"There are now. All of these lights will have to be replaced with compatible beach mice lamps."

"I do not think there is a beach mice product available in the lighting industry."

"That is your problem, not mine. I want them replaced with lamps that meet my requirements. I don't have any more time. You come up with a plan that meets my requirements. Until then, the construction of the inn is red-tagged and cannot move forward."

"Why didn't you bring Jan to this meeting?"

"I did not need her. I have total responsibility for the administration of the Habitat Conservation Plan from the regional office in Atlanta. You will answer to me."

Without further discussions, Troy got in his truck and drove away. The meeting lasted less than ten minutes.

Quinn and George watched him depart. "I hope you're going to tell Brad about this. I think he would fire me," George said.

"Yes, I'll talk to him. What do you make of Troy's mandates?"

"I think he is f...ing out of his mind. There is no scientific data or even sound precedence for either of these requirements. I think he has pulled them off the top of his feeble mind. Am I to assume we will replace certified turtle lights that are already installed on the building with a lighting product that has not even been developed yet? What candlepower of illumination is required? What proof is there that the mice will be threatened by the small amount of light that reach their foraging areas on the dunes. Most of their movements on the dunes take place in the early morning hours and illumination is at its lowest during that period...it is his GD attitude that pisses me off more than anything else. I think Brad is perfectly willing to discuss the scientific merits of any additional habitat protection, but to have untried or thoughtless ideas thrown at us as ultimatums is infuriating."

"I'm going to talk to Jan about it and also give the FWC regional administrator a call. Something does not feel right about this. Maybe they can shed some light on the issues. In the meantime, I need to give Brad a heads up on this meeting. Are you sure you do not want to come along?"

"I'm so damned frustrated that I need to get back on the dunes. I've called Forestry Suppliers to get some more traps for the feral cats. They tell me there has been a run on traps and they only had one left in stock. Get this—the traps were sent to this area. Someone else is apparently having cat problems as well. When I receive this one trap from the supplier, I'll have five. If I am going to get the cats out of the preserve; I need to be working the trapline all the time. I am becoming more and more convinced it is the cats that are ravaging the mice population. What I don't know is where they are coming from. It is not uncommon for me to trap three cats a night."

"What do you do with them once you have trapped them?"

"I take them to the SPCA to be euthanized. The trip up there with the cats means my trapline is out of the field for the day. I need another six traps minimum to make a dent in that cat population. Either that or I work around the clock."

"Let me know if I can help. I'll call our Tampa office and see if they have any traps. In the meantime, I have got to talk with Brad."

"Okay, let me know how it goes."

Quinn walked across the street to Brad's office as George burned rubber out of the parking lot with his muddy four-wheel-drive truck.

After the WaterColor meeting, Troy had organized a conference call between himself, Jan, and the regional administrator to lay the groundwork for his enforcement case. "Everyone knows the big bad developers are trying to get away with something," he smugly told himself. "It will also give me another chance to show them how dedicated I am to protecting the damn mice."

Jan Adler was a dedicated Fish and Wildlife Service officer who had risen through the ranks to become assistant supervisor of the Panama City Field office at age 32. It was only a brief post for her, as she continued to advance due to her efficiency and administrative talents. She felt lucky to have Troy on her staff. He was senior to her in the number of years with Fish and Wildlife Service and had received a number of commendations, some of which Jan had recommended herself for his efforts to protect the Choctawahatchee beach mouse. The call took place in her office.

"Thanks for taking the time to talk with me about the Choctawahatchee beach mouse Habitat Conservation Plan," Troy said with his best conciliatory tone. "I wanted to discuss the St. Joe Company's activities in compliance with the provisions of the plan. I have reasons to believe that the plan to protect the mice is failing due to their blatant disregard for its provisions. The last few quarterly reports have shown a drastic decline in the mice population. This comes after a population increase at the WaterSound Preserve with the relocation conducted under my supervision. I have put them on notice that any further decreases in the CRM population would result in a jeopardy determination from this office. I have also inspected the WaterColor Inn project to see if they have violated the provisions of the plan. As you recall, the inn impacted about 1.4 acres of the Grayton Beach colony of Choctawahatchee beach mouse."

"Yes, I recall the provisions of the plan. That 1.4 acres was a marginal habitat area and the developer had offered the 1.5-mile section of beach as mitigation. You did an excellent job on that negotiation and I am glad to hear you are staying on top of the developer and making sure they comply with the provisions of the Habitat Conservation Plan," the administrator said.

"Thank you and, yes, that is correct, sir! I have continued to monitor the plan and think the developer is failing in their responsibilities. I wanted to let you and Jan know where I am on my enforcement efforts and to warn you that there may be some complaints from the company or their consultants. I do not think they will take kindly to my efforts to make them tow the line and do what they have committed to in the Plan, so you can expect a call from them, complaining about my enforcement actions."

"Excellent work! I'll be happy to take their call. You and Jan keep everything under control on the coast. I wish all of our field offices were as diligent on enforcing the Endangered Species Act as you are. Keep me informed of your progress."

"Thank you, sir. I will keep you informed."

Jan wrinkled her brow as they hung up the call. "You know, this does not sound like the St. Joe Company. They have always been diligent on following through with their commitments. I have met with Brad Garner on several occasions and have come away feeling confident that they are good stewards of the environment."

"Excuse me for saying so, but I think you are being naïve. You allowed them to sweet talk you into trusting them, so they could get away with murder. I've watched them for a long time before you got here and I can tell you, they are not to be trusted," Troy said with self-righteous indignation.

"Well, I have not seen that and I am usually a very good judge of character, so keep me informed as you go forward on this."

Jan was not comfortable with Troy's zealous attitude. She sat thinking as he left the room and then reached for the telephone to call Quinn Wilson. However, she decided not to call, but to place her trust in Troy. After all, he was a senior officer with a great track record.

CHAPTER 10

COMPLIANCE

Quinn walked across the street to Brad's office and found him just coming out of a meeting.

"How did it go?" he asked.

"Not good—we need to talk."

"Come on into my office," Brad said as he headed down the hallway.

"Troy has given us some ultimatums. He believes the cabbage palms in the landscaping plan are not indigenous to the county and should be removed from the habitat along the dunes. Secondly, he says our turtle lighting plan is not sufficient and does not provide protection for the Choctawahatchee beach mouse habitat. He wants it replaced. The third condition is the hardest. He has red-tagged the construction of the inn until these items have been taken care of to his satisfaction."

Brad was quiet for a minute then spoke. "Troy actually said that cabbage palms are not indigenous to Walton County? They are all over the place! We have 40 palms either in the ground or ready to be planted and he wants them removed? The same with the lighting plan—we have installed certified turtle lights and it will take thousands of dollars to remove and replace them. You know better than I do, but I do not recall there being any beach mice lighting fixtures."

"You are right on both issues. His requests seem arbitrary. I'm going to call Jan and see what is going on with Fish and

Wildlife Service. I will also call the regional administrator. Troy's attitude seems out of line. There is something going on here that I cannot put my finger on," Quinn pondered.

Brad was quietly reflecting on some inner thoughts. "You know what? Let's do what he wants. We will comply with his mandate and not complain. And we will do it quickly to avoid delays in construction."

"Are you sure that is what you want to do?"

"You have to remember, we are developers. We are totally unappreciated within the environmental community. They see us as the villains destroying the natural environment and, in some cases, they are right. There are some unscrupulous people in this industry and we have to set ourselves apart. The last time we talked, I told you that it was about the environment—correct? Well, now it is time for me to back up my words with actions."

"I can appreciate that, but Troy's demands are arbitrary at best. There are cabbage palms growing in Choctawahatchee beach mouse habitat to the east and west of us, so it does not make sense that he claims there are no palms in Walton County. Ecosystems never follow political boundaries. Give me a few days and I'll prove this point. Palm trees are common among beach dunes throughout northwest Florida and they are not detrimental to beach mice."

"I hear you and I agree, but I am trying to make a stewardship statement here. We will take out the palms and develop new lighting fixtures that will protect the mice. WaterColor will be the most environmentally compatible project on the Gulf Coast. Before we are finished, I want to have Fish and Wildlife Service acknowledge our efforts and make us an award-winning project. So let's get started and let's do it fast. It is the construction delay that worries me more than the cost."

It would take three months to remove and replace the cabbage palms and exterior lighting on the inn. The landscaper grumbled and charged thousands to remove the trees, while the lighting contractor had a field day developing new lights and installing them for hundreds of thousands. Those lighting fixtures that were not replaced received lower wattage bulbs and were fitted with rheostats so the candlepower could be reduced as needed. The total cost for the retrofit was well over $300 thousand, plus the time lost in construction of the hotel.

In late March, Brad, George and Quinn met at the inn late in the evening to review the lighting plan. As the sun went down and the lights came on, they all sat and intensely watched the results.

"Damn, it's dark out here," said George. "Any darker and we are going to be putting our guests at risk."

"Those low bollards along the walkway are the only light on the path and they are spaced twenty feet apart," Brad offered. "Also, notice the dark tinting on the hotel room windows. They give very little light with the curtains open and it will be inn's policy to draw the curtains in every room as part of the "turn-down service" offered to guests.

"The red rope lights on the edges of the dune walkovers are a nice touch. They at least let you see the steps before you fall over them," Quinn offered. "Let's walk over to the beach and see what it looks like from there."

Once on the beach, Brad said, "There is more phosphorescence in the surf than there is light from the inn." George had disappeared and they found him lying on his stomach underneath the walkover.

"What are you doing down there?" Brad asked with a laugh.

"I'm checking the light sources from the mouse's point of view. There is no induced illumination at ground level within the habitat that I can perceive," George said with a measure of pride."

"George, from now on all of St. Joe's development on the coast will have this lighting package on their plans," Brad stated. Turning to Quinn he said, "Now let's get Jan and Troy out here to view the plan. Invite the regional administrator as well. Let's make a big deal about the inspection and invite them for dinner, if they will come."

"I'll call all of them in the morning and set it up," Quinn volunteered.

CHAPTER 11

SALAMANDERS AND BUTTERFLIES

Troy was surprised and a little disappointed that he or the regional director did not receive a call from the WaterColor group. He thought he had twisted the knife enough to cause them to cry and complain like little children. His demands had been outlandish and he had worked to refine his argument when they called to complain. He had driven by the project and saw the palms being removed from the landscaping and the lighting contractor working on the lights with cherry-picker trucks. This was a setback in his plans, since he had hoped they would argue the points long enough for the spring quarter trapping numbers to come in and he and Cal Summerford could lower the boom on them with the jeopardy determination and lawsuits.

Troy's girlfriend had called and said she was returning to Detroit for the summer and could not take care of the cats any longer. This weakened Troy's plan to keep the pressure on the population of mice in WaterSound. The last thing he wanted to happen was for the spring trapping numbers to come back strong and weaken his regulatory position. Cal was counting on him to bring this developer to the altar and then slaughter them in court. He had to make sure that happened.

He had one more card to play. Since the adoption of the WaterColor Habitat Conservation Plan, yet another northwest Florida species was to be added to the ESA endangered list. Little was known about the life cycle of the flatwoods salamander until John Palis' research on the species. The salamander was a habitat specialist living most of their lives under the pine debris of flatwoods forests and breeding in ephemeral ponds and wetlands. Since all of the Florida Panhandle was pine flatwoods, Troy planned use this newly listed amphibian to stall the WaterColor project and cost the developer more time, effort, and money.

So on the first day of listing the salamander as a federal endangered species, Troy sent a registered letter to St. Joe stating:

> Please be advised that the flatwoods salamander (*Ambystoma cingulatum*) has been listed as an endangered species under the federal Endangered Species Act (ESA). Presence of habitat suitable for this species' survival have been observed on the WaterColor project. Without data pertaining to the existence of this species on your project site, it is assumed to be present. Therefore, you are hereby notified that all work within pine flatwoods, pine savanna, and wiregrass communities is to cease immediately. No further work may be conducted in these areas until field surveys, by creditable experts familiar with the life cycle of this species, have provided data regarding the presence of this species. Failure to perform these surveys to the satisfaction of the Fish and Wildlife Service will result in fines or imprisonment of responsible parties in accordance with the provisions of the Endangered Species Act.

Brad took a deep breath after reading this latest letter from Troy Pinkham and picked up the telephone to call Quinn. "I've gotten yet another cease-work order from the Fish and Wildlife Service. This one is on the flatwoods salamander. Are you familiar with this species?"

"Well, they certainly did not waste any time getting that letter out. Flatwoods salamanders were listed as a federal endangered species just today," Quinn noted.

"They have asked for a credible field survey to be conducted. Who do we have that can perform this survey?" Brad asked.

"I suggest we call John Palis directly. George can certainly do the work, but John has the credibility with Fish and Wildlife Service, specifically Troy."

"That Habitat Conservation Plan has really done nothing at all for us. If anything, I feel like we have a target on our forehead. Well, let's get started. Call John today and see if he has time for us," Brad said with a rare show of exasperation.

Prior to European settlement of the southern coastal plains, the flatwoods salamander lived among the litter of longleaf pine and wiregrass savannas, where their habitat was maintained by periodic lightning fires. The harvesting of these forests in the early 20th Century and the resulting change in habitat to agriculture, pasture, and silviculture caused the extirpation of a sizable breeding population of salamanders before anyone knew they were present in the habitat. Further degradation of habitat occurred with the suppression of wildfires, draining of ephemeral ponds and ongoing land development that fragmented the habitat and isolated breeding colonies from one another, similar to what occurred to the beach mice.

In addition, the salamanders had a particularly interesting breeding process that was inadvertently disrupted by humans. Adult salamanders spend most of their lives isolated under pine litter in burrows. From September to December, adults migrate from surrounding pine and wiregrass habitat to their natal wetlands during rainfall events associated with passing cold fronts. Courtship among these isolated members of this species occurs on land where the female accepts contributions left on the ground by passing males. At no time is there ever any physical contact between the male and females of the species. Females lay fertilized eggs in clumps of moist wetland vegetation. Eggs hatch in response to inundation by rising water levels in the ponds and larva remain in the ponds for approximately three months before returning to the pine litter habitat in the early spring and continuing their isolated life cycle.

While the concern for the species was real, the targeted enforcement of the Endangered Species Act to the WaterColor project was conducted for other reasons. Since WaterColor had an Habitat Conservation Plan, they became the first project to be evaluated by the Fish and Wildlife Service for the presence of flatwoods salamander.

Fringe environmental advocacy groups started to make their presences known on WaterColor in various ways. A number of letters were being received at the WaterColor office calling for the protection of their favorite environmental issue or species, coastal dune lakes, burrowing owl, red-cockaded woodpecker, sea turtles, water quality, bald eagle, Florida black bear, piping plover, or manatees. Even the Ivory-billed woodpecker, which had been declared extinct for the last 60 years, was brought up as an issue by the Audubon Society. Many of the species did not occupy habitat in northwest Florida, let alone WaterColor. Yet the requests were similar in asking for all development of the property to stop immediately, because of irreversible impact on habitat for this increasing list of species. One morning a group of six people arrived in a van and picketed the inn construction site. Their signs demanded all construction to stop to protect the flyway of the monarch butterfly.

"What do you make of this, Quinn?" Brad asked, while the picketers chanted on the street below.

"I think there is some organization behind this effort. We are hearing a lot more from the environmental organizations than we did during the Development of Regional Impact (DRI), and environmental permitting process. I do not think Troy would organize these groups, but it looks like he is at least a part of the effort. There is another chapter out there to be written. I just do not know where it will come from."

"I have another question for you."

"Okay, shoot."

"Are we in the flyway for the monarch butterfly? If so, is the inn in any way impeding their travel?"

"The monarchs do migrate to the Gulf coast from the central U.S. They rest for a short time before flying across the Gulf or along the coast to their wintering hibernation colonies in the mountains of Central Mexico. We are on the fringe of the migratory corridor, so I don't think we have a direct impact on the flyway. Also, we have left significant amounts of native vegetation in place that should support their short stay."

"Central Mexico! You have got to be kidding."

"No, I'm not kidding. The monarch is a phenomenal insect. Did you know that the average life span of a monarch is four to five weeks? But once a year a Methuselah generation is born that lives seven to eight months. That is the generation that migrates to Mexico and back to the U.S. before dying."

"A Methuselah generation, now that is interesting. That is the kind of thing that would intrigue our guests. We could do an informational plaque in the landscaping and we could plant some flowering vegetation in our native landscaping for the butterflies. You know, maybe I should go join the picket line."

"Maybe we both should go!"

"No, don't bother. We both know the answer. We are the evil developers out to destroy the world and every living thing in it," Brad said with a discouraged tone. "I cannot get over the fact that all of these environmentalists live in houses, shop in stores, drive cars, have air conditioning, use the toilet and make other demands on resources. Where do they think those conveniences come from? At some point in time, all the infrastructure they take for granted was part of a development that more than likely displaced natural habitat. Yet, *we* are the bad guys. They give no thought to the amount of risk we take to bring quality development to reality. I'm sorry. I'm on my soapbox again. You are one of the few people I can complain to without impacting our stock price, so you just have to put up with my ranting."

"I am happy to help where I can. I would like to figure out what is going on and who is orchestrating these environmental groups. If we knew, maybe we could be more proactive," Quinn said as he rubbed his chin in thought.

"I think we will know before long. I just have a feeling it will come to a head in the near future," Brad added.

Other environmental advocacy groups showed up at WaterColor with less obvious agendas. One group wore black tee shirts, berets, and camouflage pants tucked into combat boots. They spoke to no one as they blatantly toured the project, often marching in ill-formed platoons. They ignored the restrictive habitat signs and climbed over the dunes, swam in the Western lake and stood in groups talking on the beach. Contractors reported finding them at home construction sites when they arrived for work before the sun came up. When approached, they would not divulge their affiliation or their objectives. They set up camp in the Point Washington State Forest immediately adjacent to the WaterColor project and their numbers increased as members throughout the U.S. came to the camp. The group had its roots in the Oregon disputes over harvesting the virgin timber stands in the national forests of the northwest. They called themselves the "Soldiers for the Environment." The Gulf Coast was a great place to wage an environmental battle, since it was springtime on the beach.

Eugene Siedmann was a junior member of the Soldiers. He had joined after flunking out of his first semester at the North Oregon Community College. His score on video games was much more important to him then attending classes. Also, he was overwhelmed by academic requirements of college life and intimidated by the learned professors who taught the few classes he did attend. His professor of Introductory Biology ranted about the destruction of the environment and condemned developers, whom he held responsible for all of the environmental degradation occurring throughout the United States. Eugene remembered one salient comment the professor had made, "No one can own the environment. Just as the birds are free to fly from tree to tree, we are free to life in the environment. Developers may buy the land, but they do not own the environment. That belongs to all of us." Eugene thought that was the most profound statement he had ever heard and struggled to wrap his mind around the concept. Upon leaving college after a few short months, he joined the Soldiers for the Environment, who were staunchly protesting the exploitation of the national forests around the campus. While his stay at the college was short, he prided himself in talking about his college days. Those who listened were not aware that they were, in fact, just days. He was proud of his newfound knowledge and association with an important organization like the Soldiers. He hoped to be able to prove himself a worthy member.

The Soldiers were one of the more extreme environmental organizations. They were structured similar to Green Peace, but without the vision and objective defined by their leadership. They were the clenched fist and combat boots, where environmental groups gathered to protect destruction of the environment. Their mode of operation was to observe, intimidate, and protest noisily. They did not nurture, cultivate, understand or bring scientific reason to the debate. They only protested any perceived environmental impact that was worthy of national attention. "No development anywhere at any time," was their time-honored motto. They liked the cameras and public attention. Their military bearing brought a certain tension to the protests. They were the veiled threat of forceful action that got the attention of the national press.

They found that their services were in demand and it was no surprise when Cal Summerford approached them about the WaterColor project in Florida. The potential of spending the summer on a Florida beach was a no-brainer for the leadership. The lucrative fee was an added incentive, so a platoon of Soldiers was immediately dispatched and a company of 40 was promised by midsummer. Eugene was a member of the first platoon.

CHAPTER 12

SALAMANDER SURVEY

After a few calls, Quinn was able to settle on a date that John Palis would be available to assist with the flatwoods survey for the salamander. John was a noted expert in salamanders and wrote the book on both their endangered status and the protocol for field monitoring for the species. He was onsite within a week. John, Quinn and George Mott met onsite to get acquainted and discuss the survey techniques as they prepared for the field work.

"John, it is good to meet you. Have you met George Mott, our wildlife biologist?" Quinn asked as they shook hands.

"Yes, we have had some time to talk about the conservation program you have here at WaterColor. I must say I am impressed. How can I help?"

"Well, we have received a letter from the Fish and Wildlife Service asking for a survey of WaterColor for flatwoods salamander habitat. Since it was just listed as endangered a few days ago, we needed your expertise in conducting the survey and providing the necessary documentation. I've brought these aerial photographs of the project and surrounding areas to give you a feel of the area. So, where should we start?"

"We survey for suitable habitat first. The combination of flatwoods and ephemeral ponds must be present before we can start looking for the species," John said with authority as they reviewed the aerials.

"The land plan for WaterColor reserves over 50 percent of

the habitat in natural condition," George offered in orientation. "That includes both pine flatwoods and wetlands. A few of the ponds have cypress, however, most are overgrown with titi. I'm sure you have seen titi dominate the wetlands throughout the region. Without natural occurrence of fire, both the flatwoods and wetland systems become overgrown. The ground litter within the older pine stands gets very thick. Do you ever look for individuals under the litter matte?" George asked as he pulled on his field pack.

"I almost never look for individuals. I'm supposed to be an expert on the species, but I have seen very few specimens in the field. Larvae are easier to spot in the ponds. In the fall and winter, I net for them. However, we are in early spring now and if the salamanders are in the habitat, they have probably returned to their burrows. Still we should be able to determine whether there is habitat that will support the species and whether or not they are in the habitat."

John talked as they walked, "The lack of fire in these systems has allowed the titi to dominate in these isolated wetlands. I think at one time these areas would have supported suitable salamander habitat, but not anymore. The silviculture operations with planted pines on ten-foot centers, plus the protection from wild fires, have allowed the habitat to deteriorate. I think we can safely say that this project does not have suitable habitat for flatwoods salamanders."

"Well, tell me this. If the titi was mechanically thinned out and the fringes of the wetlands periodically burned, would the area be restored to a good breeding habitat?" George asked.

"Yes and no! The restoration of the habitat would certainly help. Left unattended, this titi will continue to spread into thickets with little wildlife value. But the salamanders, if they were here before, have already abandoned the area due to the deterioration of the habitat. If you wanted to restore the habitat, plan on maintaining the systems for 30 to 40 years and maybe the salamanders will find it suitable for breeding and return. Are you willing to make that commitment? If so I would be happy to help."

"You know…it is not entirely out of the question. Brad has a strong commitment to conservation, plus the titi is basically a blight on the landscape. We will be doing some restoration work, either thinning or eliminating the titi in favor of pond cypress, so I think the habitat will start trending towards the open ephemeral ponds that the salamanders need for breeding. We will come back in 40 years and do this field inspection again and see if we have been successful," Quinn said with a laugh.

"OK, guys, I'm leaving you," George said. "I've got to go check the feral cat traps out at WaterSound. So far I have trapped over a dozen feral cats and they just seem to keep coming. I'm getting a little paranoid about it. They are impacting my Choctawahatchee beach mouse population and the Fish and Wildlife Service has told us they will issue a jeopardy determination if the population falls during the spring trapping, so John, it has been great working with you. I have to go." George shook hands with both John and Quinn and headed out of the woods with long strides.

On returning to the office later in the afternoon, John and Quinn called Troy Pinkham to report on the field work. "Troy, this is Quinn Wilson. I am here with John Palis. We have just completed the field work on the flatwoods salamander habitat on WaterColor and wanted to give you a report."

"Let me hear it from John, so I have an unbiased report."

Quinn glanced at John, who had a quizzical look before he spoke, "This is John Palis. I do not know if we have met or if you are familiar with my work, but I am a specialist in the flatwoods salamander and I was retained by the St. Joe Company to evaluate habitat on the WaterColor project for flatwoods salamanders. I was accompanied in the field by George Mott and Quinn Wilson. The bottom line was that the habitat on the project was not prime for salamanders. The ephemeral ponds necessary for breeding were too overgrown with titi and most of the flatwoods are now pine plantation. The silviculture operation is over 60 years old and the plantations are already in their fourth rotation of harvesting and replanting. Therefore, what I am saying is the habitat is *not* suitable to sustain a population of salamanders."

"I want both a biological opinion and environmental assessment describing your field work and findings in detail. There will be no more development on WaterColor until I have accepted those reports," Troy stated with a measure of attitude.

"Biological opinions are typically not required unless the species is present in the habitat," John stated.

"I said that I wanted them. This is a new species on the endangered list and I want to make sure the documentation is in the file."

John looked at Quinn, who stated, "We will get you the reports, Troy. Since John has attested to conditions in the project; can we continue development in areas that are not potential habitat?"

"No, I have issued a cease-and-decease order and there will be no work conducted until I say so. Have a good day." Troy abruptly ended the call.

"What is up with that guy? I've done these surveys for other Fish and Wildlife Service offices all over the southeast and they have always accepted my findings without a formal biological opinion. I think my credibility has been challenged," John said with concern.

"I think, in this case, you are guilty by association. Officer Troy Pinkham has a dislike for developers, especially the St. Joe Company. He has made our life difficult from the beginning.

However, lately he seems to be even more disagreeable. I have to assume his leadership is backing him up, because we have not heard a peep from them. His attitude is becoming increasingly disrespectful and distrustful. As a result, we are required to provide documentation at every step. It's a shame because WaterColor is conducting some innovative conservation projects and it would be great if Fish and Wildlife Service participated with us, instead of snipping from the sidelines. So in regards to the biological opinion, we will prepare and have you review it before it is submitted to FWS. I'll have Dr. Pam Latham start work on it. She did the Habitat Conservation Plan for the beach mice and has all of the project background information."

CHAPTER 13

THE IN-BASKET

The reports requested by Officer Pinkham were coming in daily now. First, the changes to the WaterColor lighting plan, including the relocation of light fixtures, candlepower of lamps, extent of illumination, special applications of red string lights along the interior stairs on the dune walk offs, and models of the background glow or, lack thereof, expected from the revised lighting plan. Within the week, Quinn delivered the report on the salamander field work, biological opinion and biological assessment. Troy diligently logged the reports into the office and stamped them with the date and time of their submittal. He carried the bundled reports and plans to his office and dropped them into his in-basket, then sat down and put his feet on his desk and smiled. He had accomplished his immediate objective of shutting down construction at WaterColor. Now it was time to twist the knife and cause delays in the project. He knew that federal regulations required his review of these reports, but there was no statutory timeframe required for his response, so he planned to leave the reports where they were, in the in-basket, for as long as he could. After he had delayed as long as possible, he would prepare a series of question and send them back to St. Joe for response. Then he could restart his review timeframe again and make maximum use of his in-basket to delay the project and cost St. Joe more money.

Meanwhile, back at WaterColor, the contractor was furloughing workers and requesting liquidated damages from St. Joe under the provisions of their contract. He had staffed up to accomplish the work within the scheduled timeframe and the work stoppage was beyond his control. The subcontractors, including plumbers, electricians and dry wall contractors were particularly hard hit. Work was scarce on the Emerald Coast and the WaterColor project was the biggest job going at the time.

CHAPTER 14

ON THE DUNES

George turned his four-wheel truck onto the forest road leading to the backside of the dunes at WaterSound and immediately thought that something was very wrong. Yet another feral cat ran across the road, stopping briefly to look in his direction and disappeared into the ilex thicket at the base of the dunes.

"God damn it!" George shouted to himself. "What the hell is going on here? I've gotten over a dozen cats off the dunes and there are still more out here. There are so many that they are all starting to look alike."

George jumped out of the truck and walked in the direction the cat was traveling. There, about ten yards off the road, he found a neatly arranged feeding area with cat food and a watering bowl. With a string of curses, George kicked the two bowls and stood in bewilderment with his hands on his hips. "Who the hell would be feeding the cats in the center of this tract? It's private property for God's sake." As his anger subsided, he began looking around, trying to figure out what was going on. He knelt down and looked at some weathered footprints leading from the road to the feeding area. They were windblown, but from the impressions visible, George could tell that they were made by a small tennis shoe. *These look like they were made by a female,* he thought. He returned to the road and walked back towards County Road 30A. His truck had disturbed most of the tracks along the narrow access road, but he could still see tread marks from what appeared to be a passenger car. Most vehicles accessing the forest roads throughout northwest Florida had off-road tires. These were road tires.

Before nightfall, George had a cable stretched across each of the three forest roads leading into the project and had placed a no trespassing signs on the gate posts. With over 1,000,000 acres of forested land in St. Joe's ownership, all of the forest roads could not be locked. St. Joe trusted the local residents to respect the land and, in turn, they could hunt and fish on the property. Rarely had they experienced any abuse that would require the gates to be locked. This was one of those occasions when the abuse had dire consequences. The spring quarter trapping was scheduled for the April new moon in about ten days, and the feral cats were still running wild in the Choctawahatchee beach mouse habitat.

Later that afternoon, a female beach mouse with one toe missing from her left hind foot sat pensively at the opening of her burrow and looked out at the tiny patch of sand as the sun slowly set to the west. Three feet below her, down a well-maintained tunnel, was a brood of two baby mice. It was imperative that she get something to eat tonight. Foraging attempts for the last two nights had been aborted due to a new aggressive predator on the dunes. She could smell them and hear them prowling past her burrow during the night. The odor of this new enemy had sent shivers down her spine. She had no choice tonight. The demands of her young meant that she must eat or die trying. As darkness fell she slowly edged out of her burrow and sniffed the air. With a rush of courage, she dashed towards a clump of sea oats about six feet down the dune to her right. She did not make it. A feral cat crouched behind the burrow grabbed her torso and sank his teeth deep within her body. Death came quickly. Her brood would die a slower death in the burrow for the lack of the nutrients their mother would provide. The population of beach mice had effectively decreased by three. The cat prowled on across the crest of the dune for yet another meal.

Seven days later, George Mott was found dead with three bullet holes in his chest. He was leaning against a pine tree near his truck in the staging area that he and Quinn used for the quarterly mice trapping. The area surrounding the staging area was littered with empty feral cat traps. That same night, a fire destroyed one of the model homes on WaterColor. The volunteer fire department suspected arson, put had no proof. The next day Brad Garner received a hand-delivered letter from Troy Pinkham informing him that the Fish and Wildlife Service had found St. Joe's actions had placed the Choctawhatchee beach mice in jeopardy of extinction. The FWS would be conducting an investigation and considered criminal prosecution for violations of the Endangered Species Act. Two days after that letter was sent, $25,000 was deposited in Troy Pinkham's offshore banking account in the Cayman Islands.

CHAPTER 15

THE ARREST

Quinn flew into Panama City on the U.S. Air flight in the late afternoon. He was to join George to assist on the quarterly trapping event. Quinn drove by the monitoring site and walked past the newly installed cable to the staging area to see if George was making preparations for the quarterly event. There was no sign of him at the site, so Quinn walked back towards the rental car that he left parked in the highway right of way. As he was leaving the site, a Buick turned into the forest road and stopped abruptly at the cable. The woman at the wheel looked surprised to see another car, but she waved and smiled as she backed out. It appeared to Quinn that she was simply turning around. After driving a half-mile down the road, he forgot about seeing the woman. He stopped for dinner at a little seafood restaurant in Mexico Beach that he and George liked to frequent. He arrived at the Quality Inn on 24th Street in Panama City a little after 11:00 p.m. and went straight to his room. The next morning he woke early and went for a run to clear his head. At 7:00 a.m. sharp he entered the dining area in the lobby of the hotel and was having breakfast when he heard of a police investigation near WaterSound Beach. The television news team panned the area and Quinn saw Troy's Fish and Wildlife Service truck parked among the sheriff's vehicles. He thought the place looked familiar and then they mentioned George's name.

The monotone voice of the reporter continued, "Walton County Sheriff Clay Pritchard has just confirmed that George

Mott was the victim of multiple gunshot wounds and was found dead this morning by Clara Fullerton while she was making her rounds for the local Sea Turtle Watch organization. Ms. Fullerton reported hearing gunshots around 5:00 a.m. while passing the site and had stopped to investigate on her return trip along the beach at 6:30 a.m. She called 911 and reported finding the body at approximately 6:40 a.m. The sheriff is still investigating the crime scene and has one person of interest that they would like to interview. We have been informed that person is Quinn Wilson, who works with Mr. Mott. At this time the sheriff is ruling it a homicide."

Quinn was on his feet when he heard George's name mentioned and almost in shock when he heard that he was a person of interest. He immediately grabbed his cell phone and dialed 911. "Yes, give me the sheriff's department please!"

"Walton County Sherriff, how may I help you?"

"This is Quinn Wilson calling. I just heard on morning news that I am a person of interest in a possible homicide!"

"Mr. Wilson! Where are you located?"

"I am at the Quality Inn on 24th street in Panama City, right across from the community college."

"Please remain at your location and I will dispatch a deputy immediately. Please stay on the line to respond to other questions."

"Sure, what do you need?"

While still online, Quinn collected his briefcase and walked to the entrance of the motel and sat on a bench and waited for the sheriff's deputy to arrive. He still could not believe what he had just heard. George Mott had been shot while out in the field preparing for the quarterly beach mice trapping. How could this have happened? He had driven by the site on his way to the hotel last night, just to see if George was there. He saw no activity, even after parking the car and walking into the site.

Blink-Out

"Mr. Wilson, are you still on the line?"

"Yes."

"Please continue to hold. The deputy will be at your location momentarily."

He could hear the sirens of an approaching patrol car and wondered why they were going to such extremes to reach his location.

An hour earlier, Troy heard on his mobile radio that a body had been found in the dunes near the WaterSound project. He knew the body would be identified as George Mott and beads of sweat popped out on his forehead as he heard the news. *Shit, things are getting way out of control. I better call Cal before he hears this on the news,* Troy thought as he picked up the phone to give him a call. After three rings, a sleepy voice spoke from the other end.

"Hello."

"Cal, this is Troy....What did you do?"

"What are you talking about?"

"George Mott's body was found on the WaterSound dunes this morning...he had been shot. Did...did you have anything to do with this?"

"Oh, my God! You are asking if...I could be asking you the same question. He was not one of *your* favorite people!"

"Are you saying that you or one of the militant environmental groups you asked to participate in this shakedown did not have anything to do with this?"

"...I did not...but I can't speak for all the groups...I gave a pep talk to them last night to get them fired up, so they would stay the course. But...God I do not know, Troy. One of them may have gotten the wrong message. I was really railing against the bastard. Christ, we could be implicated in this murder!"

"Shit, if you and I have to question each other to see if we committed murder, eventually someone else might figure that out as well. We need a plan and fast."

"Yeah, yeah you're right, I have to think. We have to buy some time to get our alibis worked out. We need time...OK, how about we blame someone else and make a lot of noise about it? That would sidetrack the investigation and give us some breathing room.

"Yeah, that may work...but who would have a motive to kill George?"

"Wasn't that consultant coming in to town to work with George on the quarterly trapping? What was his name? Wilson was his last name. Wilson... Wilson, oh, yeah—Quinn Wilson was his name."

"I remember that George said he was coming to town, but what would be his motive?"

"I don't know...he is a consultant, isn't he? They're all money-grubbing bastards. We could say he was stealing money from St. Joe and George found out and confronted him on it. That would work, wouldn't it?"

"Yeah, Cal, that may work!"

"Troy, you are a trusted member of the law enforcement community. Give Sheriff Pritchard a call and make the allegation and, Troy, make a big deal about it! George was your best friend and technical advisor—right?"

"Yes, he was. I'll call right now!"

Troy hung up the phone and stared at the wall of his living room. *Shit, shit, shit...*he thought as he picked up his handheld emergency radio that he carried on his service belt and switched it to the sheriff's frequency. *No*, he thought, *I'll drive to the site. My comments will have a lot more impact if it is delivered straight to them by a fellow law enforcement officer in person.*

Troy got to the preserve just as the television news team arrived and was pleased to have his picture taken as he talked to the sheriff. "Do you know this man, Troy?" The sheriff asked.

Blink-Out

"Yes, I do, that is George Mott, a wildlife biologist with St. Joe, and I think I know who may be responsible."

Quinn was sitting on the bench in front of the Quality Inn when two patrol cars raced into the parking lot from different directions and slammed on their brakes. Two deputies jumped out of each vehicle and took cover behind the open doors. The closest deputy began to shout, "Raise your hands! You heard me, drop everything and raise your hands so we can see them!"

Quinn was holding a coffee cup in one hand and his cell phone in the other, still connected to the sheriff's dispatcher, and could not figure out why the officers were looking at him. He stood up and looked over his shoulder to see who they were addressing. His actions were seen as threatening and the officers braced their guns and shouted again. "Drop that weapon now and raise your hands or we will open fire!"

Weapon! What weapon? Quinn thought as he once again looked back into the lobby of the motel for the person the officers were addressing. The guns were definitely pointed in his direction, so he thought it best to comply with the officer until he understood what was going on.

The officers shouted again, "Put down your weapon and raise your hands, NOW!" Since Quinn had no weapon, he raised his hands, still holding his coffee cup and cell phone.

"Drop them, drop then now!" The officers shouted in unison.

Quinn reluctantly dropped both and cringed at the noise his cell phone made hitting the concrete.

"Get down on your knees! Now! Get down!" The officers shouted as they raced towards him. He did not have time to comply with the order to kneel before the first officer tackled him and they both landed in the heavily landscaped area alongside the motel entrance. His face was buried in the mulch as his arms were twisted behind his back and handcuffed.

"Officer....what is this all about?" Quinn asked from his prone position in the landscaping.

"You are under arrest for the murder of George Mott. You have the right to remain silent. If you chose to speak, everything you say can and will be used against you in a court of law. You have the right to an attorney. If you cannot afford one, an attorney will be appointed to represent you."

"There has got to be a mistake. George was a friend of mine. I just heard about it on the local news and called the sheriff's office immediately. I did not kill him."

"Save it for the judge, scumbag!"

Quinn was placed in the back seat of the patrol car and transported to the sheriff's office in DeFuniak Springs. There he was place in a shabby interrogation room and left unattended for two hours. *How can this be?* he thought. *George is dead. It does not make any sense. Why would anyone want to kill George?* These were repeated questions that ran through his head.

It was 11:00 a.m. when Walton County Sheriff Clay Pritchard entered the room and dropped his broad-brimmed hat on a hanger by the door. He was the spitting image of a long-serving small-town southern sheriff. His stomach strained at the buttons of his cowboy-style shirt and his patrol belt hung low on his hips.

Clay Pritchard had been sheriff of Walton County for 15 years. He had started with the department as a rookie sheriff's deputy after graduating from high school, when the population of Walton County was only 14,000 people. In these earlier times, the county was largely agriculture with DeFuniak Springs at the center of population in the northern portion of the county. There was very little development along the coast and the majority of the lands in the southern portion of the county was owned by the St. Joe Company and was planted in endless miles of pine trees. Deputy Pritchard patrolled these southern territories for much of his early career and was lulled into debilitating boredom from driving the long deserted highways. With little law enforcement duties to occupy his time, he had learned to stake out remote sections of Highways 20 and 98, where it was almost impossible for motorists to maintain the low speed limit of 55 miles per hour. Here was the chance to turn on the siren and bully the drivers with threats of being carted off to jail in handcuffs for their grievous violation of the county's speed limits or any other law that he could make up on the spot. He liked that part of the job and refined his act through the years. He had risen through the ranks of the department mostly by attrition, as smarter, more educated deputies left for better paying jobs in other counties of Florida and Alabama. He became sheriff after 22 years in the department and he lived the job. His physical presence, attitude and bearing said to the world that he was the ultimate law enforcement officer of the county and respect was mandatory. New deputies learned to bow down in his presence and to do exactly as they were told for fear of long and painful retributions from perceived lack of respect.

In his early career there had been an occasional bar fight, domestic disputes among the farm laborers and a few murders—none of which required any investigative work. The guilty party was so obvious that it was a simple matter to apprehend and convict the perpetrators. Those few that did resist soon buckled under his bullying style of interrogation. He believed in the law enforcement edict that all murders were about three things, money, sex or drugs. You just did not have to dig deep for a motive.

Walton County changed as development began along the coast. At first it was individual homes and small developments along the beach. Then came the summer resort developments of San Destin and Seaside with the seasonal spikes in population as the area began to cater to vacationers from Atlanta and Birmingham. With them came more variations in criminal activities and more demands on his department, as he trusted no one but himself to deal with these criminal vacationers.

This proud attitude and superiority complex came with him as he entered the interrogation room. *This is going to be easy, just like all the rest,* he told himself as he walked down the hall and opened the door to begin the questioning of this latest piece of scum.

"You're in a heap of trouble, young man. You have picked the wrong county to commit murder. Your ass is mine. Now we can do this the easy way or the hard way—the choice is yours. You can save us both a lot of time if you can give me your confession now."

"Sheriff, you have the wrong man. George was a friend of mine and I had no reason to kill him."

"All right, we will do this the hard way."

"Where were you this morning between 4:30 and 6:00 a.m.?"

"I was at the Quality Inn until about 4:45 or 5:00 a.m. Then I went for a run through the community college and got back to the hotel at about 5:45 a.m."

"Was anyone with you on this run?"

"No, I was alone."

"So, you have no witness to collaborate your whereabouts this morning?"

"The hotel clerk may have seen me leave on the run."

"We have already talked to the clerk. Other than your credit card charges at check-in, they have no record of your activities. So, I'd say you have no alibi. How well did you know George Mott?"

"He was a friend and client."

"You say he was a client? What does that mean?"

"George worked for the St. Joe Company. I am a consultant to them on environmental issues."

"Is it true you were in town to meet with Mr. Mott?"

Blink-Out

"Yes, he and I were scheduled to perform a quarterly Choctawhatchee beach mice trapping event starting this evening."

"Beach mice? Why were you doing that?"

"We are required to monitor the beach mice population, in accordance with an agreement with the U.S. Fish and Wildlife Service."

"Mr. Wilson, let me get to the point. We have it on good authority that you were stealing from the St. Joe Company and you killed Mr. Mott to keep him from turning you in."

"Stealing? I...on whose good authority did you hear that?"

"I'm asking the questions here. How much money were you paid over the last three years for work on the St. Joe WaterColor project?"

"I do not think my company's business dealings with St. Joe have anything to do with this situation."

"Well, of course, you don't. Guilty men always try to cover up the truth. How much?"

"I don't have the exact figure, but would estimate it was in the two and a half million range."

"Did you say two and a half million dollars? Shit, that is outrageous! I am the sheriff here in Walton County and I make sixty-two thousand a year. What could you possibly have done to earn two and a half million?"

"Well, it wasn't just me, I've managed a team of scientists, planners, and engineers who did the permitting, engineering design and construction management for the project. An accounting of charges is available from both St. Joe and my firm, if you need them. I can assure you there was no misappropriation of funds."

"Misappropriation my ass, two and a half million is a lot of money! Get me the records and I'll make those determinations myself if there was misappropriation. Now tell me more about this trapping. Hunting during this time of year is illegal in my county."

"George and I do quarterly trapping of beach mice under the provisions of our approved Habitat Conservation Plan through the U.S. Fish and Wildlife Service."

"What the hell do you do with the mice? Eat them?"

"We catch them, record their vitals and release them. Basically, it is an inventory of the population. We use these quarterly trapping events to calibrate the model and estimate the mice population in the habitat."

"Who the hell cares? They're rats!"

"They're an endangered species on the list for both the state and federal governments. The Florida Fish and Wildlife Conservation Commission and the U.S. Fish and Wildlife Service care quite a bit about them."

"So you are telling me that the two of you get together once a quarter to trap mice for a weekend?"

"We trap for four days actually, during the new moon."

"Where do you stay during these trapping events?"

"We usually catch a nap in the pick-up truck between trap inspections. I stay at various motels. George lives in the area and goes home."

"You both sleep in the truck? Vagrant activities are illegal in my county. Are you two homosexuals?"

"Sheriff, you're out of bounds."

"You let me be the judge of that. I'm telling you that your activities are highly suspicious. Two grown men sleeping in a pickup truck and trapping mice is not normal activities in my county. You are guilty as hell and I am going to prove it and lock you up for the rest of your life. I don't know if you were ripping off St. Joe, waiting on illegal drugs to be dropped off on the beach, or were just two queers shacking up. But you are guilty of murder and I intend to prove it!"

A knock on the door interrupted the staring match between the two adversaries. "God damn it! I'm conducting an interrogation here!"

The door opened and Jan, in her Fish and Wildlife Service uniform stuck her head through the door. "Sheriff, we need to talk to your suspect. I have Agent AJ Lindall with me from the Pensacola FBI office."

"FBI, what the hell are they doing here? This is a simple murder and I can handle the investigation without interference from the Feds! Hell, I already have the murderer in custody."

A tall dark-haired woman nudged Jan aside and entered the room in one long stride. She was at least 5 foot 10 inches or taller with long black hair. "Sheriff, I am here investigating the fire at the WaterColor development last night. I'm not here about the murder. We think your suspect may have information to assist my investigation. The fire is suspected to be a terrorist activity."

"Terrorist! Well, boy, your ass is in even more trouble than I thought. You have ten minutes ladies."

As the sheriff left the room, Agent Lindall slid into his chair and tossed her long hair across her shoulder with a flip of her head that seemed more like a nervous twitch. Two industrial-strength hair barrettes held her tight curls in place on the side of her head. Her features were angular, even gaunt, and her large hands looked out of proportion to her thin arms. She organized a legal pad in front of her and then cast a discerning look at Quinn before she spoke, "I'm Agent Lindall from the Pensacola FBI office. Jan contacted me about the fire last night at the WaterColor development. I understand from Jan that you are a consultant on that project. Is that correct?"

"Yes, I have been a consultant to the St. Joe Company since the beginning of the project."

"Where were you last night between 2:00 and 3:00 a.m. this morning?"

"I was at the Quality Inn on 24th Street. I checked in around 11:00 p.m."

"We have already verified that you checked in, but did you leave the hotel after that time?"

"I went running, around 5:00 a.m. and was back at the motel before 6:00 a.m."

"How long would it take you to drive to WaterColor from the motel?"

"It would probably take an hour to make the trip, maybe 45 minutes without traffic."

"Have you noticed anything unusual going on at WaterColor in the past month?"

"Unusual? In what way?"

"Mr. Wilson, we suspect the fire at WaterColor was an act of environmental terrorism and the murder of St. Joe's wildlife ecologist may be related. Jan called our office with her suspicions and I am here to check out the facts. I also think that you are a key person of interest in these events. We are asking for your cooperation on this investigation."

Quinn pondered her statement for a moment and then turning to Jan said, "Jan, have you talked to Agent Lindall about our ongoing work with Troy on the Habitat Conservation Plan?"

"I've given her the basics about the project and suggested she talk to you."

"Actually, Jan, I wanted to come over and talk to you while I was in town for the quarterly trapping event. Things seemed to be getting out of hand."

"Then talk to us, Mr. Wilson," Agent Lindall interjected as she scribbled a note on her legal pad.

"We have been working with Officer Pinkham from Jan's office to resolve some issues with our Habitat Conservation

Plan for the Choctawhatchee beach mice. Recently some conservation organizations have shown up on WaterColor and the timing seems odd."

"What organizations are you talking about?"

"There have been the usual ones, the World Wildlife Foundation, Audubon, Sierra Club, Walton County Friends of the Environment, and even a group advocating the protection of monarch butterfly habitat. One organization refers to themselves as the Soldiers for the Environment. Their members wear black tee shirts, fatigues pants, berets and combat boots. Unlike the other groups, they do not seem to have a specific environmental agenda. The interesting thing is that they all showed up about the same time, as if someone was organizing the effort. We have not published notice of any regulatory action, so there has been no notice in the local paper or the *Federal Register*. Also, we think that militant group came from Washington state or Oregon. I have no idea how they showed up along with the local groups."

"So you think this militant group may be responsible for the fire?"

"I can't say. I've read about environmental terrorism on the West Coast but we have never experienced anything here in northwest Florida. I would suggest you talk to them." Quinn hesitated before continuing as he looked at Jan.

"Is there something else you wanted to tell us, Mr. Quinn? Agent Lindall asked as she noted his hesitation.

"Well...Jan, I wanted to talk to you about Troy. We have a long working relationship with him and I'm sure you know that he is zealous about his job and the protection of beach mice populations along the coast. We understand that, but recently he seems to be much more intense. The situation with the beach mice lighting at the WaterColor Inn seemed to be out of line. There were no studies, science, or lighting protocols to back up the demand to change out the turtle lighting on the inn that had been agreed on in the Habitat Conservation Plan. Also, the letters notifying us of perceived violations are coming rather fast and without advance notification. My question to you is whether he seems more intense that usual?"

"Jan, these technical issues with lighting packages are foreign to me. Do you understand what he is saying?" Agent Lindall asked.

"Yes, I understand—it's all part of the Habitat Conservation Plan. They willingly changed the lighting on the inn. I thought they had reached an agreement with Troy. St. Joe has been a willing and trusted participant in the process and Officer Pinkham holds them to the letter of the Plan and their commitments. He is a senior officer with the Service and is given a measure of latitude on his enforcement duties. As his supervisor, I have had some concern about the disrespectful way he has been treating St. Joe, but beach mice are his responsibility and he takes it seriously."

"So, you do not think his actions have been out of line?" Agent Lindall asked.

"Oh, no, Troy is just intense. He is an outstanding officer."

The sheriff opened the door to the interrogation room abruptly. "Ladies, your ten minutes are up. I am hauling this scumbag in front of the judge in the morning. In the meantime, he is staying right here in my jail."

"Sheriff, it is too early for an arraignment. You do not have enough evidence to charge him with the crime," Agent Lindall said.

"You let me be the judge of that missy. The last time I checked, the FBI has no standing in this murder investigation."

"We should all be interested in the truth. The fire at Watercolor and the murder may somehow be linked—we should be investigating that connection," she noted.

"You go right ahead with your little investigation. I've got a murderer to prosecute," the sheriff said as he put the handcuffs back on Quinn and hauled him from the room.

Jan and Agent Lindall left the sheriff's office and discussed the case as they drove back to the Fish and Wildlife Service office. "Jan, how did Mr. Wilson sound to you? Was he answering the questions truthfully?"

"Yes, he was. In the two years I have known him, he has been honest and straightforward, just as he was today."

"Do you think he is capable of murder?"

"I do not know what to say! I deal in wildlife issues, not murder cases, but my gut instincts tell me he is not a murderer."

"Um, well, we'll see, won't we?"

At court the next morning, the judge agreed that there was enough evidence to hold Mr. Quinn Wilson as a suspect in the murder and agreed to release him on a one-million-dollar bond. The St. Joe Company promptly paid the bond and Quinn was free to go. The judge issued a stern warning. "Mr. Wilson, you are a suspect in the murder of George Mott. While you are released on bail, you will remain in Walton County. Any attempts to leave the county will result in a revocation of your bond and you will remain in jail pending your trial. Is that understood?"

"Judge, I am a resident of Pinellas County and request permission to return home to await trial. I have a family and employment responsibilities that need attention. I am not a flight risk."

"Request denied."

Brad Garner met Quinn at the door as he departed the courtroom. "I cannot believe this kangaroo court. There is a murderer running around out there and they are holding you as a suspect!"

"Thanks for the vote of confidence and bailing me out. Things have somehow gotten out of hand and I am not sure what to do about it all."

"Well, for starters, we will get you a place to stay at Seaside, until the inn is finished. I've called David Pardue and while he is not a criminal lawyer, he is a straight thinker. We will find the truth in this mess."

"Brad, have you talked with George's wife? I can only imagine what she is going through."

"Yes, I have spoken with her and offered what assistance I can. She believes the newspapers and thinks you are guilty."

"That hurts more than hearing the judge say it," Quinn said as they walked to the car.

Quinn rented a room at the Seaside Motor Court. It was an out-of-way motel tucked in back of the sprawling Seaside resort. Quinn preferred the motor court to the more conventional hotels in the area and often stayed there when he was in town. It was a takeoff of the first motor courts constructed in the 1920s when people first began touring by motor cars. It was a low one-story building with a single parking place directly at the front door of each room and a roofed patio between adjoining rooms. Each unit had a small sitting room, a compact kitchen, and bedroom. A small bathroom had been constructed as if it was added to the original structure. Pipes were exposed to add authenticity to the design. The end effect was an offbeat quaint accommodation that was a long way from the commercial hotel rooms of today. The motor court was behind the commercial buildings of Seaside and few people knew about them, so Quinn was happy to be alone with his thoughts and away from the prying questions of the sheriff and press.

CHAPTER 16

THE CALL HOME

It had been a busy day and it was time to call home and explain things to his wife. He stared at his cell phone before dialing, wondering how to break the news that he was being held for murder. After some thought he decided on the direct approach and dialed the home number.

"Hello, honey, how are you doing?"

"How do you think I am doing? You're all over the news and the reporters keep calling me to ask what it's like to be married to a murderer! Will you tell me what is going on?"

"George Mott was murdered this morning and I was arrested and am being held for his murder. It is all a mistake, of course, I didn't kill anyone."

"Then why are you being charged?"

"The sheriff thinks otherwise and he is calling the shots at the moment."

"Well, I don't have time for this right now. You know I have that operation later this week and I need you here."

"Nancy, I can't come. The court has released me on a one-million-dollar bond with the provision that I remain in Walton County. If I leave, St. Joe will lose their one million and the sheriff will put me in jail as a flight risk."

"Well, you just have to decide what is more important, me or your client."

"Nancy, they would put me in jail if I left the county right now and revoke the bond! I want to be there for you, but I just can't make it home."

"It is always this way, isn't it, Quinn. Your job always comes first. I'm lucky if I am even considered second place in your life."

"Nancy, this is very serious stuff. I'm sorry, but I just cannot leave."

"Well…I'm trying to understand. How could they possibly think you are a murderer?"

"It is all circumstantial! I'm up here to meet with George. I was in the vicinity of the crime scene about six hours before he was shot and I have no alibi for my whereabouts at 5:00 a.m. this morning. That is the sheriff's case."

"I guess I could have one of the neighbors take me to the hospital. It's just embarrassing to ask. They will all want to know what my husband is doing on the front page of the paper. What do I tell them?"

"Just tell them it is all a big misunderstanding and I will be home soon. I will call you in the morning…and again, I'm sorry."

"Okay, I just hope you haven't gotten yourself into real trouble this time. I'm not waiting 20 years for you to get out of prison, so take care of things on that end and come home to as soon as you can."

"I will. Good night and I love you."

The only replay was a click in his ear as she hung up the phone.

CHAPTER 17

FBI

It was late afternoon when he hung up the phone and sat staring into space for an indeterminate length of time when he heard someone checking into the adjoining room across the patio. He glanced at his watch and was surprised to note that it was 7:00 p.m. His stomach was starting to protest, even though he did not feel hungry, so he thought he would go to his favorite Bud & Alley's restaurant for a beer and something light to eat. As he stepped out of the front door, Agent Lindall emerged from the adjoining room.

"Agent Lindall, this is a surprise."

"Yes, I guess it is. Jan recommended this place as being out of the way and generally deserted," she said with another nervous toss of her head. "I was just going to get something to eat. Can you recommend a place?"

"I was just heading over to Bud Alley's Restaurant. They have good seafood."

"That sounds good. Can you show me the way?"

"Sure, we can walk over together. It is on the other side of the County Road. That is if you don't mind being seen with a murder suspect."

"Well, now that is an issue, isn't it? You can show me the way and I think that should be sufficient."

"Sure, just go around in front of Modica Market and stay on the sidewalk until you cross CR 30A. Bud & Alley's is just past the maze of commercial stalls on your right."

"Okay, thanks."

What followed was an awkward effort to avoid one another on the walk to the restaurant. Quinn stopped to window-shop at the retail shops as Agent Lindall passed him looking straight ahead. At the restaurant, they were seated two tables apart. Both ordered a beer as they both looked over the menu.

Agent Lindall took a deep breath and looked around a nearly empty restaurant. "This is ridiculous. Can I join you? I realize this violates law enforcement rules and protocol, but screw it, I'm off-duty. However, I do have to remind you that you are under investigation and anything you say can and will be used against you in court."

"Please have a seat. I understand and will be careful of what I say."

She settled into the seat across from him and stared at him intently, before returning to the menu. "Everything looks so good. I see that they have grouper as the entree on several of the dishes. Do they serve real grouper in this section of Florida? In New Orleans, it often means mystery fish. Oh, they also have mahi-mahi. I love seafood. Did you kill that man? The desserts look good too."

Quinn tried to mask his surprise at the line of questions. "Is this the new style of FBI interrogation techniques? You just reminded me that anything I said could be used against me, so is this the FBI agent asking this question?"

"No, this is the young lady, wondering what kind of a man is sitting across the table from her."

"Well, regardless of who is asking, the answer is no. I did not kill George Mott. He was a friend and colleague. I will miss him a great deal. Everyone liked George; he was one of the good guys."

"Okay, so you are not a murderer?"

She noticed a look of anguish pass briefly over his face.

"You are slow to respond to that basic question? Is there something you need to tell me?"

"Oh, sorry, I'm not use to being a murder suspect…I was a Marine captain during Desert Storm and led my company against one of the strongholds of the Republican Guard. There was intense fighting…I can remember too many men falling in front of my M-16. So sometimes…sometimes I wake up at night feeling like a murderer.

"That was war! It makes a big difference."

"Does it really?" Quinn said softly with a look of deep introspect that took Agent Lindall by surprise.

To change the subject, she returned to her menu. "I think I will have the broiled grouper with yellow rice and black beans," she said with another nervous toss of her head and what appeared to be a fleeting smile or at least a softening of the professional façade that had marked her appearance up to now.

"Ah…yes, the menu. I'm not too hungry, so I guess I'll order the shrimp salad and another beer. Are you up for another one?"

"Let's get another thing straight. It's bad enough that we are sitting together, but this is not a date. I'll do my ordering and there will be separate checks. Understood?"

"Yes, Agent Lindall. I am confused by some of the questions, but I fully understand our relationship."

"Good. Waiter, can we have another round of beers?" she ordered as she emptied her bottle with gusto.

Quinn was cautious to maintain the awkward relationship between a suspect and law enforcement agent during dinner. Agent Lindall was less professional, as her questions varied from personal to an abrupt interrogation style. Quinn remained uneasy and wondered if she was inexperienced or highly clever with her far-ranging questions. She was particularly interested in the WaterColor project and the work done with the Fish and Wildlife Service on the beach mice. Despite her earlier comments, the dinner was feeling like a date.

"I can't believe you're putting so much effort into protecting mice. How much value did you say St. Joe placed on the beach mice habitat?"

"The coastal dunes were valued at $85 million and the developed value would have been much higher."

"Whoa, that is an amazing commitment for a mouse!"

"How long have you been with the FBI?" he asked as she finished off her third beer and ordered a fourth.

"I've been with the Agency for 18, no 20, months now. This is my first field assignment. Up until now, they have kept me locked in the office going over accounting ledgers and acting as a secretary. They figured that the fire at WaterColor was a good chance to get me in the field. The fire was probably accidental, so they did not want to waste a senior agent's time. I'm a graduate of Louisiana State with a degree in economics. I bummed around for a few years working at one accounting firm or another. While at Price Waterhouse, I became intrigued with an FBI investigation on one of our clients. One thing led to another and I ended up accepting a job with the Bureau."

"It seems the environmental issues and murder investigations are a long way from accounting. Are you comfortable with the facts you have heard so far? There is some connection between these events. I just have not been able to put them together."

"I need to remind you that you are a suspect. It is up to us trained professionals in law enforcement to figure it out."

"Thanks for that perspective. I think the Endangered Species Act and the Habitat Conservation Plan have something to do with the series of events. I know those issues and maybe can help you understand the connection."

"Murder is always about sex, drugs or money. I can't see how your Habitat Plan plays a role in any of the three."

"Money...uhm?"

On the way back to the motel, Agent Lindall was much less standoffish. "Oh, God, I drank too much," she said as she wrapped her hands around Quinn's arm. "Can you get me back to my room and don't tell anyone you saw me like this?"

"Anything you say, Agent Lindall."

"You can call me AJ while I am off-duty. My name is Alice Jasmine, after my grandmother and great aunt and I do not feel like an Alice or a Jasmine. Both sound so old-fashioned, so AJ works for me. That sounds modern and hip don't you think?"

"Okay, AJ, it is and, yes, that does sound professional."

"Back on the patio between the two rooms, AJ was slow on releasing Quinn's arm. "My woman's intuition 'tells' me that you are not guilty of murder or anything else for that matter." She punched him in the chest with her forefinger and said, "I'm really going to be mad if you prove me wrong. You got that?"

"I got it and thanks for the vote of confidence."

Sleep came slowly as Quinn mulled over the events of the day. Being charged with murder was not something to be taken lightly. As was his custom, he drifted awake at 5:00 a.m., splashed water on his face and pulled on his running shorts and shoes for a jog before breakfast. He stepped out of his room, just as Agent Lindall came out of hers. "Where are you going?" she asked.

"I was going for a run. I go every morning when I can."

"So do I. I don't know the area, so I am going to shadow you. How many miles do you run?"

"Oh, I usually run for half an hour, so it is somewhere between 5K and 5 miles."

"Perfect. Let's go."

They ran in silence for the first part of the trip, down the internal streets of Seaside and out the back pedestrian gate onto the nature trails around Western Lake in WaterColor. She ran with the long, casual stride of a trained athlete. Quinn could hear her measured breathing behind him and wondered if his pace was too fast or slow. About 2K into the run, something seemed wrong and Quinn slowed to a walk and sniffed the air.

"What is it?" AJ asked.

"I smell smoke and it does not appear to be a woods fire. The odor is different." Then through a clearing in the trees, he could see a faint glow of orange across Western Lake. He immediate reached for his cell phone and dialed 911. "Hello, this is Quinn Wilson, calling from WaterColor north of Seaside, there is a fire in the new residential area just west of CR 395. Can you dispatch a fire truck to the area? Thank you and, yes, I will be available at this number." He disconnected the call and looked at AJ.

"We have got to get into that area. Do you know the way?" she asked.

"Yes, follow me," he said as he ran towards one of the conservation trails around the lake. The pace was faster now and he could hear AJ breathing hard close behind him. A mile further, they emerged from the trail in back of the new subdivision. Across the street, one of the newly framed houses was now fully enveloped in flames. AJ stepped forward and drew her weapon that she carried beneath her sweatshirt.

"You wait for the fire truck," she said as she moved toward the fire.

Quinn continued to run towards 395 and within a few minutes, directed the fire truck into the subdivision. A sheriff's patrol car was not far behind. Quinn followed the vehicles to the fire and joined AJ near the fire truck.

"We will have to wait for the fire investigation report, but this looks like arson to me. I think this is definitely environmental terrorism. Someone is in for a big surprise when we enforce the new Homeland Security Act and send them to Guantanamo Bay. Do me a favor. Don't tell the sheriff that we were together this morning. I want to see how he responds. Okay?" She said as she returned the gun to her holster.

The firemen seemed to be moving in slow motion as they connected to the new fire hydrant and began fighting the fire. In the meantime, two more patrol cars arrived and then the sheriff himself arrived in his big Suburban with sirens blaring. He stepped out of the patrol car, took his time putting on his Stetson hat and hitched up his pants as he watched the firemen fight the fire.

Quinn thought he would take the direct approach and talk to the sheriff. The sheriff's response was anything but cordial. Quinn found himself handcuffed and seated in the back of the patrol car, while the sheriff took his time watching the fire before returning to the car to question him.

Agent Lindall had watched the sheriff's actions with interest while she talked to the fire chief and investigated the site. She was not surprised to see a Fish and Wildlife Service truck pull into the area and park near the sheriff's patrol car. She could see the starched uniform from a distance and knew immediately that it was Officer Pinkham.

Troy had slept little the night before. He was increasingly worried that Cal would figure out who was responsible for George's death and he would be implicated. If so, their well-planned scheme could blow up in his face and Cal would make sure he was responsible. He heard the call coming from the fire truck over his police scanner and had sat thinking about it before realizing that he could use it as another diversion to lead the sheriff in the wrong direction and away from his and Cal's plans.

Troy glanced at the sheriff's car and noted with satisfaction that Quinn was seated in the back seat. *Oh, this is even better than I hoped,* he thought. He walked over to the sheriff and asked, "You caught the bastard red-handed?"

"Well, not red-handed, but it is very suspicious to find him here. How are you reading the situation?"

"I think this is a diversionary tactic to confuse the investigation and make us think that there are other suspects. It's an act of desperation, if you ask me, but we are just too smart to fall for it."

"Yeah, that is the way I see it too," the sheriff responded as he headed back to interrogate the prisoner.

"Now, I may be just a country sheriff," he started after making an elaborate display of calling in his location to the dispatcher and organizing his notepad, "but I think it is very suspicious to find a murder suspect standing at a crime scene at 5:30 a.m. in the morning. I am going to haul your ass in and charge you with arson. By the time I'm finished, you will be spending the rest of your life in an eight by ten cell. Now do you want to tell me what this is all about, pretty boy?"

"Sheriff, I was out running this morning and smelled smoke and saw the fire in the distance. I called 911 at about 5:15 and directed the fire truck to the fire. That is about all I can tell you."

"Do I look stupid to you, son? That is the same lame running alibi you used on the murder investigation and you saw how far that got you. I would think a man of your intelligence could think up a better story without any trouble. So impress me, boy. What were you doing this morning and who can verify the story?"

"I'm afraid I do not have any further information, sheriff. As I said, I was out running and saw the glow in the sky. When I investigated, I found the house on fire."

"Suit yourself. We are just going to take a little ride into DeFuniak Springs to give you time to think about telling me the truth."

Agent Lindall watched them go and thought she noted a fist pump from Officer Pinkham as he headed back to his truck. *That is interesting*, she thought.

Quinn spent another four hours in the interrogation room

before the sheriff returned to continue the questioning. "Have you had time to think it over, son?"

"I've told you what I know, sheriff. I was on an early morning run, saw the fire and called 911."

"I find it very suspicious that you traveled all the way over to Seaside to shack up in that dilapidated motor court after your release. I suspect you wanted to be close by the crime scene to cause a diversion in our investigation—isn't that right?"

"No, sheriff, I often stay at Seaside when I'm in the area. The motor court is a change from the typical motel rooms, plus it's close to WaterColor and the St. Joe administrative offices."

"Can anyone vouch for your whereabouts around 5:00 a.m. this morning?"

"Well…I think…"

There was a knock on the door before Quinn could answer.

"Damn it!" The sheriff grunted as he rose to open the door. "You again? Let me remind you, when this door is closed…"

Agent Lindall strode into the room with her long gait and stood eye-to-eye with the sheriff. "No, let me remind you sheriff, I am in charge of the FBI investigation into the terrorism at WaterColor. You will not interrogate this or any other suspect without my presence. Furthermore, I want this suspect released. I was on the trail this morning and can vouch for his actions from 5:00 a.m. until you placed him in the patrol car." She took another step closer to the sheriff to make her next point and caused him to back step. "You will not make any further arrests on this case without coordinating with me. This is a federal case, sheriff, do you understand?"

The sheriff was beat red in the face and huffing before he could bring himself to respond. "I'll be God damn if a f…ing little girl is going to order me around in my own office…shit!" was his parting shot as he grabbed his hat and blundered noisily through the door.

AJ watched him go and turned to Quinn, "Oh, that felt so good. He is such a self-righteous bastard! I am sorry it took me so long to get here, but I have been watching things from afar and have gained some new insight into this case. One confirms my female intuition that you are not a murderer. Another suggests that this case is much more complicated than I had imagined. We can talk more on the way back to Seaside."

"You are the only one in law enforcement who thinks I am innocent of murder. Do you know who the shooter is?"

"No, not yet, but I have some ideas. Let's get out of here."

The sheriff was nowhere to be seen as they left the interrogation room and Quinn picked up his battered cell phone and meager belongings from the clerk's desk. Agent Lindall's staff car was parked out front.

"So what makes you so sure I am not the murderer?" he asked as they turned south on State Road 331 and headed back to the Emerald Coast and Seaside.

"I searched your room this morning."

"You searched my room? Weren't you supposed to have a warrant to do that?"

"You gave me permission to search."

"I did? When was that?"

"Well, technically, you are about to give me permission—but you will."

"I...Okay, I have nothing to hide, so yes, you have permission to search my room."

"I knew that."

"You just knew that! What did you find that was so convincing?"

"Oh, I think it was your correspondence files on your laptop."

"You went through my computer files?"

"I told you I searched your room. You left your computer on and I am an expert on computers. I found your email messages to George. It was obvious that you two were close friends. You talked so earnestly about the mice and your conservation efforts. I was impressed. Officer Pinkham's messages, on the other hand, were inflammatory—even caustic. Yet your responses were very even-toned and conciliatory. I don't see how you did it. Hell, he made me mad just reading them."

"So, let me get this straight. Last night your women's intuition convinced you that I was innocent. So this morning, you break into my room and read my computer files, just to prove that your instincts were correct?"

"Hey, I was looking for leads, okay!"

"I suspect your woman's intuition is working in overdrive. It's going to get you in trouble one day."

"You have no idea how powerful women's intuition can be. And besides, you men are open books to us and so easy to read."

CHAPTER 18

THE FUNERAL

George's funeral was held two days later at 2:00 p.m. that afternoon. It was a somber affair and well-attended. Quinn did not feel welcome, since he was considered the prime suspect. However, out of respect to George, he attended, but arrived after everyone was seated and stayed at the back of the church. He noticed that Troy Pinkham attended in his full Fish and Wildlife Service dress uniform. He sat in back of the family and Quinn was surprised to see that he was very attentive to George's widow and his parents. He also offered one of the eulogies and choked up when he described his and George's friendship. Quinn was perplexed by his sincerity, especially after the two had almost come to blows over Troy's disrespect at the last meeting. To avoid a scene, Quinn slipped out of the church and sat in his rental car at the back of the parking lot as the procession departed for the cemetery.

CHAPTER 19

BLUE FUNK

The sheriff had everyone in the department on edge before he left for the day at his usual 7:00 p.m. They could feel the blue funk through the closed door of his office and see it in his red face as he stalked the halls. No, this was not the time to approach him unless it was an issue of dire public safety. "A damn skinny girl, not much older than a high school kid, ordering me around in my office," he would repeat to himself, with a various series of adjectives, while he sat at his desk.

He was still in that mood when he left the office and drove the 12 miles north to his ranch on the outskirts of DeFuniak Springs. The ranch had been in the family almost sixty years now. He had grown up there while his dad attempted to make a living raising cattle. He lived alone and leased out the pasture to local ranchers to supplement his sheriff's salary. They paid a premium rental fee for the land in the hopes of staying on the sheriff's good side.

He did not bother to change clothes when he got home. In fact, his closet was lined with neatly starched uniforms and little else. He grabbed three beers from the refrigerator and sat down in his favorite chair next to the police scanner. Two beers were gone before the first call came in over the radio. It was a traffic stop in Destin with a drunk college coed in the backseat. "Nothing the deputy can't handle," he thought as he twisted the cap from his third beer.

CHAPTER 20,

SEA TURTLES

Quinn and AJ had just gotten back to the motor court and were standing in the patio between the rooms when Quinn's cell phone rang.

"Hello, this is Quinn."

"Quinn, this is Clara Fullerton."

"Clara, it's good to hear from you."

"I saw you at the funeral today, but you got away before I could talk to you. I am so upset about George and you being arrested! Has the world gone crazy?"

"Yes, I believe it has. I am doing what I can to get it back to normal."

"The reason I called was to see if you were interested in going with me on the turtle patrol tomorrow morning. I am nervous about having a murderer running loose on the beach and would like to have some company."

"Clara, you know that I am a suspect in the shooting?"

"Oh, that is just the sheriff barking up the wrong tree like he usually does. Anyone who knows you does not think you are a murderer. I would really like you to come tomorrow, if you can."

"Thanks for the vote of confidence. I would love to come. Do we meet at your place in Grayton Beach?"

"Yes, at the usual place on the beach. Say about 4:30 a.m.?"

"Great I'll be there. Oh, also Clara, can I bring one additional passenger?"

"The ATV can carry two people so bring them along. And thanks for coming, Quinn. I said I was nervous, because I did not want to admit I was scared to be out there alone. I thought about skipping a few days, but we are just starting to see the turtles coming ashore this spring and I don't want to miss a nest."

"You don't have to thank me. I'm looking forward to it. See you tomorrow morning."

Quinn disconnected the call and found AJ looking at him intensely with her arms folded across her chest. "Who is Clara?" she asked.

"Clara Fullerton is our local sea turtle watch coordinator. She called to ask me to go with her tomorrow morning. Basically, she drives the beach and looks for turtle crawls and records nesting activities. Would you be interested in going? We start at 4:30 and should be back to Grayton Beach by 9:00 or 9:30."

"Hell, yes, I want to go! I was hoping I was the passenger you mentioned. That sounds like a blast. You environmental types get to do some cool stuff. So where do you want to go to eat tonight, so you can tell me more?"

Once again Quinn was taken aback by her response. She seemed to move rapidly from being an FBI agent to a hip out-of-control teenager and he was having trouble keeping up with the swing between the two personalities. Was this some kind of a female Colombo act?

At dinner it was his turn to study the individual sitting across the table from him. Her height was the most obvious feature. She was probably 140 pounds and at least six feet tall, maybe taller. Because of her height, her arms and legs seem to be disproportionately long. She walked with a long stride that made it difficult to keep up with her on the few times they had walked together. As with her hands, her feet appeared to be large and she wore flats that looked anything but female, in a size 10 or larger. She almost always dressed in black slacks and jacket. Quinn had noticed several times that the jacket covered a small automatic handgun and a clip case that she wore in the small of her back. She carried an oversized purse slung casually over her shoulder and from it came what seemed to be an unending array of gadgets, including two cell phones, an iPad, flashlight, Garmin GPS, and a FBI badge and identification, plus the ever-present hairbrush and an assortment of barrettes. Her hair always seemed to be on the verge of being out-of-control and she would often brush and pin it back in what seemed to be more habit than necessity. Then she would toss her hair over her shoulder with a rapid flip of her head, a movement that suggested that she kept a nervous energy barely under control. She wore no makeup and those who appreciated beauty would not find her attractive, but she wasn't bad looking either.

There was one other personal trait. She liked beer. She finished her first in a few gulps and ordered another before the waitress left the table to get water.

As he casually surveyed her with glances while looking over the menu, he became aware of a steady stare from her side of the table. "What?" he asked acknowledging her stare.

Tell me about Clara. How well do you know her?"

"Clara? I have known her for probably two or three years now—ever since she took over the sea turtle watch. She is a volunteer, but knows sea turtles better than some of the biologists I know."

"Is she attractive?"

"Attractive? Why would you...well, yes, Clara is an attractive lady in her early sixties. She has white hair and weighs probably 200 pounds. She is a retired school principal from Ohio, I think. But, as you will see tomorrow, she is full of energy and excited about sea turtles."

"So, tell me about tomorrow and what we are going to be doing."

"We will meet up with Clara and drive the 25 miles of beach on the ATVs looking for turtle crawls and nesting sites. If we find one, we will take pictures, record the location and species of turtle, if observed. We will be driving past the WaterSound project where Clara found George a few days ago. Other sections of beach are developed and we will be driving on the recreational beaches adjacent to hotels and condos."

"Are there a lot of turtles out there?"

"We may get from 20 up to 25 nests along this section of coast during the spring nesting season. There are five species of turtles in the Gulf and they return to the same section of beach to deposit their eggs."

"Five species?"

"Yes, there are loggerheads, they are the biggest, hawksbill, green, Kemps ridley, and leatherbacks. All the species range widely throughout the Gulf of Mexico, Atlantic and Caribbean Sea. Scientists who specialize in sea turtles continue to be amazed at their ability to navigate long distances and return to the beaches of their birth to deposit the next generation of eggs."

"I heard you and Jan talking about 'turtle lighting'—what does that mean?"

"When the turtles are coming ashore they will avoid areas that are brightly lit. So, over the years, a low-level turtle lighting program was developed that removes direct light from the beach and avoids the glow in the sky that would discourage the turtles from coming ashore. Also, baby sea turtles can become disoriented in brightly lit areas. Apparently, their first instinct after being born is to head for the sea. If the lighting confuses them, they could crawl away from the water and die from dehydration. The turtle lighting packages on new construction work pretty well. It's the old development with bright lights still visible to the open beach that are problems. When we finish dinner, we can walk out on the beach and I will show you what turtle lighting looks like."

"You all are very serious about these endangered species. I had no idea there was so much effort and money being spent to protect them."

"We are very serious. Brad Garner has a strong policy in place about protecting the resources and cooperation with the resource agencies."

"Yes, I saw the correspondence between you two. He seems sincere."

"You said earlier that murder is always about sex, drugs, or money. I think we can eliminate the sex and drugs, so where does the money trail take us."

"Well, I'm not ready to give up on the sex angle yet. This is my first case in the field and I was hoping for a little excitement."

"Uh…we were talking about money?"

"Oh yes, money! Despite what the sheriff said, I seriously doubt you are stealing from St. Joe."

"That was a shock. I wonder where he got that idea?"

"I think it was from your good friend, Troy Pinkham."

"Troy? Where would he get that idea? He has no insight into our contract with St. Joe."

"Tell me how your contract works."

"We have a master contract in place with St. Joe. Under that contract, we submit task orders for their approval. The orders include a scope of service and a budget. With a signed task order, we conduct the work and invoice monthly. We have done all the environmental permitting and civil engineering under this contact process."

"So, you never go over budget?"

"I did not say that. There are often new tasks that surface or unforeseen obstacles that are not covered by the task orders. In those cases, we talk to the client and create an amendment."

"Give me an example of an 'unforeseen obstacle,' that may come up."

"Troy's issue with the lighting package on the WaterColor Inn is a recent example. Our scope could not have anticipated that the standard agreed-upon turtle lighting package would be rejected and have to be redone. Based on our agreement with St. Joe, we conducted this new design work on a time and materials basis."

"Time and materials, means your multiplied labor costs and expenses right?"

"Right, I forgot that you were an accountant."

"I understand what you are saying, but I think that you would be in jeopardy if this went to court."

"How so?"

"The opposing attorney would make a big deal of the fact that the task order says you will do it for this amount, but you billed this much more. They would say it is black and white. You are stealing."

"What I described was the standard operating contract between a client and an engineering consultant. Everyone operates the same way."

"I know…I know! I'm just telling you what an opposing attorney would say to make you look sleazy. And he might succeed in the eyes of the jury. Then you would be screwed."

Quinn rubbed his chin in thought, "I think I need another beer."

"Oh, yeah! Waitress, can we have another round of LandSharks and two checks please? Let's go out on the beach and you can show me the turtle lights," she said.

"Okay. Are you sure you won't let me pick up the check?"

"Hey, mister, are you trying to bribe a federal officer?"

"I was just asking."

They took the last two LandSharks and walked out of Bud & Alley's and down the long corridor of empty commercial stalls to the Seaside pavilion. From the elevated platform, they could see the coastal beaches for many miles in both directions.

"Oh, this is beautiful."

"Way to the east, you can see Panama City Beach. Those high rises are beach condominiums with the lights of the city in back of them. You can see the glow in the sky from the urbanized areas. Now look to the west toward WaterColor. Notice the few lights that are visible? They are a lot lower candlepower and there is no glow in the sky. Now let's go down on the beach and look back towards Seaside."

"It is so dark! I can't see the stairs. Hold my hand. This is so romantic! Have you ever brought your wife here?"

"No I haven't. She does not like to travel with me while I'm working. She claims I ignore her too much."

They reached the bottom of the stairs and walked straight towards the sound of a moderate surf rolling onto the beach. "Okay, turn around. Seaside was built before turtle lighting became required, but many of the private owners have not toned down the exterior lighting on their residents. You can see the effect here on the beach. Even though some lights are not visible from where we stand, you can see the glow in the sky from the beach. WaterColor will have much fewer visible lights than you are seeing here in Seaside and no glow in the sky."

Quinn turned back towards the Gulf. "Right now I am willing to bet there are sea turtles cruising offshore looking for their section of beach. Too much light and they stay out there. If we do not manage our coastal environment, the turtles will lose nesting habitat and their numbers will continue to diminish until they blink-out."

"Blink-out? That is an odd term."

"That is a term we environmentalists use to describe the end of the line. When the last of a species dies, they are said to have blinked out and become forever extinct. No biologist wants to witness a blink-out, especially if it is a species under your care."

"How sad! It seems to carry a lot more weight standing here in the dark listening to you talk about the sea turtles. I understand more now. You have described a passion that is strong enough to kill for. All I have to do is figure out who gains and why. Now take my hand and get me back into the light where I can see my feet."

Quinn knocked on AJ's door at 4:00 a.m. the next morning. The shades were drawn and he could see no light from inside. A moment later, the door opened and AJ walked out onto the patio. She wore blue jeans and a sweatshirt under her FBI jacket. Her hair was rolled up into a bun and covered with a New York Yankee baseball cap.

"You didn't think I was going to sleep in and miss this trip, did you? Let's get going. How far is Grayton Beach from here?"

"It's only five minutes west of here. I'll drive. I'm sure the chamber of commerce would appreciate not having an FBI car parked on their beach."

"You're the boss."

"I am?"

"Just a figure of speech—you're still a suspect and I'm the cop, so don't forget it," she said flippantly.

"Here, I brought a couple of energy bars for breakfast. I'm hoping Clara has a pot of coffee brewing. I could use a cup. It's going to be chilly for the first couple of hours."

Grayton Beach is an old beach village located on the west side of Western Lake and adjoining the state park that bears the same name. The cluster of old-style beach homes were clapboard bungalows with screened-in front porches and picketed fences. All the roads within the village were narrow and many were unpaved, giving the village a quaint look, as if time had passed it by. At the center of the village was a small commercial area that included the Red Barn Restaurant and a real estate office that mostly handled the beach house rentals. A few of the homes closer to the beach had been built under the new federal emergency management flood elevation requirements. These houses were built 15 feet off the ground and soared above that base elevation up two or three stories, giving this section of the village an austere vulnerable look of homes that were in the path of danger.

Clara and her husband owned a bungalow near the center of the village. Quinn drove by the house and noticed a light in the back. He continued for another block to the unofficial beach parking area, for those individuals who were not part of the community. Quinn turned off the car and felt the early morning chill seeping through the door. He and AJ sat in silence for a few minutes as she munched slowly on her energy bar.

"We have a quarter moon this morning. From where it is in the sky, it probably rose shortly after we turned in last night. That will give us some light for the trip. I think it is about 52 degrees this morning," he said passively as he checked the weather conditions of the day.

"Are you ready?" He asked as AJ finished her energy bar.

"Yes, I'm not fully awake, but I'm ready," she replied. "Find me a cup of coffee"

They walked the short block back to Clara's house in silence and knocked softly on the front door. Clara's husband greeted them with a friendly smile and waved them into the small living room. The smell of coffee brewing wafted in from the kitchen. "Clara's in the kitchen. Can I get you both a cup of coffee?"

"Yes, we would love to have a cup." They responded almost in unison. Clara appeared in the doorway wiping her hands with a dish towel and crossed the room to give Quinn a hug. "Good morning, Quinn. So glad you could join me this morning."

"The pleasure is all mine, Clara. I'd like to introduce you to Agent Alice Lindall, from the Pensacola FBI office, and she will be our third crew member this morning."

"The FBI? I was hoping for a little protection this morning, but I was not expecting the FBI," Clara said as she extended her hand to AJ and then gave her a hug instead. "It's nice to meet you agent…?"

"It's nice to meet you, as well. Just call me AJ. I'm not really here on official duty. It's just that the FBI jacket was the only one I had for field work."

"Either way, it's nice to have you along. Let's have some coffee and get underway. I have a feeling this morning that the turtles are on the beach waiting for us."

CHAPTER 21

THE ARRANGEMENT

When Virginia Stratford decided to return to Detroit for the summer, she was concerned about her responsibility to Officer Pinkham and the stray cat program they had developed. She had enlisted the help of some ladies in Seaside who loved cats, but there was no one dedicated enough to make the morning trips to WaterSound to put out the food and water for the cats that roamed the isolated dunes. She just could not leave until they were taken care of properly.

She had noticed the environmental groups that had been collecting in the WaterColor project and asked Troy about them after one of their late afternoon liaisons. "They are environmental watchdog groups that keep an eye on unscrupulous developers. When they heard that the environment is in danger at WaterColor, they came to do what they could to protect the fauna and flora. If the situation is bad enough, they file suits to stop development."

"Oh, that is so reassuring to know. It is nice to have such dedicated people around watching after the environment," she replied.

The next day she approached the platoon of environmental storm troopers as they made a show of marching in front of the WaterColor administration building. "Excuse me!" she shouted from the sidewalk. "Can you help me?"

"Platoon, halt," shouted the leader. "Can we help you?"

"Yes, I am looking for some help caring for the stray cats. Is that something you'll do?"

"Lady, if it involves the protection of the environment we are available. What do you need us to do?"

"I am going back to Detroit tomorrow and I would like to have someone go out on the dunes every other day and leave food and water for my cats. It would have to be done in the morning before daylight, so the cats are well fed for the day. I'm going out tomorrow morning and can train someone, if they are available."

"Eugene, this looks like a perfect opportunity for you. Take care of it! Stay here and get the details, while we finish the training exercise. Good day, ma'am."

Eugene stepped out of line and stood still, watching the platoon march away.

"Your name is Eugene?"

"Yes, ma'am, Eugene Siedmann at your service."

"It's nice to meet you. My name is Virginia. Do you have a vehicle?"

"Yes, ma'am, I have the best pickup truck anybody has seen in these parts."

"Oh, well...good. Can you meet me in front of Modica Market at 5:00 a.m. tomorrow morning? I will show you what needs to be done."

"Yes, ma'am, 5:00 a.m. I will be there. Are there bears in the woods where we are going?"

"I don't know, but I carry my gun just in case. Bring one, if you have it."

"I will. See you tomorrow morning at 5:00 a.m."

That evening Eugene and the rest of his platoon sat around the fire enjoying some rather good weed they had scored from one of the construction workers. He was very mellow when he finally turned in for the evening. He set two travel alarms his mother had given him to make sure he woke up on time. He knew his mind was not going to be totally clear until tomorrow, but it did not matter. *How sharp do you need to be to feed cats?* he thought as he turned in.

CHAPTER 22

TURTLE CRAWL

They fired up the ATVs and headed down to the beach. Clara followed a well-established route through the deeper sand along the edge of the dunes to the rack line on the beach where the sand was wet and compact from the surf. There she turned east and accelerated to around 15 mph. AJ cuddled up close behind Quinn and put her chin on his shoulder. She slid her hands into the pockets on his jacket and settled in for the ride.

"This is so cool," she said only inches from his ear. "What are we looking for?"

"Turtle crawls, where they leave the water and make their way to the edge of the beach. You can't miss them."

"It's so beautiful out here! I have never seen so many stars in my life."

"That hazy area above us is not a cloud—it is the Milky Way with billions of stars. It's the first celestial body to disappear when you get near the lights of the city," Quinn said in his best professorial voice.

"I can see why Clara does this. It feels like we have the world to ourselves," AJ said as she took a deep breath of fresh salt air.

"You have to hand it to Clara. She is out here every morning during nesting season. Rain or shine. During some of the tropical depressions in late summer, conditions can be pretty bad. She is tough."

They rode in silence for a while, until Clara slowed to a stop and turned her lights off. Quinn pulled up behind her and fumbled for the light switch. Silence surrounded them as he turned off the engine and seemed to demand they speak in whispers. "What is it, Clara?"

"We have a fresh crawl about ten yards ahead. Let's walk up. Keep it quiet."

AJ almost leaped off the ATV in her excitement. "My heart is beating so fast, I'm so excited," she whispered with girlish enthusiasm. They walked the ten yards up the beach and found a crawl trail that appeared to be made by a moderate-sized turtle. Probably a green turtle, Clara mused half to herself as they followed the trail towards the dunes. "There is no return crawl yet, so the mom is still on the nest. Don't make any fast moves to distract her."

Up ahead, near the base of the dunes, they could hear the dull thud of flippers beating the sand and the exhale of breath from the laboring turtle. As their eyes became accustomed to the dark, the image of the turtle began to emerge. AJ grasped Quinn's arm as she leaned forward and strained to make out the details. As she did, the turtle finished her work covering the nest and began moving awkwardly back towards the surf line.

"Oh, my gosh! That is the biggest turtle I have ever seen," AJ gushed in a high-pitched whisper.

The turtle stopped when she got abreast of the team and cast a look in their direction, as if judging their threat to her nest. Having satisfied her curiosity, she continued on towards the surf. She had fulfilled her obligation to the next generation and would provide no further assistance to her offspring. As she disappeared into the surf, Clara got busy. She examined and photographed the nest and recorded the GPS coordinates. "It was definitely a green turtle. We only get a couple of their nests per season and this is the first one this year. I'm excited," she said in the casual tone of an experienced turtle watcher. "Let's keep moving. I'll come back to this nest later today and put some hog wire over it to keep the predators from digging up the eggs."

The night was again filled with the sound of internal combustion engines, as they fired up the ATVs and continued east on the beach. AJ again cuddled close to Quinn and shivered a little as she tried to warm her hands in the pockets of his jacket. They drove for another 15 minutes when Quinn spoke.

"We will be at our WaterSound beach mice preserve shortly, so we will be driving along the 1.5 miles of beach that George and I survey every quarter. Also, I guess you would call it the crime scene, since Clara found George's body at our staging area."

"I definitely want to see that area. Point it out to me when we get close," AJ asked.

Clara slowed again and came to a stop. Quinn idled up alongside of her and could see the turtle crawl up ahead. "Two in one night, that is a good sign."

"Yes, it is. This one has already returned to the water so leave your lights on the ATV and turned towards the dunes so we can see the nest."

Quinn swung the ATV up the beach and scanned the dunes until he saw the area of disturbance. He left the vehicle on and he and AJ joined Clara, who was surveying the crawl.

"It looks like a small loggerhead to me. They're not as heavy and move faster than the green turtle we was earlier. Let me get a GPS reading on the nest and then we'll keep moving."

"Clara, are you sure this is a nest or just a false crawl?"

"What makes you think it's an aborted nest?"

"Take a look at the nest area. It does not look like she dug very deep. Do you think something could have scared her off?"

"Each species digs a little differently. There is only one way to tell if it is an active nest and that is to dig down to the eggs. Are you up for that?"

"Sure, let's do it." Quinn said, as he and AJ dropped to their knees and began moving the soft sand with their hands. "How deep do you think they are buried, Clara?"

"Usually they are about 15 to 18 inches, depending on the species and size of the mother. You are almost there."

"Okay, I found an egg," AJ said.

"Stop right there. That is all the proof we need. Cover them back up and let's get moving. We still have a long way to go," Clara replied.

They covered the next few miles of the beach without noticing a crawl. Quinn pointed out the property line and areas he and George regularly monitored. Once again Clara slowed to a stop and immediately turned her headlights out. "There is a really big crawl up ahead and I think she is still on the nest," she whispered. All three walked in silence up to the crawlway.

"Oh, my gosh! It looks like the trail was made by some prehistoric creature. It has got to be twice as wide as the first one we saw and that was the biggest turtle I had ever seen," AJ whispered with excitement.

"It is big! Let's follow it to the nest," Clara said as she walked purposefully towards the dunes.

It was a loggerhead and a large one. "That is one of the biggest ones I have seen in my years of patrolling the beach. It has got to be 200 or 300 pounds," Clara said with a trace of surprise in her voice. "But look, there's a cat setting on her back, and there is another one eating something over there!"

Both Quinn and AJ move a little closer and saw that Clara was right. There were two feral cats hanging around the nest eating the eggs.

"Oh, this can't be happening," Clara said. "George told me that he was seeing a lot of cats on site. But these are eating the eggs as the mother lays them. I can't take it!" She rushed the nest and swatted the cat off the back of the loggerhead and then kicked it as it attempted to run away.

Immediately there was a popping sound from the adjacent

dunes followed by a hissing sound of something hitting the sand. Clara winced and fell to the ground in front of her ATV. AJ was surprised by the noise and stood looking at the dunes wondering what had happened. However, Quinn had been there before and knew that they were under fire.

"Get behind the ATVs," he yelled, "someone is shooting at us." He helped Clara get behind the ATV as he tried to assess the threat. *That was a small caliber handgun, probably a 9 millimeters and not very accurate at over 10 meters,* he thought as he used his previous military experience to gauge the threat.

The first shots were followed by another volley. These were louder and kicked up a six-foot plume of sand when it hit the beach. "There are two shooters, the second with a larger caliber, something like a .45 or .357," Quinn whispered as he took cover next to AJ. "Not much more accurate at this distance, but deadlier if someone takes a bullet." He became aware that AJ was cowering next to him behind the ATV and screaming something unintelligible.

"AJ, are you okay?"

"No, I am not okay, someone is shooting at us!"

"Clara, are you okay?"

"I…I think I have been hit in the shoulder. It felt like a bee sting and now it is bleeding pretty badly. Help me, Quinn!"

"AJ, you are going to have to return fire!"

"What…I can't…someone is shooting at us. I'm only an accountant. I've never been shot at before. I don't know what to do!"

More shots rang out. These were more accurate than the first and Quinn knew that the shooter was adjusting his aim. The last one hit the left fender of Clara's ATV. He knew they would be sitting ducks unless they could put some pressure on the shooter.

"Give me your gun!"

A sixth shot hit the rear tire of their ATV as Quinn checked AJ's field weapon. It was a light .25 MM with a nine-shot clip and one backup, 18 shots total. *Not much of an assault weapon*, he thought as he levered a round into the chamber and took the safety off the gun. *It will have to do,* he thought as he looked over at AJ. She was on all fours next to the ATV. Quinn raised the weapon and zeroed in on the area that he thought the gunfire was coming from and fired three shots. He immediately left the cover of the ATV and charged the target area. Running in a low crouch, he fired three additional shots as he ran.

Eugene had been standing at the edge of a dune with Virginia when they had seen the lights coming down the beach from the west. At Virginia's behest, they had walked closer to the beach and remained hidden by the dunes to watch the vehicles pass. In the light of the quarter moon, they could see the two ATVs come to a stop and three figures walk toward the dunes where she and Eugene were hiding. They were close enough for her to overhear the comments about the sea turtle and stray cats. She was incensed when she saw the shadowy figure try to kick one of the cats. She drew her gun and before she could even think, she had fired three rounds at the shadows on the beach.

Eugene was caught off-guard and since he was still high on the marijuana from last night, he had not made the mental observation that these were people on the beach. Therefore he followed suit, drew his trusty .44 magnum and began firing as if he was at the firing range. With each shot, he zeroed in on the target and was pleased with himself when he heard the clang of a bullet striking metal. "Good shot," he thought in an abstract manner as he took better aim for the next round.

He saw the muzzle flashes and felt more than saw the shots impacting the sand around him. He lost his balance at the shock and fell backward onto the sand. As he fell, he caught sight of a figure running towards him firing more shots as he ran. *Oh, my God, they are shooting at me,* he thought as he scrambled to his feet and started to run towards his truck. In the distance, he could see Virginia's Buick pulling onto the highway. She had started to run after the recoil of her handgun brought her back to reality. Now he was alone with a gunman chasing him and he was stumbling and falling out of fear, as he ran in panic towards his truck.

Quinn moved cautiously until he reached the top of the dune near where the shooters had been standing and quickly surveyed the area as he lay on his stomach with the small weapon trained at the shadows in front of him. In the distance he heard a large engine start and hear it race down the dirt road towards the highway. It was probably 50 yards from him and out of range when he turned and headed back to the beach. Clara needed his help.

Both Clara and AJ were still hiding behind the ATVs when he got back to the beach. He went to Clara first. "Where are you hit?" he asked as he reached her side.

"My right shoulder. Why would someone be shooting at us, Quinn? Are they gone?"

"Yes, they're gone, I saw them drive away. We are safe. AJ, can you turn on the ATV lights and give me a hand? Clara, have you got a first aid kit?"

"Yes, there's a kit in my equipment bag. Is it bad, Quinn?"

"No, it does not look bad. You are going to be okay, but we need to stop the bleeding and get you to the hospital."

AJ finally found the nerve to leave the protection of the ATV and crawled over with the first aid kit to assist. "I'm so sorry, Quinn. I've never been shot at before. I froze."

"It's okay, AJ. Right now we need to get some help. Call 911 and ask for an ambulance. Also contact the sheriff and ask him to meet us at the Mexico Beach pavilion by the Pass.

He will know where that is."

"Okay, okay, I'll call," AJ said as she fumbled with the phone in the headlight of the ATV.

CHAPTER 23

THE ESCAPE

Virginia pulled onto the highway in a daze. She could not believe she had fired her gun at those shadows on the beach. They had made her so mad kicking at one of her cats and they were her responsibility. Officer Pinkham was counting on her to take care of them and she could not let him down, but she had overreacted and now she had to get out of there. She was already packed to return to Detroit, so she developed a plan. "I will go back to the house and pretend nothing has happened. She would smile and say good-bye to everyone and head back to Detroit just like nothing was wrong. However, that moron from the environmental group—I'm sure he will get caught. I heard him firing shots after I ran to the car. He will identify me to the police and they will put me in jail!" I cannot go to jail! I was only protecting my cats. They will understand that, won't they?"

Eugene raced down the dirt road towards the highway, his big truck tearing up the road, as he swerved around the tight corners. Being shot at had a strange sobering effect on him and he was coming out of the marijuana haze from last night's party and was beginning to realize what he had just done and how much trouble he was in. Out of desperation, he stopped on the bridge over one of the coastal dune lakes and hurled his revolver into the water. All he could think of was to get on the road back to Oregon. He would be safe once he got home.

Virginia's plans were beginning to gel. She had to talk to Eugene and make sure he would not identify her to the police.

Blink-Out

There was only two ways out of the WaterSound project and she was sure he would be coming along Highway 98 behind her. She had no sooner had that thought when she saw the red pickup truck coming up fast from behind. She slowed down and waited for him to catch up, then blinked her lights and waved desperately for him to pull over. Together they pulled into convenience store parking lot along the highway. She pulled up alongside of the truck.

"Eugene, we have to get our stories straight. You can't let them know that I was involved."

"Oh, no, you don't—this was all your idea. I am not taking the fall for this. I was only along to feed the cats," he said as his face got red and his eyes bulged. So f...you lady, I'm getting out of here."

In dismay, Virginia returned to her home in Seaside, finished packing and headed for Detroit. Eugene also returned to camp and packed quickly. He was heading home to Oregon and wanted to be on the road as soon as possible. On leaving the camp, he pulled the truck off the road near the fence between the State Forest and WaterColor. Out of anger, he retrieved a roll of toilet paper from his camp gear, poured some Coleman lamp fuel on it and set it on fire. He threw it as far into WaterColor as he could, where it landed in a patch of palmetto. "That will keep them busy," he thought as he spun his truck onto the highway and headed for I-10.

The manager of the Publix's supermarket on SR-395 noticed the smoke and called the fire department. The Forestry Division brush fire trucks were slow getting to the site and the flatwoods and blackjack oak habitats were fully ablaze by the time they arrived. The fire Eugene had set would threaten the newly developed subdivision and scorch the last remaining segment of pine flatwoods salamander habitat on the project.

CHAPTER 24

THE RESCUE

Quinn held a compress on Clara's shoulder as he helped her onto the ATV. She was bleeding worst and was showing signs of going into shock. "I need you to hang in there Clara. We are about a mile and a half from Mexico Beach and the ambulance is on the way." AJ was still badly shaken, but was able to get the ATV in gear. Quinn ran alongside as he steadied Clara and kept the compress firmly in place on her shoulder. The sun was coming up as they reached the pavilion. Quinn could hear the wail of the sirens in still morning air, but knew that it would be five minute before help would make it to the Pass. Clara was fading fast.

The local sheriff's deputy arrived first and immediately recognized Quinn from his participation in the arrest two days before. On seeing the blood on Clara and Quinn, he jumped from the patrol car with his gun drawn. "Get…get your hands up where I can…"

"Cut the crap here and put that gun away. We have an injured woman who needs help immediately," AJ said as she stepped in front of the deputy and pulled her ID out of her jacket pocket. The stalemate between the two was broken as the ambulance turned off the highway and headed for their location. The sheriff's SUV was right behind the ambulance.

The early morning sunlight cast long shadows over the beach and the seagulls foraged along the shoreline for their first meal of the day, as the surf rolled gently to the shoreline. The affairs of men were much less tranquil than the natural environment of that early spring morning. The flashing red and blue lights reflected the tension the group that collected at the pass that morning. Paramedics worked feverishly to stabilize Clara, while the hulking figure of the sheriff stood with his hand on his gun, glaring at the tall thin woman who stood facing him. Quinn knelt down to comfort Clara as the paramedics prepared to load her into the ambulance.

"I'm sure glad you came along this morning," she said. "I'd be lying dead on the beach right now, if you had not been there. I don't know why anyone would want to shoot at us."

"Neither do I, Clara. Once we get you safely on the way to the hospital, AJ and I will talk to the sheriff and see if we can come up with some answers."

"Quinn, can you call my husband and tell him I'm okay. He will be worried to death, so assure him I am out of danger."

"I will," he said as he reached into his pocket for his cell phone.

Nearby AJ and Sheriff Pritchard remained in tense conversation. "Look, sheriff, just because he is covered with blood does not mean he is guilty of anything. We were shot at from the dunes and Clara was hit. He knew what to do. He chased the shooter away and kept her from bleeding to death. So take your hand off your gun and put the handcuffs away."

"This is the third time in two days that I have found him at a major crime scene. He is either the perpetrator or is in back of these crimes somehow. Either way, his ass should be in jail."

"I agree that he is a link to these crimes, but not in the way you think. If we are going to solve them, we have to listen to him—not put him in jail."

"I plan to put him in my interrogation room and do just that—listen while he spills his guts. I'll get him to talk."

"He doesn't know what is going on any more than you or I do. But we can't make any progress without him. What is happening is somehow linked to the environmental work he has been doing for years. So let's listen and learn what we can."

"Shit!"

"Yea, well, that is very profound of you, sheriff. You have gotten to the core of the issue now, haven't you?" AJ said as she wheeled around and walked back to where Quinn was standing at the rear of the ambulance.

She stood next to him for a moment as she watched the sheriff take his hand off his gun and walk back to the patrol car. "I'm screwed," she said to Quinn in a low voice.

"What do you mean?"

"I'm going to be kicked out of the Bureau."

"Why do you say that?"

"Oh, nothing! I just froze under fire and cowered behind the ATV. Then I gave my gun to a murder suspect who fired at a sniper. That is just a few of the issues that are going to surface when my boss starts asking the questions. They make a very big deal when an agent reports that their weapon has been fired."

"What do you suggest?"

"I should go ahead and resign. That will make things a little easier."

"No you shouldn't."

"Look, let me tell the story, okay, and don't be surprised if you hear me say I fired the gun."

"AJ, I suggest you tell the truth. Things are confusing enough without lying about events that took no more than one minute of time. Your boss will understand."

"Yeah, I doubt it. Look, I got the sheriff to stand down and not haul you back to jail. I think he will listen and be a little more cooperative. Go talk to him. I have got to call the office and tell them what is going on. The Bureau does not take kindly to their agents being shot at."

Quinn walked over to where the sheriff stood talking with his deputies. "Sheriff," he said in greeting.

Clay turned to face Quinn as he hitched up his belt and spit a chew of tobacco at his feet. "I should be hauling your ass back to my jail, but your girlfriend says you have something to tell us. Do you want to clue me in?"

"I don't know what to tell you, sheriff. I'm as much in the dark as you are."

"Huh, I thought so! This is the worst crime spree in the history of my county. I've had a murder, arson, and now a shooting with injuries. You are still a suspect in the murder and I find you at the other crime scenes and you don't have anything to tell me?"

"I think they are all related. I know it doesn't make sense, but all these events are somehow related to the beach mice and our Habitat Conservation Plan."

"Beach mice! That is the most ridiculous thing I have heard in my entire career in law enforcement."

"Well, you asked me what I thought. I have not figured out all of the angles yet or who may be involved, but there is a connection."

AJ walked over as she put her cell phone away. "So, you two are friends now?"

"Just as I thought, this scumbag doesn't have anything to say, except he thinks the beach mice are the cause."

"I'm beginning to believe him, sheriff. Let's go back to the crime scene and see what we can find."

"Suits me, get in the patrol car."

"Sheriff, vehicles are not allowed on the beach during turtle nesting season," Quinn reminder.

"Don't tell me what I can't do in my county. Law enforcement takes precedence over any damn turtle."

"I'll take the ATV and, sheriff; turtles aside…the beach sand is *very* soft."

"You don't worry about me. I have been driving these beaches since I was 12 years old."

"AJ, are you riding with me?" Quinn asked.

"I'll go with the sheriff. I have to talk to him about my call to the office."

Quinn fired up the ATV and followed their previous tracks back along the beach to keep from having any more impact. Behind him, the sheriff put the big SUV in four-wheel drive and immediately sunk six inches into the beach sand as he followed Quinn.

"Sheriff, my boss and two special agents from our Pensacola office will be here by midmorning. There must be an investigation whenever shots are fired at a federal agent. They will want the crime scene roped off and left alone until they get here," she said. "It's a Bureau requirement, you understand?"

The sheriff glanced in her direction with an exasperated look, but did not say a word. The big SUV was laboring through the sand and was beginning to fishtail, so he steered towards the surf line where the moisture would compact the sand and make driving easier. But the tide was high that morning and the compacted sand was being washed over by breaking waves. After another quarter mile, the patrol vehicle sunk up to its axles and no amount of gear shifting or cursing was going to move it from its location.

Quinn had already reached the crime scene and winced as he watched the sheriff tear up the beach. Waves were breaking against the driver's side as Quinn pulled up alongside in the ATV. AJ stepped out without saying a word and jumped on the back of his ATV. Quinn could hear the sheriff barking orders on the radio.

"Let's get out of here! He is going to be tied up for a while," AJ suggested.

It was a much more subdued sheriff who finally arrived at the scene. His heavily starched shirt was soaked with sweat and he glared at Quinn as if to dare him to make a comment. "Okay, tell me what happened here," with a small measure of humility.

Quinn glanced at AJ and she understood that he would expect her to relay the truth about the shooting, even if it meant her job.

"Sheriff, we were riding with Clara Fullerton this morning. She does the survey every day to record new nests. There was a loggerhead turtle on the nest up there by the dune. Clara was standing about ten feet way when shots were fired from that direction. I think she was hit by one of the first shots. We got in back of the ATVs and the shots continued until we charged the shooter and he ran. That is when we called it in and got Clara to the pavilion as quick as we could."

"Why the hell were you out here looking for turtles in the first place?"

"Sheriff, Clara asked us to come along. She is the volunteer turtle watch coordinator for this section of beach. She drives it every morning and records any nesting sites she finds. This information is reported to both the state and federal wildlife agencies that are responsible for protecting turtles."

"That sounds like more of that environmental shit that you are involved with."

"Yes, sir, it is all required by the Endangered Species Act," Quinn added.

"Do you have anything to add to Agent Lindall's account of this incident?" The sheriff said looking at Quinn.

"That is the way it happened. I would add that there were two shooters or at least two weapons fired by the same shooter. Based on the firing patterns, I think there were two different individuals. The first fired three rapid rounds with a small-caliber automatic. The second was a larger caliber, maybe a 44 magnum or a 45. Those shots were fired much more deliberately and with more accuracy. I believe the shooter reloaded once and probably would have continued, had we not returned fire and flushed him out. By the time I reached his position, I could see a pickup turning left onto the highway. It was too far away and still dark, so I can't give you a description of the vehicle."

"You returned fire?"

"Yes!" AJ and Quinn both waited for the next question, but it never occurred to the sheriff to ask who fired the shots.

"Let's walk up to where you think the shooter was standing," he said with a glance down the beach to see if the wrecker had arrived to rescue his patrol vehicle.

Quinn walked the path he had followed into the dunes. He and AJ pointed out the obvious evidence. Footsteps made as he ran towards the shooter, expended shell casings, areas where he had taken cover. Finally they reached the area where the shooter had a clear elevated view of the beach.

"We better leave that area alone until the crime scene team arrives," AJ advised, as a reminder to the sheriff that this was now federal jurisdiction.

Quinn suggested, "Let's walk along the valley between these dunes and go to the access road where they would have entered the site."

The sheriff was sweating profusely and breathing hard as they climbed the last interior dune and walked into a stand of stunted sand pines. The forest road paralleled the dunes and it was easy to walk back to where George usually staged his trapping events. There were signs of a rapid departure with the soft ground chewed up by a large-wheeled vehicle spinning its wheels as it headed back toward the highway. To the right was the tree where George was found shot just three days before.

Quinn's attention was drawn to a stack of large animal traps that George had used to catch the feral cats. He felt that something was not right, but at first he could not figure out what it was. Then it hit him—eight traps were in the stack! George had said he only had five, just a few days ago. Someone else was trapping cats, but who?

"What is it? AJ asked when she saw Quinn looking at the traps.

"There are eight traps here. George told me just a few days ago that he could only get five traps. So, where did the other three come from?"

"Where do you buy traps like that?"

"We typically order from the Forestry Supply catalog. They are the main supplier for field equipment."

"Forestry Supplies, that is so cool. I'm learning so much on this case. Who would ever have thought that there would be a catalog for forest equipment?"

"Well, yes, you can get survey instruments, firefighting equipment, wildlife management gear, and even clothes for outdoor work in various climates."

"If the extra traps were ordered from a catalog, we could check and see who received them. Do have a copy of the catalog?"

"They have a web site. We can look it up when we get back to the computer."

The sheriff came up to them as they were talking. "How can I get back to the beach from here? The wrecker should be here by now."

"There are two ways back to the beach from here, sheriff. The way we came or go to the east along this road and you will come out near the pavilion. We avoid crossing the dunes directly to the beach, since it's part of the preserve, plus the dunes are pretty steep along this section."

"Sheriff, Quinn tells me that he is concerned with the number of traps stacked up here."

"Why would that be an issue?"

"George told me he could only get five traps and I see there are eight here. I just don't know who else would be trapping cats on private land."

"I thought you were only trapping mice. What does that have to do with cats?" he asked.

"Feral cats eat mice. So we catch them and remove them from the dunes."

A black sedan pulled off the highway. Two men in suits and ties stepped out and surveyed the area before walking in their direction.

"Oh, Christ, here comes the Feds," the sheriff said, half under his breath. "I'm going back to the beach. Do not leave the area without checking with me. Is that understood?"

"Yes, sheriff, we understand," AJ said with a little attitude. "Quinn, that is Special Agent Mark Thompson to the right. He's my boss and agent in charge of the Pensacola office. Let me introduce you."

Mark Thompson was a no-nonsense career agent who had taken over as chief of the Pensacola office about one year ago. He was a 35-year-old native of Princeton, New Jersey, and had joined the Bureau after a short stint with the Philadelphia Police Department. He had a degree from Penn State in law enforcement and was married to a public defender. Quinn's first impression was that he was a sharp, driven individual who liked dealing with the facts and not the philosophy of crimes. AJ had been his first hire and he continued to have mixed feelings about her progress with the Bureau. The house burning assignment had seemed simple enough to see if she could function as a field agent. If it did not work out, he was going to reconsider her employment status before she embarrassed the Pensacola office and raised questions about his administrative skills.

"Nice to meet you," he said after AJ introduce him to Quinn. "Is he the murder suspect?"

"According to the sheriff he is, but I…"

Blink-Out

"Show me the crime scene and tell me what happened," he said as he cut AJ off in mid-sentence.

"Okay, the shooters parked their cars here and the shots were fired at us from the dunes about 50 yards down the road. Let's walk down there and I'll show you the site."

"Tell me what happened first. Mr. Wilson, I want you to talk to Agent Wilkes. He will take your statement. Then we will secure this area before going to the site on the dunes. So, start taking pictures and look for evidence."

Turning back to AJ, as Agent Wilkes took Quinn aside, Thompson said, "All right, Agent Lindall, let's hear it."

"Okay, I was riding with Clara Fullerton and Quinn on the morning turtle watch."

"Who is Clara Fullerton?"

"She is the local turtle watch volunteer. She surveys the beach every morning for new nest."

"Why were you on this survey? You were here to investigate the house fire."

"I…I have found out that the house fire had a lot to do about the environmental issues and I was doing research."

"What kind of research?"

"Any ties I could find between the environment and the house fires."

"And you were going to find this at 5:00 a.m. in the morning here on this beach."

"I don't…I don't know. I was looking for leads and staying close to Quinn Wilson. He is a key to both the murder and the house fires."

"Yeah, he is a suspect in the murder."

"However, he is not the murderer. This bumpkin of a sheriff grabbed the first person he could find and charged him with murder. He has the wrong man."

"And you know this how?"

"I have interviewed him and reviewed his computer files and…"

"Did you have a warrant to access his computer?"

"No, I had his permission. I did not need a warrant."

"Oh, so he cleaned up his file and let you look at them. How convenient was that."

"It was not that way at all. Will you let me finish the story?"

"This is the story, AJ, but go ahead."

"Well, we stopped at this site to record a loggerhead turtle nest and shots were fired at us from the dunes. Clara was hit with one of the first rounds and we took cover behind the ATVs. Quinn tells me…"

"I do not want to hear what anyone told you. I want to know what you saw."

"There were a lot of shots fired and the second series of shots made more noise than the first ones."

"Two guns, okay. Then what happened?"

"We were pinned down and the shooter kept getting closer and closer with the shots. So, Quinn took my gun and charged the shooter."

"Wait a minute. Did he take the weapon from you or did you, in fact, give your service weapon to a murder suspect! Be very clear on this."

"No, I did not give my weapon to a murder suspect! I gave my weapon to a former Marine captain who had been in Desert Storm and knew what to do. He saved our lives. I…I did not know what to do. I was scared, okay. He took charge and saved our lives."

Agent Thompson was silent for a moment as he wrote and then said, "Discharging your weapon during the act of a felony is a serious situation in the Bureau. There are going to be a lot of people who will want to hear about this. You are aware that you are relieved of active duty during this investigation. We will get to the bottom of this and then we will talk again about any indiscretions you may have exhibited in the field. Are we clear on that?"

"Yes…I am clear on the procedures."

"Fine, let me talk to Mr. Wilson."

Quinn and Agent Wilkes were standing near the area where the shots were fired when AJ and Agent Thompson walked up.

"Mr. Wilson, do you confirm that Agent Lindall gave you her weapon and that you fired the gun at a fleeing suspect?"

Quinn glanced at AJ before answering. He was relieved that she told the truth. "Yes, AJ and I had only a few seconds to assess the situation and take action. I have been under fire before, so I took the weapon and charged the shooter. We knew Clara had been hit and we needed to get her assistance as fast as possible. We can make a big deal about it or start asking the important questions—who was shooting at us and why?"

"A murder suspect taking a weapon from a federal agent is a big deal, Mr. Wilson. We will be talking more about that, but since you have questioned the shooter's motive, I am interested in your opinion."

"I really do not know. It wasn't homeless squatters, since they came in cars. They were under-armed for drug dealers, as they prefer assault rifles. Local hunters would be using shotguns this time of year. Anyone with a vendetta against St. Joe would not be on this site that time of morning. Those shooters were here for a reason and we got in their way. So, I think this all has something to do with George's murder and our Habitat Conservation Plan."

"I'm not making the connection."

"I'm not either, but the clues are starting to add up. As Agent Lindall states, murder is about sex, drugs and money. Sex and drugs seems like a reach, so it's the money trail that will lead to those responsible."

"All right, we will talk more later. AJ has been relieved of duty pending an investigation of the shooting. I suggest you go back to your hotel and wait to hear for me."

AJ and Quinn walked back to the beach. "Will you look at that? The sheriff has got his entire department out on the beach trying to rescue his patrol car. Damn, there must be six vehicles. And look, Officer Pinkham is with them. Are we the only ones who are supposed to honor the Habitat Conservation Plan? Troy knows that vehicles are prohibited on the beach. I have got to say something about this."

"You're not going to win any friends by bringing that up now with the sheriff or Troy."

"Yeah, but I can't help it," Quinn said as he turned the ATV around and headed back down the beach. The wrecker had dug a deep hole in the sand and attached a tow cable to the axle of the sheriff's SUV. The driver had set the truck's jacks and was operating the wench as the wrecker's wheels dug deeper in the sand. Troy and three deputies were standing by watching the wrecker as Quinn and AJ pulled up on the ATV. Quinn went to Troy first.

"Troy, what are all these vehicles doing on the beach. You know the rules during turtle nesting season."

"Shit, I think it is obvious. We are helping the sheriff get his patrol vehicle out of the surf."

"I see you and three deputies standing around watching. The sheriff should not have taken his vehicle on the beach to begin with. By the time you finish, there will be an acre of disturbance. I suggest you get your vehicle and those three sheriff's patrol cars off the beach and let the wrecker do its job."

"You don't have any authority to be telling me what to do. I'm an officer of the Fish and Wildlife…!"

"The hell I don't. I am an agent of this property owner and I am charged by him to administer the Habitat Conservation Plan. The rules on beach access are consistent with the Endangered Species Act. You know that. So get these vehicles off the beach."

Blink-Out

The deputies overheard the conversation and came over. Two of them unbuckled their gun strap and rested their hand on their service weapon. Troy was red in the face and so mad he could not speak.

"I...I, shit. I...don't have...to listen to this," he mumbled.

Quinn turned to the deputies, "I mean no disrespect, but I need you to get these vehicles off the beach. This is sea turtle nesting season and disturbance on the beach can disrupt their nesting patterns, so please move these vehicles back to the parking area. The wrecker will be able to get the sheriff's car removed without your assistance."

The deputies were unaccustomed to being ordered around by a civilian, especially one they had arrested for murder just two days before. Nevertheless, they recognized authority from both the body language and Quinn's tone of voice. They milled around, cursed and spit tobacco on the beach and then sullenly walked towards their patrol cars. The sheriff's SUV was now sunk up to the bumpers and the wrecker was straining to break it free, as the jacks dug deeper into the beach sand.

Quinn turned back to Troy and asked. "I have another question for you, Troy. There are eight traps at the staging areas where George's body was found. I know that he only had five and was working overtime to get the cats off the dunes. Do you know where the other three traps came from?"

Troy hands were defiantly on his hips as he paced in circles muttering to himself, his face still flush with anger. Quinn's question caught him off-guard and the blood drained from his face and he drew a quick breath, as if he had been hit in the stomach. He caught himself and tried to recover quickly.

"I don't know what you are talking about! The cats were George's responsibility. We never talked about the traps."

Both Quinn and AJ, who had been standing 20 feet away noticed the change in his demeanor and made a mental note to add to the growing list of evidence. Troy was still standing on the beach, silently refusing to move his vehicle out of defiance, when Quinn and AJ headed back to Grayton Beach on the ATV. They could see AJ's fellow FBI agents in the dunes busily collecting evidence and taking notes as they past.

"I'm screwed," she said as they passed. "This is going to be a big deal and then I'll have to go before the board and they will fire me. Field agents are never supposed to relinquish their weapon to anyone, especially an accused murderer. This is going to be very messy."

"We both know it was the right thing to do at the time. We will just keep telling the truth and they will come around. Also, did you see Officer Pinkham's response when I asked him about the traps?"

"I did! He looked like he was going to faint for a second. If I were a real FBI agent, I'd say he was guilty of something. Then again, you had all kinds of emotions stirred up. I'm surprised one of those red neck deputies didn't try to arrest you out of belligerence."

"Well, I was in the right to ask them to get off the beach. Sea turtle protection is no joke. The plan says 'no vehicles on the beach,' and they had six. The Endangered Species Act is federal law. It applies to everyone, law enforcement agencies included. Also, did you notice that they had not even made it to the crime scene? If it wasn't for your FBI team, no evidence would be collected."

It was midmorning when they returned to Grayton Beach. Even though the temperature was cool, there were a number of people walking the beach and lounging in the morning sun. They looked with curiosity as the ATV motored into the little town. The two riders looked very serious and out of place to the festive atmosphere of the community.

Quinn could see the smoke rising in the northeast as they

approached Grayton Beach and feared the worst. "*Not another fire at WaterColor,*" he thought with concern as he parked the ATV behind Clara's house and he and AJ ran back to the car and headed towards the smoke to investigate. They drove through Seaside and turned north on County Road 395. Up ahead they could see the clouds of smoke obscuring the road and the flashing lights of the county fire truck. When they got closer they could see the trail cut through one of the project's natural areas as the firemen accessed the fire and began to cut firebreaks to contain the blaze.

"Look at that! I think those firebreaks are as destructive as the fire itself. I need to walk in and see how much damage has been done. Are you going to wait here?"

"Not on your life. I'm going with you. These fires are what I came to investigate in the first place," AJ said.

They walked together along the freshly cut fire line and Quinn cringed as the bulldozer track cut directly through a cypress conservation area leaving deep ruts in the soft organic soil. Once at the fire line, Quinn stood surveying the damage. Fire, in a natural system is not all together a bad thing, so long as it does not burn too hot. When the forest fuel moisture level is right, a prescribed fire can burn through the litter on the ground and release nutrients back to the soil, but this fire was far too hot. It had burned intensely through the understory of vegetation and leaped into the canopy of sand pine, where it raged through approximately 60 acres of habitat, killing everything it its path. Quinn and AJ stepped aside as the Florida Division of Forestry water truck rumbled along the fire line and began spraying hot spots that were still on fire in the smoldering habitat.

"What do you think?" AJ asked, breaking the silence.

"Well, it was a hot fire that burned rapidly and destroyed everything in its path. The conditions were very dry and the fuel moisture was low, so it burned hot and reached the treetops very quickly. There was no stopping it after that."

"How do you think it got started?" she asked.

Quinn turned and looked back towards the highway. "I don't know. We are a quarter mile off of 395, so it could not have been started from a discarded cigarette. There have been no atmospheric conditions that would have caused it to get started. My guess is arson and the nearest point of access is the forest road in the Washington State Forest that runs just north of the property line. Let's walk up that way."

As they approached the northern property line of WaterColor, they could see that the bulldozer had cut through the fence and was now cutting firebreaks through the oak scrub habitat within the state forest. There adjacent to the fence was a well-worn forest road that connected back to County Road 395. "That is the road that leads to the Soldiers' camp site," she said with excitement. "I need to talk to those boys again."

CHAPTER 25

PANIC

Troy called Cal Summerford on his cell phone as he was leaving the beach. "Cal we have to talk."

"Sure, what's the problem?"

"That consultant, Wilson, the one we framed for shooting George, is about to figure out our plot."

"No, no, no, we are too insulated from the murder for anyone to think we are involved. You have the sheriff in your back pocket and that FBI agent they sent could not investigate her way out of a paper bag. I'm telling you, we are safe, so calm down."

"Quinn Wilson is the smartest one of the bunch. He asked me where the three cat traps came from at the site where George was shot."

"Cat traps? What does that have to do with anything?"

"He said George only had five traps and was working overtime to get the cats off the dunes. There were eight traps at the scene. The other three were ours. Virginia must have left them there after she released the cats I brought to her."

"Well, that is easy to explain. George was a resourceful guy. He found more traps. End of the issue. You make sure Virginia backs us up on that."

"She is back in Detroit for the summer. They won't take time to locate her."

"All right then, what are you worried about? You need to settle down. The money is starting to roll in by the basketsful.

I'm almost finished with the complaint and will be filing soon. I am asking for the revocation of the Army Corps permit, the removal of all structures in any habitat occupied by a listed species and $200 million in damages. I'm going to bleed those bastards for every cent of profit they would make on this project and drive them out of business. It is all part of my 'scorched earth' policy. My legal fees will be at least 40 percent. You will get a cut of that, so I need you to take a deep breath and relax. Tell you what I am going to do. I'll put another 50 thousand dollars in your offshore account. Will that makes you feel better?"

"Thanks, Cal. I'm sorry. I guess I just panicked. I'm okay now."

"That's my boy! Let me know if anything changes." Cal hung up the phone and stared out the window of his hotel room. *"That weak ass son-of-a-bitch is going to crumble before this thing is over. I've got to distance myself from him before he drags me down too. And while I am at it, I might as well silence that consultant. Troy is right about him—he is the smart one."*

CHAPTER 26

REFLECTIONS

Once they were back at the motel, Quinn left AJ and walked towards Western Lake, lost in thought. Firing that gun brought back an avalanche of memories that he had suppressed. His company of Marines had been in the thick of battle in Desert Storm. They had followed the mine-clearing tanks through the fortifications built by the Republican Guard outside of Kuwait and had become the tip of the spear for that section of the line. The opposition had been fierce, but they had routed the Guard from their bunkers and trenches and sent them running in retreat. Overhead the Air Force and Navy fighters had flown low over the battlefield and fired their missiles with deadly accuracy. More men than he cared to remember had fallen in front of his M-16. *Too many,* he thought. The noise and images of combat were again in his mind because of the events that morning. He thought he was finished with firearms when he was discharged from the Marines, but here he was again with a weapon in hand, charging an enemy position.

He exerted all his will power to force his mind off those events and the fire by concentrating on the physical environment that he knew so well. Western Lake was calm with the tannic-colored water lapping gently at the spatterdock and softly rushing along the shore. Across the lake he could see the dark green and purple hue of dense pickerelweed, backed by giant bulrush against the shore. A snowy egret, intent on catching lunch, flew as he approached. Along the path were dwarf saw palmetto, slash pine and ilex. "*Serenoa repens, Pinus elliottii,* and *Ilex vomitoria,*" he recited to himself, as if addressing old friends by their proper name. Purple pitcher plants grow in the low-lying areas along the lake. He stopped on the suspension bridge near the BoatHouse and reflected on the design and permitting of these shoreline structures that were such important issues at the time and now seemed such a minor footnote in the history of the project. Up the hill towards Cerulean Park, he could see a lot of activity, so he began heading in that direction.

AJ, who was out on her own reflective walk, joined him near the Bait House Restaurant and they walked together towards the activities. "What is going on in the park?" she asked.

"I don't know. It looks like some kind of festival."

"I have got to tell you, this place is beautiful. The open space and views of the lake through the trees is breathtaking. I would love to live here. And you had something to do with this project?"

"Yes, I did the entitlement planning and environmental permitting. The design was done by a famous landscape architect out of New York, by the name Jacque Robinson, based on what is referred to as the new urbanist concepts. It is an effort to recapture the feeling of community. Seaside is one of the earlier examples of this design discipline. If we go into the Seaside bookstore, you will find all kinds of literature on the project's design and history. As Jacque would say, we stopped designing projects for people around 1918 and started to design for cars. The subdivisions that most of us grew up in had two-car garages and no sidewalks, typical of this design orientation towards the automobile. As a result, people became more and more isolated from one another and it has impacted the fabric of the community and possibly the nation. New urbanist designs try to get back to the people. The residential lots are smaller and there is less room between units. All the space that would have been taken up in yards and setbacks between houses are moved to common open space for

Blink-Out

everyone's use and not just the private property owner. All units have front porches that are close to the sidewalks, so that you can talk to your neighbors as they walk by. The commercial areas are always within walking distance, so it minimizes the need for automobiles. Then you add early 20th Century housing design to the mix and it creates this strange feeling of nostalgia. It's funny, because none of us grew up in these neighborhoods, yet we feel a longing to be in these types of communities. Do you feel it?"

"I do! Actually, I wasn't sure what I was feeling until you explained it. This is so cool!"

"Jacque looked closely at Seaside and felt that they ignored the cars and did not incorporate enough open space in the design. So here in WaterColor, we put the cars in alleys in back of the residential units and left 50 percent of the project in open space."

"Quinn, I am very impressed! I have learned so much on this case. Apparently, I have spent too much time with my face buried in spreadsheets to see the environment. I want to thank you for opening my eyes."

"Well, I'm glad you find it interesting. Let's go see what is happening in Cerulean Park."

There were a series of small tables and booths lining the sidewalk along the park. Each bore the name of an environmental organization espousing the protection of one or more environmental habitat or species. The monarch butterfly people were still there, even though Brad had donated $2500 and agreed to modify the landscape plan throughout the project to include butterfly forage. The Sierra Club and Audubon Society were also there with displays. As Quinn talked to the monarch butterfly group, AJ wandered down the line of exhibits.

"Hello, would you like to make a donation for the protection of the Choctawhatchee beach mice," a rather rugged-looking outdoors guy asked as she walked by.

"Oh, I love those little guys," she said. "I would like to make a donation, but can you tell me how my money would be used?"

"All donations will go to protect the beach mice habitat, of course. Developers are destroying beach sand dune habitat at an alarming rate and they need to be stopped."

"So, my money would be used to...?"

"It will go to sue developers like St. Joe and force them to set aside the beaches for the mice and keep people out of the habitat."

"Oh, well, isn't that what they are doing here at WaterColor?"

"I've read their signs. It's all lies. They are not doing anything to protect these precious mice. We need to force them to do the right thing. There is no way a developer will protect the environment unless he is under a court order and the watchful eyes of my organization."

"Can you excuse me for a minute?" AJ walked back to Quinn and said, "I need to talk to you."

"What is it?

"For starters, what do you think of these environmental organizations?"

"There are a lot of variations in their purpose, organization and expertise. Some are far more zealous than others and sometimes their knowledge does not keep up with their objectives. Others are very credible and responsible organizations that do a lot of good."

"I just talked to the guy down the way who was collecting donations to protect the beach mice. And he intended on doing that by suing St. Joe."

"That is interesting, but not unusual. Developers get threatened with lawsuits all the time for a variety of reasons. Many times the problems are overblown, but resolved once the facts are known. However, let's talk to some more of these organizations and see if that's a common theme. I've got friends in the national organizations of the Sierra Club and Audubon Society that I can call. Also, I see The Nature Conservancy down at the end. I have a lot of respect for their work."

"What does The Nature Conservancy do?"

"They purchase land and act as intermediaries for other governmental and private groups that want to set up conservation programs. They also manage the lands they own, which is where other organizations fall short. If they are collecting donations, it would be for the purchase of coastal dune habitat. I'd be all for that effort. Beach property is the most expensive real estate in Florida and it is in high demand for uses other than protection of habitat. I think I mentioned that St. Joe's beach mice preserve was valued at $85 million. Not many property owners can make that kind of commitment."

They walked along the displays and played the role of a vacationing couple. All of the environmental groups were recruiting members and soliciting for donations. Quinn was proud of AJ as she used her newfound knowledge of the environment. She talked intelligently to each of the representative and asked detailed questions about their intended use of donations. Beach mice were the leading conservation effort among the groups.

"So, let me get this straight," AJ said to the woman in the Green Peace tee shirt. You are collecting donations for the protection of beach mice. Why should I donate to you? The Sierra Club is also collecting to protect the mice."

"Forgive me for being so direct," she said with passion and pride for her organization, "but the Sierra Club is a group of old ladies in tennis shoes. They produce a very nice magazine, but that is about as far as they go. Green Peace gets things done. We are the ones who challenge the whalers on the open sea and stopped the slaughter of baby seals. We will be on the beach and in the courtroom forcing the developers to protect the mice. We will be in their face demanding action."

"Okay, I'm going to give you a check for $100, how much of that will go directly to protect the mice?"

"All of the donations will go directly to protect the mice. Not one cent will be used for other purposes. And for a donation of $200, you get a one-year membership, our bi-monthly magazine, and a Green Peace tee shirt and hat. I'll even throw in an authentic Green Peace whalers mug, if you donate today."

"Oh, I want the hat," Quinn said with a smile. He was snickering under his breath as they walked away from the booth.

"So you want the hat that I just paid $200 dollars for?"

"I do!"

"Here you go. I hope you're wearing it when you meet the Green Peace squad on the dunes at 2:00 a.m. in the morning. Did you believe her when she said that the entire donation was going for the protection of the mice?"

"Not for a minute. These organizations all have overheads they have to cover, some as high as 60 percent. The funds go to salaries, insurance, travel expenses and of course, tee shirts. Sometimes their overhead costs are higher than that."

"So she lied!"

"Yes, but I'm sure she was a volunteer and has no idea about the inner workings of the Green Peace organization. It was a sales pitch and an effective one—she got an extra $100 from you."

"I'm calling it research and will include the donation on my expense report."

"Look, there is Earl Talisman, the state director for The Nature Conservancy. Let's go talk to him."

"Hello Earl, it's good to see you."

"Hi, Quinn, it's nice to see you. Are you with Green Peace now?"

"We just got a good deal on the hat and could not resist."

"I can give you a great deal on a hat from The Nature Conservancy for $50."

Can we get two for $75?"

"Sure, I'll make an exception just for you."

Earl, I would like you to meet AJ Lindall. She is a field agent with the FBI, here to investigate a house fire we experienced here on WaterColor last week. Also, I'm sure you heard about George Mott."

"I did and was very sorry to hear it. George was a friend and an exceptional conservationist. He will be missed."

"Earl, can you tell us who organized this environmental get together?"

"I am not sure. We got word through the grapevine and didn't pay any attention to it at first, but then we heard about it from our national headquarter and decided to attend. After all, The Nature Conservancy is the only one of these organizations that is actually working with St. Joe on their conservation programs. The theme seems to be the protection of the beach mice. The consensus is that St. Joe is the bad guy and needs to be held accountable. They don't listen to me when I tell them how good the program is that you and George put together to protect the mice. Their minds are made up."

"Mr. Talisman, we heard about a lawsuit from some of the other organizations. Is that what your donations are funding?" AJ asked with interest.

"Please call me Earl. In answer to your question, we don't participate in that kind of environmental advocacy. Our donations go directly to the purchase and management of conservation lands.

"Just out of curiosity, what percentage of your donations goes to pay overhead costs?"

"We watch that number very closely. Right now we are at about 25 percent overhead. The organization stays very lean. Since we're talking about money, you were serious about the hats, weren't you?"

AJ and Quinn walked back to the motor court with an assortment of pamphlets, magazines, tee shirts and hats. "So let me get this straight, St. Joe puts a conservation easement on a mile and a half of prime beachfront property worth $85 million, releases mice into the habitat and regularly monitors the mice population to make sure they survive. Am I right so far?"

"Yes, those are the facts."

"You have done all that, but the environmental organizations that have done nothing to protect the species are collecting money to sue St. Joe. They are going to spend all the money on lawyers and in the end the beach mice have no more protection than they do right now. Do I still have it right?"

"Yes, you are correct on both counts."

"Well, what I can't figure out is why you are not upset about this. I'm infuriated."

"I guess it is all part of the game we play. Developers are always the rich bastards who are raping the land for profit and the environmental groups are the zealous protectors. You may have heard the term *NIMBY*?"

"No, what does that mean?"

"It stands for *Not in My Backyard*. It's the rallying call for local environmental and civic groups opposed to development. They are always present at public hearings that are required for approval of projects like WaterColor. You will hear that any specific project will destroy the environment, reduce property values, increase traffic, overload schools and on and on. I guess we are used to it and expect to deal with it on any given project. The point is, there are always conflicts, disagreements over impacts and the consequences of development. When these issues cannot be resolved by local government, they end up in court. There are even some environmental organizations that do nothing but litigate." Quinn stopped dead in his tracks.

"What is it?"

"That is what this is about. If you follow the money from these donations, it will end up in the hands of one of these mega-environmental litigators. These guys are the great white sharks of the environmental organizations. They ferret out conflicts and sue for millions of dollars. They use ruthless, slash-and-burn tactics, subvert the interest of local environmental groups and walk away with a fat payday, all under the guise of environmental protection. I wasn't too concerned about the threats because one environmental group could not pool enough resources to launch a suit, but if all the national organizations joined in, they could have hundreds of thousands of dollars."

"If you are right, there would have to be someone behind the scene pulling strings."

"Yes, there would be. We need to find that person and this whole situation will start making sense."

CHAPTER 27

EXONERATION

Mark Thompson was sitting in his black Ford Taurus when Quinn and AJ made it back to the motor court.

"Mark, we have a theory we need to talk to you about." AJ said with enthusiasm.

"I have some more questions for the two of you before we talk about theories. First let me give you a quick rundown on the crime scene. There was a considerable amount of disturbance at the scene. Although the loose white sand did not retain any footprints, we were able to discern that two individuals were at the scene. One was either a woman or a juvenile, based on the size of the indentations. The other wore heavy hiking or work boots. There were two vehicles, one a truck that largely obscured the tracks of the second vehicle when it departed the site in a hurry. There was a lot of tire spinning and fishtailing, as the vehicle raced back to the paved highway. We found three shell casings from a 9 mm automatic and six from a 44 magnum revolver. The shooter with the revolver apparently fired six shots and reloaded. So the shooter could have fired up to 12 rounds. The variations in caliber tell us there were two shooters. The sheriff finally got his vehicle out of the surf and made it to the scene. He had very little to offer and made no effort to collect evidence on his own. Since you were among those being shot at, he could not accuse you of being the shooter, even though he tried. On further questioning, it was obvious that his case against you was flimsy at best and at worst, a total fabrication.

I suggested to the sheriff that he drop charges against you. Nothing he had would stand up in court. So, AJ it was obvious to me that you had already come to that conclusion and you were not collaborating with a murderer. The question about you relinquishing your weapon will still have to be addressed by the board, but in the meantime, I am returning you to active duty. I'll need both you and Mr. Wilson in this investigation. Now, what is your theory?"

"Quinn, why don't you tell him?"

"Well, we think that George's murder and the fires at the two homes here in WaterColor are somehow linked to the Habitat Conservation Plan and the protection of the Choctawhatchee beach mice."

"That seems to be quite a reach—I'm not making the connection."

"We think someone is organizing the environmental groups to launch a lawsuit against St. Joe over the protection of the beach mice and the murder and arson are either directly related to that effort or are secondary causes."

"I'm still not getting it. I suspect there is a far simpler explanation for these events and that is the direction on which this investigation is going to center. Now, I am going up to the hospital in DeFuniak Springs to interview Clara Fullerton. We'll talk more about your theory over dinner this evening."

"We need to see Clara too. We'll go with you."

"Okay, but I want to interview her alone to corroborate the stories of the shooting. Understood?

AJ and Quinn followed Agent Thompson up State Road 331 to DeFuniak Springs. AJ took advantage of the time to get better acquainted.

"You have never mentioned your wife and I noticed you do not wear a wedding ring. Are you married?"

"Yes, I've been married for 23 years and have a daughter

who will be graduating from high school in the spring. How about you?"

"I'm between boyfriends right now. Oh hell, I don't have to be coy with you. I have not had anyone interested in me for the past two years. I don't know if you have noticed, but I am not the most attractive female in the dating pool. I'm 6'2, skinny, my hands and feet are too large and my hair is way too curly. Most girls are much shorter with perfectly groomed hair. They really piss me off. My mother always said that someday someone would like me for who I am and I would be happily married. I think that 'someone' is going with the cute redhead with the big breasts."

"Well, I'm glad you got that off your chest."

"That is another thing. My chest is too small. You would think God would have given me one feminine feature that was at least normal size. But, no!"

"AJ, I think your mother is right. Someone will…"

"Oh, no, don't you start sounding like my mother. I won't put up with it."

It was late afternoon when they pulled into the hospital parking lot. A chill was settling over the city as the sun began to set. Clara had spent most of the day in the intensive care unit under observation. She had just been transferred to a private room and was there with her husband when the three of them entered the room.

"Quinn, I'm so glad to see you," she said as she raised her good arm to give him a hug. "I have been thinking all day that I needed to thank you for saving my life. I was having this nightmare of being out there by myself. They would have just walked up and shot me and there was nothing I could have done to stop them."

"There is no need for thanks, Clara. AJ and I were glad we were there to help. This is Special Agent Mark Thompson with

Blink-Out

the FBI. He has got some questions he wants to ask you. But first, tell me the truth, how are you really doing?"

"Well, I have never been shot before. My job as principal of the middle school back in Ohio was hazardous at times, but nothing like this. Agent Thompson, this man saved my life! You should give him a medal. Here someone is shooting at us and I see him running into the gunfire just before I passed out. When I came to, here was Quinn running alongside the ATV holding a compress on my shoulder. I would have died out there if he wasn't along. You go tell that old fool of a sheriff that Quinn is *not* a murderer..." Clara coughed and the pain it caused in her shoulder made her stop to catch her breath.

"AJ, can you and Mr. Wilson wait outside for a few minutes while I talk to Ms. Fullerton?" Agent Thompson asked. "Mr. Fullerton, you can stay if you like."

"Sure," said Quinn. "Clara, we will be back in a few minutes. Okay?"

"Don't you leave without talking to me again. I'm not finished thanking both of you."

AJ seemed nervous in the hallway. She crossed her arms over her chest and paced back and forth in deep thought. Finally she sat down next to Quinn and busily adjusted her oversized hair pins. "Quinn, I'm sorry for my outburst in the car. I never talk about my personal life and I don't know what came over me, especially when I heard myself talking about my breast size. That is so embarrassing. From now on, I will keep our relationship strictly professional."

"AJ, in my years in consulting, I have found that it is not the projects or the successes and failures that stand out in your memory. It's the personal relationships you have with the people with whom you work—the friendships you form that sometimes last for a lifetime. I will, of course, defer to you, but I am fine with some personal discussions."

"It's just that you are so easy to talk to. You're very knowledgeable and not judgmental like my father."

"Oh, so I remind you of your father?" he said with a smile.

She playfully hit him on the arm, "That's not what I meant!"

"That's right. You said in the car that I sounded like your mother."

"Cut it out. You're making me laugh and my boss can see me through the window. He already thinks I'm a ditz."

They settled into the hospital chairs and she leaned over until her shoulder touched his. They were no longer just an FBI agent and a murder suspect. An understanding and trust had evolved between them and they carried on a casual conversation as they waited for Agent Thompson to finish talking with Clara.

"I'm getting hungry and I am not in the mood for hospital food. Do you know a restaurant here in DeFuniak Springs?"

"There are a couple of choices. Are you familiar with the term 'meat and three,' for country restaurants?"

"Sure it means a meat and three vegetables all cooked with a lot of grease. You don't grow up in Louisiana and not know that term. I love country cooking, but Mark is a city slicker and won't even know what a 'meat and three' restaurant means."

"There is another place just a few blocks from here that we can try. I can't remember its name, but it's located in a turn of the century hotel and offers what I call, high-end country meals, mostly steak and potatoes. How does that sound?"

"That sounds better. I'm sure Mark is going to spend some time interrogating you, so be prepared."

"I'm so happy not to be a murder suspect that I won't mind at all. What is my status now anyway? If I was just a person of interest, I am sure you would just question me and tell me not to leave town."

"Okay, you have convinced me that the environmental issues play some role in this case, so you are consulting with the FBI."

"So, do I get my usual pay rate for consulting?"

"Don't push it, mister. I can make you a suspect again with just a flick of my pen."

"That is reassuring and here I thought I was out of the woods."

Mark stepped out of Clara's room. "She wants to see you again and be prepared for some hero worship. I had to tell her twice that the FBI does not issue medals for bravery."

Quinn went in to say goodbye and AJ and Mark caught up on the case. "She confirms your story up until she passed out. It appears that two shooters were waiting for you in the dunes at 5:00 a.m."

"That is highly unlikely. We would not even have stopped at that location, if it had not been for the nesting sea turtle."

"Well, I do not have an explanation or a motive for the shooting. What do you suggest?"

"Let's talk more to Quinn over dinner and see if he has any ideas."

"Oh, so it's Quinn now—you are on a first-name basis with a suspect?"

"He is a former suspect. And yes, we are on a first-name basis. He saved my life too."

CHAPTER 28

THE CONSPIRACY THEORY

The restaurant was in the old DeFuniak Springs Hotel located on U.S. Highway 90. It was constructed in the early 1900s and was now a preserved historical building. It was built to accommodate travelers who would come by train for the warmer weather of Florida. The grandeur of the hotel slowly faded as the center of tourism moved to the coast and travelers came to the area by car rather than train. The old photographs on the walls told of a more genteel time when southern charm was in abundance. The town and hotel itself was named after DeFuniak Springs, a near perfectly round lake that was the central feature and primary tourist attraction for the town.

Their table at the restaurant overlooked the lake and served as a pleasant backdrop as they settled in to a table by the window and reviewed the menu. "That is a very round lake. Is it man-made?" Agent Thompson asked as he gazed out of the window.

"No, that is a karst lake. It is a natural feature occurring in areas of limestone substrata," Quinn said in explanation. "It basically is a very well-defined sinkhole formed when solution cavities in the limestone collapsed."

"Does he always talk like this?" Mark asked, glancing over his menu at AJ.

"Yes, he does! Just stick around and you'll learn a lot. I know I have."

"Well, I don't know about you FBI types, but I'm having a beer. It has been a long day," Quinn said as the waitress came for their drink order. AJ looked longingly over the top of her menu at the mention of beer.

"No, we are on duty. No beer for us," Agent Thompson said without looking up. Quinn and AJ exchanged glances and he knew she was disappointed.

The waitress took their order and the conversation turned to the events of the day as Agent Thompson retrieved his notebook. "I still cannot grasp the connection between your Habitat Conservation Plan and this wave of crime. Can you enlighten me?"

"I know! I am still having trouble piecing it together. Here is what we know so far. All of this started when the population of beach mice began to decline during the quarterly monitoring events."

"Oh, please, we are talking about murder and arson! How can these crimes possibly be associated with mice?"

"Just hear me out. The short version of the theory is that the declining mice population got the attention of the U.S. Fish and Wildlife Service. They started writing letters of violation to St. Joe. George thought the decline in mice population was directly attributed to feral cats and he started trapping and removing them from the habitat. Environmental groups showed up at the same time, collecting money for lawsuits. Two new homes are burned at WaterColor, George is murdered preparing for the next quarterly monitoring event and we are shot at from the dunes three days later. I'm starting to get the picture of some organization behind these events."

"So, this is a cat and mouse game?"

"Clever, but yes, that's what I am saying."

"AJ, do you go along with this theory?"

"I am beginning to believe Quinn is on to something. We walked through the environmental booths at WaterColor this afternoon and there appears to be some organization and purpose behind their efforts. Money is changing hands, passions are running high, and people are motivated to take action. I still can't see how this resulted in murder, but it is worth further investigation."

Agent Thompson busily jotted down notes before he spoke again. "I'm still not buying it, but who would we question if I took the investigation in that direction?"

"I would start with Jan and Troy with U.S. Fish and Wildlife, then with the environmental groups, especially Soldiers for the Environment."

"Why the Soldiers?"

"They came out of Oregon, where the battles over clearcutting virgin forest included some apparent environmental terrorism. Plus, they don't seem to have any environmental reason for being here, except for the intimidation factor. If there is any organization behind these events, you should be able to find out from them. We talked to some of the other environmental groups and they are not sure why they are here. Direction or suggestions from the national organization was the common answer."

"So, what kind of an organization would be behind this and why?"

"The answer came to me this afternoon. You are looking for an environmental advocacy group that specializes in litigation. If these national environmental groups are all sending their money to one litigator, there could be hundreds of thousands of dollars in play."

Agent Thompson looked at AJ as if he was starting to understand the logic. "Do you think the FWS is involved?"

"Troy Pinkham has been extremely difficult lately. Also, he signed the regulatory letters we have been receiving. His actions have cost St. Joe a considerable amount of money and caused delays in construction. That has made the company more vulnerable to litigation. But he is an FWS officer and I find it difficult to believe he has a role in this conspiracy.

"Okay, it is a stretch, but I do not have any other theories. So, AJ, you and I will talk with Fish and Wildlife. We'll meet tomorrow afternoon and compare notes. Now let's eat."

The next morning AJ and Quinn met for an uneventful run around Western Lake and had breakfast at the Great Southern Café while they planned the day's activities. "We learned a lot from the environmental groups yesterday, but now we have to get serious about the interviews. We will need a series of questions. What do you suggest?" AJ asked as she stirred her grits.

"AJ, I have been going over our discussions with Mark last night and there are a few legal things I am still confused on. While I hate to sound dense, tell me what specifically are we looking for? Is it just for leads in the house fires and murder or are we investigating my beach mice conspiracy theory? The sheriff still has jurisdiction over the murder, unless there is a conspiracy—isn't that correct?"

"Well, technically yes, but he has asked for our assistance because we think all the events are interrelated. Of course, when shots are fired at a federal officer, we take charge."

"Okay, aside from the shooting, I realize not everyone is buying into the idea that these events are related. But tell me this, if one of the environmental litigious organizations is orchestrating these events, what crime would they have committed?"

"What do you mean?"

Would they be guilty of shaking down St. Joe for money or land? What criminal laws apply? Would it be racketeering, extortion, collusion, or conspiracy?"

"Crimes have been committed. We are talking about murder, arson, and attempted murder of a federal officer. Where are you coming from?"

"I was thinking that a national organization got the ball rolling to protect an endangered species and solicited support from other environmental groups. So far, no crime has been committed—right? The murder and arson may have been unrelated events caused by passions that were stirred up. Under that scenario, would any of the national organizations be committing a crime?"

"I see what you mean," AJ said, as she cradled her second cup of coffee. "It all depends on their level of involvement. If they said, 'Let's do what we can to protect the beach mice,' then they are not guilty of anything. But, if they say, 'Go burn down that house,' or 'Murder that biologist,' then yes, they would be behind all of these events and guilty. In either case, the individual who committed the crime would be charged."

"Okay, here's another question. We had talked about Troy, excuse me, Officer Pinkham, being overly zealous in his enforcement of the Endangered Species Act. What if he is working with a national organization to discredit St. Joe and prepare the way for a lawsuit?"

"You have been watching too many criminal shows on television. I seriously doubt that a federal Fish and Wildlife Service officer would be involved with extortion under the guise of the ESA. But to answer your question, again it would be dependent on his motives and level of involvement. If he is saying, 'I am going to enforce the Endangered Species Act to the letter of the law,' then he is fulfilling his responsibilities as a Fish and Wildlife Services officer. But, if he is sabotaging the Endangered Species Act or taking actions to subvert the law for financial gain, well then he may be guilty of something. Of course, there are still the crimes of murder and arson. If he or anyone else was involved with those felonies, they are guilty. You're just full of questions this morning, aren't you?"

"Yeah, well, here's another one—St. Joe is held to a standard of care for the beach mice under the 'incidental take' provisions of the Endangered Species Act."

"Oh, I like that term, 'incidental take!' What does that mean?"

"It basically means that we have the ability to take or kill an individual beach mouse while conducting activities necessary for the protection of the population. In other words, if a mouse dies in a trap during the quarterly monitoring, we are still within the authority of the Habitat Conservation Plan. However, if others take or kill a mouse, they would be guilty of violating the Endangered Species Act. My question to you is whether the violation of that provision of the Endangered Species Act, a federal law, would involve the FBI?"

"You must have stayed awake all last night thinking up these questions. I think the answer is that the Fish and Wildlife Service is responsible for enforcement of the Endangered Species Act. The FBI may make note of that violation in the report of other criminal activities, but we would not charge anyone with that alone. Criminal prosecution for the violation of an environmental law is pretty rare. It would have to be very blatant. Where are you going with these questions?"

"I don't know. I was thinking about those three additional traps at WaterSound and it occurred to me that maybe someone was bringing cats to the preserve and releasing them. George and I could not figure out where all of the cats were coming from. He had captured over a dozen and they kept coming. If someone was purposely releasing cats into an area protected by the ESA, they would be violating the 'incidental take' provisions, correct? Also I can't help thinking how enraged George would have been if he caught someone releasing cats at WaterSound."

"You are hurting my brain. It is too early in the morning for questions. If you are right, you are talking about a major conspiracy to shake down a developer. Is that what you are saying?"

"That is exactly what I am saying. We just need to be asking questions to see if there is any truth to my theory. So we not only need to find out who is involved, but at what level of involvement."

"I guess we start with the obvious questions: the name of their organization, their purpose of being at WaterColor, who within their national organization sent them and why. We could ask if they were aware of the house fires and whether they have seen anything suspicious. I would be curious to know more about their concerns for the beach mice. That seems to be the common theme among the groups. I suspect we won't be able to get all of the facts without interviewing some of the people in the respective national organization, so we need to know who to contact and where."

"There is a group of well-meaning ladies at Seaside that take care of stray cats. We need to talk to them, as well. In fact, let's ask around here at the restaurant and see if we can locate them."

CHAPTER 29

THE INTERVIEWS

They walked across CR-30A to the commercial area that lined the boardwalk along the dunes. The owners were opening their shops and getting ready for the day. Vendors were pushing hand trucks loaded with soft drinks and supplies for the restaurants and refreshment stands. Towards the rear of Bud & Ally's Restaurant, they found an elderly woman carrying a bag of cat food and a jug of water.

"Look what we have here," Quinn said, half under his voice.

"You let me handle this," AJ said as she approached the woman and smiled. "Hi, are you one of the ladies that take care of the cats here at Seaside?"

"Yes, I am," she said returning the smile.

"I just love cats. I have two of them myself. Would you mind if I asked you a few questions? Is there a place we can sit in the sun for a few minutes? I'm just a little chilly in this morning air."

"Why, yes, it is still chilly. There is a bench near the boardwalk to the beach where we can sit."

AJ passed Quinn and said, "Get lost for a few minutes, will you? I think she will talk easier just to me." And then to the lady, "We are enjoying our stay here at Seaside so much. One of the waitresses said that there was a group of ladies taking care of the cats and I was hoping to meet one of you. Can you tell me what you do?"

"We have a dedicated little group of about six ladies that take turns caring for the cats. We leave food and water for them.

When we can catch them, we take them to the vet and have them spayed. Once they recover, we release them back to the dunes. We also watch for any litters that the unspayed cats may have and we take those to the vets and have them vaccinated. Once they are old enough to be on their own, we turn them loose."

"How do you catch them? The ones I have seen won't let me get near them."

"Most of the cats get used to us and are easy to catch, but some of them are wild and we can't catch them. When we can, we put them in a cardboard box and take them to the vets."

"Are you the leader of the group?"

"No, Virginia Stratford is our unofficial leader, but she went back to Detroit about a week ago. The rest of us are just carrying on in her absence."

"Do you take care of cats at any place other than here at Seaside?"

"You know, I think Virginia may help at other places. I see her coming back some mornings with her cat food in the car. But the rest of us stay here at Seaside, as there is plenty to do here. Would you care to make a donation to protect the cats? It is a worthy cause."

"Oh, yes, I would—is ten dollars enough? I may do more after I talk with Virginia. You say she has gone back to Detroit? Will she be coming back soon?"

"I'm not sure, but I think she won't be back until the fall."

"Do you know where I can reach her?"

"No, I have her phone number here, but I don't know her Detroit contact information."

CHAPTER 30

SCORCHED EARTH

On March 3rd, an otherwise sunny day filled with the promise of spring and the return of the splendor that defines the Florida Gulf Coast, Cal Summerford filed the complaint with the fourteenth Circuit Court. The complaint detailed the failure of the St. Joe Company to comply with the Endangered Species Act, and the Habitat Conservation Plan prepared and entered into voluntarily, under Section 10 of the Endangered Species Act. This blatant disregard for the ESA had resulted in the Choctawhatchee beach mice being declared by the U.S. Fish and Wildlife Service as in jeopardy of extinction. To redress these grievances, the International Natural Resource Council, acting on behalf of a long list of environmental organizations, asked for the revocation of the Army Corps permit to construct WaterColor, the removal of all structures, infrastructure and associated facilities from habitat occupied by one or more of the listed species addressed in the plan, the restoration of all habitats impacted by the development of the project and $200 million in damages. The complaint also requested immediate action by the court, since the extinction of the beach mice was imminent.

Cal chuckled to himself as he walked from the courthouse. "That should get their attention. Let the games begin. My 40 percent cut should be somewhere between $20 and $80 million. If I can get rid of the smartest member of their team, my fee goes up. That would be worth a small investment of two or three hundred thousand dollars. I'll make some calls."

Brad Garner received notice of the complaint by registered letter and had to sit down once he had read the leading allegation. He immediately reached for his phone and dialed Quinn's number. "Quinn, can you come by the office? That other shoe we have been talking about has just fallen. We need to talk."

One hour later, Quinn and Brad sat at the conference table reading the complaint. "Excuse me for being blunt, but damn, we have been set up. These allegations twist the facts and portray St. Joe as the villains out to destroy the environment for profit. We need to call David Pardue and develop a strategy. If the court honors their request for immediate action, we won't have much time to prepare."

David Pardue was among the best environmental attorneys the state of Florida had to offer. As a senior partner with Hopping Green and Sams in Tallahassee, he had been legal counsel for the St. Joe Company since they restructured the firm from a timber paper manufacturing company and became land developers. He was at his desk when Brad called.

"This is David."

"David, this is Brad."

"Well, good afternoon. How is everything at WaterColor?"

"Not so good, David. We just received notice of a lawsuit filed by a group called the International Natural Resource Council. I'm going to fax you a copy."

"Sorry to hear that. What is it about?"

"They allege that we violated the Endangered Species Act and placed the Choctawhatchee beach mice in jeopardy of extinction."

Did you say the International Natural Resource Council filed the suit? That is Cal Summerford's group. He has been very active on the West Coast and has developed quite a reputation for his aggressive style. He is an SOB and we should not take this lightly.

"I agree. Can you come over for a strategy meeting as soon as possible?"

"I'm available on Friday, if that works for you."

"Good, why don't you come over on Thursday afternoon and we can discuss this over dinner with Quinn?"

"Late Thursday will work. If Quinn is there with you, I would like to speak to him."

"Yes, he is right here. Hold on."

"David."

"Hello, Quinn, I hear you are no longer a murder suspect."

"Yes, I have been downgraded to a person of interest and have apparently become a consultant to the FBI."

"That is too bad. I was looking forward to all the money I was going to make defending you."

"Sorry to disappoint you. From the looks of this suit, you would not have had the time anyway."

"How are you reading this situation?"

"I'm looking forward to talking with you in detail about my suspicions. It feels like a setup to fleece a developer. Their demands are outrageous. Did Brad tell you about that?"

"No, what do they want?"

"They're asking for the permit to be rescinded, all infrastructure removed and habitat restored, plus $200 million in damages."

"Shit, they are not fooling around. That is the scorched earth approach—ask for the world and settle for a continent."

"Yeah, things are going to be confusing around here soon, with the FBI investigating the fire, George's murder and now this civil case."

"Can you get in contact with the FBI about this suit?"

"Yes, what are you thinking?"

"Obviously they can't work on a civil case, but they should know about it. I'm thinking there is a motive for murder in that $200 million."

"I had the same thought. I'll talk to them. We are going to miss George on this one."

"I miss him already. We will see you Thursday."

CHAPTER 31

THE CONTRACT

Cal sat on a bench near the entrance to the Pine Log State Forest and talked quietly on his cell phone as he scanned the nearly deserted parking lot and trail to make sure he was alone. "No, there has been too much shooting going on. I want it to look like an accident, a drowning or a tree falling on him, something that would be an unfortunate tragic event and not raise any suspicions. And I need it done within the next two weeks, the sooner the better. Here is what I know. His last name is Wilson and he is staying at the Seaside Motor Court, Room 2. Apparently he runs every morning between 5 and 6 a.m., so a heart attack would be great if you can arrange it. Yeah, I'll go $20K for a clean job." After listening to the party on the other end for a minute and grunting in agreement, he added, "We have a deal, but this conversation never happened. You got that, amigo?"

Cal knew that 'amigo' would take a cut off the top and pass the assignment down to an associate, who in turn would take his cut and hire a local contractor, who would pay local muscle for the hit. *There is no way this can ever be traced back to me*, he thought, *since the last two clogs in the wheel don't even know I exist. And if they did, I'd frame that dweeb Pinkham for it. These people just do not know who they are dealing with*, he thought as he drove back to Panama City Beach. *This is my biggest paycheck ever and the stage is set, so I'm not going to let any consultant get in my way.*

CHAPTER 32

THE ACCIDENT

Quinn and AJ missed connections for a few days. Quinn was working with Brad to organize the files for the lawsuit—a pretrial hearing was coming up in two weeks where both sides had the opportunity to address the allegations. At the same time, AJ had been conducting interviews with environmental groups and tracking down leads on the arson and shootings.

It was about 11:00 p.m. on Wednesday night when Quinn saw AJ pull up to her room in her black Ford Taurus, one that looked so much like a government vehicle, you might as well have painted FBI on the door in big letters. "Hey, AJ, I need to talk to you once you get settled in."

"I need to talk to you too. Give me five minutes and come on over."

Quinn returned to the small dining room table and looked over his files of the WaterColor permitting process. It was all there, well-documented and ready to review with David tomorrow afternoon. The team had not cut any corners in the process. Quinn had directed the team to do the research and conduct meetings with all the affected state and federal agencies. *No fault could be found in the process and documentation,* he thought as he rubbed the stubble on his chin and tried to think of anything he might have forgotten. Five minutes passed quickly, so he crossed the patio quickly and knocked on the door to AJ's room.

AJ answered the door with a smile. "Hi, come on in." He noticed that she had changed out of her work clothes and slipped on some gray sweats with an oversized FBI stenciled on the back. "I have had a busy couple of days and was hoping we would have a chance to catch up," she said as she tossed her long hair over her shoulder with a flip of her head.

Their conversation was cut short by a powerful explosion that seemed to come from right outside the door. Either due to the force of the impact or Quinn's hyperactive responses, he was hurled into AJ. Both were airborne for a split second before landing on the bed. Out of shock or protective instincts, AJ wrapped her arms around Quinn and held tight.

"What the hell just happened?" Quinn whispered in her ear.

"I don't know," she whispered back.

Quinn attempted get up from his awkward position on top of AJ only to feel her grip tighten as he moved. There was a fleeting few seconds when the mutually protective position in which they found themselves changed to something more. *What is this?* he thought.

When she reluctantly released her grip, Quinn rolled to the side, swung his feet to the floor and headed for the door. AJ followed, picking up her weapon that had been knocked to the floor as she passed. The door was jammed, so Quinn braced his shoulder on the door and pulled. On the third try, he was able to pry the door open enough to view total destruction. His room across the patio was gone. In its place was a pickup truck with a smashed hood and cab.

CHAPTER 33

THE HIT

As Cal had suspected, a local thug with ties to the drug ring and a rap sheet for battery was given the chance to make a quick 5K. He was known by many names over the years and was currently calling himself, Carlos. "No guns," he was told, "and make it quick."

Easy money, Carlos had thought as he was given a newspaper clipping with Quinn's picture, taken during his arrest, and the address of the Seaside Motor Court where he was staying. He had driven to Seaside that afternoon and attempted to mingle with the tourists. He found the motor court tucked away in back of Modica Market and waited. Quinn had returned to the room at about 8:30 and was busy organizing the files for the meeting with David Pardue the next day. Carlos had watched from the shadows and fingered the .38 revolver he carried tucked in his belt, while cursing the conditions of the contract.

It will be hard to make it look like an accident if the SOB sits in his room all night, he had thought. *I could just go to the door and put a couple of rounds in him. That would be an accident all right. I'll be damned if I am going to sit out here in the cold until morning and wait for him to come out. They want an accident? I'll give them one.*

He had walked along the side streets of Seaside until he found what he was looking for, a Chevy pickup with Alabama license tags that the owner had left open with the keys in the ashtray. *This will do the trick,* he thought. But he had to wait for the tourists who were wandering around the circle to leave. There were too many witnesses for what he had planned. So he had moved his car to a parking lot near CR 30A for a quick getaway and picked up a six-pack of beer and two cheap bottles of wine from Modica Market. He had planned on drinking a few beers to keep his courage up as he waited and then was going to leave the empty cans and wine bottles in the pickup to make it look like the driver was drunk. At 11:00 p.m., the streets had been empty, so he was ready to go. One more check of room number 2 had shown the intended victim still there and busy working at the table in the front sitting room. Carlos had walked casually to the pickup, opened the two remaining cans of beer and dumped them on the seat, then had driven to the western end of the circle, fastened his seatbelt and accelerated the truck. He had been going 50 mph as he passed the bookstore and angled into the motor court parking area with Room 2 dead ahead.

AJ had returned to the Court a few minutes after 11:00 p.m. and Quinn had walked across the patio to her room only a few seconds before the truck slammed into his room. Had he been in the room, he would have been buried in the debris and most certainly dead.

CHAPTER 34

DAMAGE CONTROL

AJ and Quinn surveyed the damage. The room was completely gone and the roof collapsed on the truck. The door was open on the driver's side. AJ searched the rubble around the truck for the driver. "There is no one in the cab," she shouted to Quinn, who was trying to collect his files and computer from under the truck.

"There are some empty beer and wine bottles in the truck. It looks like the driver was drunk. It was lucky you were not in the room or you would be…oh, my God."

"What?"

"This may not have been an accident. They could be trying to kill you," she said as she drew her weapon and looked at the debris with new interest.

"Why would anyone want to…" Quinn started to say, until the realization of AJ's comments began to sink in.

"We need to find the driver. He must have gone out the back after the impact. Go look to the north and see if you see anyone suspicious. He may be injured. Don't approach anyone until I am with you—got it?"

"Yeah, I got it," Quinn said as he laid his files aside and climbed over what remained of the back wall. AJ headed south towards CR-30A, as she called Mark on her cell phone. "Mark," she said with urgency as his tired voice answered the call. "A pickup truck just slammed through Quinn's room. It is totally destroyed and could have killed him. He's okay, but this doesn't look like an accident. Someone tried to kill him."

"I'll be right over. Call 911 and get the scene secured. You could be right."

"AJ reached CR-30A and found it nearly deserted. Only a few cars were on the road at that time of night. She scanned in both directions for someone on foot and found no one suspicious. She holstered her gun and dialed 911 as she watched a late model Chevrolet Malibu pass with the driver looking straight ahead.

"This is Walton County emergency response. How may we help you?" The voice on the phone said in a mechanical way, as if reading from a well-worn script.

"This is FBI Agent Lindall, there has been an accident at the Seaside Motor Court. A truck has smashed through one of the rooms. No injuries or fire, but send a deputy sheriff to secure the scene."

"I will dispatch a deputy immediately. It is also standard procedure to dispatch a fire truck to traffic accidents. You say the driver is uninjured?"

"The driver has fled the scene of the accident and no one was in the room," AJ said as the question marks continued to surface in her mind.

North of DeFuniak Springs, the sheriff stirred in his easy chair when he heard the emergency call come on his scanner. The voice and name of the caller were all too familiar to him. His anger in hearing AJ's voice quickly changed to one of confusion and bewilderment. *What the hell...I...I never saw a group of people attract so much trouble,* he thought as he pulled on his jacket and headed for the patrol car.

AJ walked back towards the motor court as she waited for the dispatcher to return and tried to reconstruct what had just happened. That truck had to be traveling at high speeds through Seaside to cause that much damage. There are some tight turns at the entrance to the motor court. It would take some skill to maneuver around the entrance sign and landscaping. That driver certainly could not have been drunk to have made those turns. If he was, the truck would have hit Room 1—it was a much straighter shot from the entrance. Where did the driver go and how did he disappear so quickly? Apparently, he had planned his escape in advance. This was *definitely* not an accident.

The dispatcher's voice came back on the phone, "Let me confirm your name."

"Yes, I'm FBI Agent Lindall with the Pensacola Bureau Office."

"Will you be available at this number if we have to contact you?"

"Yes, this is my cell phone."

"A sheriff's deputy and fire response team have been dispatched to your location at the Seaside Motor Court. Please remain at that location and keep this number open in case the responding officers need to contact you. Do you have any additional information or questions at this time?"

"No, I have nothing more," AJ hung up and stared at her phone for a few seconds in thought. *I'm sure of it. This was not an accident! Someone was deliberately trying to kill Quinn. They have a contract out on him, but why?*

CHAPTER 35

DUCK FOR COVER

When AJ returned to the motor court, she found Quinn under the truck collecting his files. She could hear the sirens in the distance and knew the sheriff would be there shortly. She looked at Quinn with a new perspective as she thought, *Who would want to harm this gentle, intelligent man? This attempt basically confirms what he was saying. There is a conspiracy going on around this project's environmental issues and someone or some group is playing hardball. I should have seen the passions and money angle sooner. It is not sex, but the passions are just as intense and a mouse is at the center of it all.*

Agent Thompson and the sheriff's deputy arrived at the motor court at the same time. As was his nature, Mark took charge immediately. "Mr. Wilson, step away from the truck. This is a crime scene and we need to secure the site. Deputy, tape off this area and call your crime scene investigators. We believe that this was not an accident. Call in that truck license number and let's find out who owns it. I want that truck dusted for fingerprints."

The sheriff's SUV pulled into the court. He stepped out of the truck and slowly adjusted his hat and hiked up his service belt as he surveyed the scene. His confusion had not diminished in his drive down from DeFuniak Springs. His grim face told Quinn and AJ that the sheriff was not a happy man.

Agent Thompson was continuing to direct the deputies as the sheriff approached. "Are you investigating traffic accidents in my county now?" He asked. "You need to step back and let my deputies do their job."

"Sheriff, we don't think this was an accident. We think someone has a contract out on Mr. Wilson and this was a professional hit that was made to look like an accident. Of course, I am open to your opinion. What do you think happened here?"

"Shit!"

"That is exactly what I thought. I am going to continue to investigate this 'accident,' until you come up with a better explanation of what is going on. Do you have a problem with that?"

"I...I... God damn it, agent, this is still my f...ing county."

"And it will be again once we finish this investigation. So, step aside and I'll keep you informed of our progress." He left the sheriff standing in the middle of the parking lot, among the flashing lights of the patrol cars, and walked over to AJ and Quinn. "Everybody okay here?" he asked.

"Yeah, we're okay, just a little in shock," Quinn said as he leafed through ravaged files.

"Tell me what happened."

"Well, AJ had just gotten back and I stepped across the patio to talk to her when the truck slammed into the room."

"What time was that?"

"It was a few minutes after 11:00 p.m. I checked my watch when AJ asked to give her five minutes before I came over."

"AJ, is that what you remember?"

"Yes, I had just left you and driven back to the room. Quinn and I were going to compare notes, since we have not talked much in the last few days."

"Did either of you see anything suspicious before the car hit the room? Was there anything or anyone that looked out of place?"

"Not that I recall, but let me think about it some more."

"AJ, we are going to place Mr. Wilson in protective custody. We will have someone with him 24 hours a day until we figure things out." Mark turned and looked for the sheriff. He was cursing out the deputy over the location of the crime scene tape. "Sheriff, we need to talk to you," he shouted as the fire truck pulled into the court, adding to the already abundant flashing lights.

The sheriff came solemnly towards them in a slow lumbering gait. When he was in range, Mark said, "Sheriff, we need to provide protection for Mr. Wilson. We need a deputy on duty 24 hours a day. Have him coordinate with Agent Lindall. She will be in charge of his protection."

"I've only got two deputies patrolling the south county and I cannot spare either one," the sheriff complained, looking at Quinn with a measure of contempt.

"Then bring in a deputy from the northern patrols, sheriff. Make it happen or I will bring in more FBI support. You don't want that, do you?"

"Shit, you just can't come into my county and order me around."

"Get used to it, sheriff. We are not going away."

It was 2:30 in the morning before things began to settle down and the flashing lights of the emergency vehicles were finally turned off. One sheriff's patrol car remained on duty at the entrance to the court. Quinn crashed on the pullout couch in AJ's room after searching through the debris for as many of his clothes as he could find. He was asleep in a matter of minutes.

CHAPTER 36

REVENGE

Carlos called the boss in the morning to make arrangement for payment of his $5K. It had been a clean hit, he was sure. No one in that room could have survived. He had a broken nose and lacerated his left hand as evidence of the impact. That old shack of a building was a lot stronger than he thought it was going to be and he had earned his money.

"Boss, I took care of business last night. When is payday?"

"You stupid asshole, I've been listening to the police scanner this morning and your guy came through without a scratch. You missed him by a mile and now the FBI and sheriff are on to us and providing round-the-clock protection to that Wilson guy. You've screwed the deal. There is not going to be any payday for either of us. I just got off the phone with our client. He said it was a one-shot deal. We can't stage back-to-back accidents without being obvious that it was a hit, so the contract is cancelled."

Cal paced the floor at his hotel and stopped to look out of the window at the Gulf of Mexico.

He was disappointed that his well-laid plans to clear the deck for the pending lawsuit had failed. Effectively removing Wilson from the case would have increased his odds of winning. Now he had to deal with him in the open court. *No matter,* he thought. *I'll just have to gut him on the witness stand. He will get what is coming to him.*

Carlos fumed over the conversation with his boss. He needed the money, but there was something more at risk. *I have a* reputation to protect, he thought to himself. *They won't come to me in the future, if I don't deliver. I'll show them what an accident is supposed to look like.*

CHAPTER 37

THE MORNING RUN

The next morning, AJ awoke to soft rustling sounds in the front room. She found Quinn setting shirtless on the couch in his running shorts and one running shoe.

"Sorry, I woke you, AJ. I was trying to sneak away quietly for a run."

"Oh, no, you don't, mister; you're not getting out of my sight. I'm responsible for your protection, so you're not going anywhere without me."

"Well, get your running shoes on. The sun is almost up."

"In case, you have forgotten, we were up late last night and I had a house guest that snored, so I did not sleep very much last night."

"May I remind you that FBI agents are supposed to exercise every day to stay in shape?"

"Oh, mister smarty pants. Okay, you get out of here and go find your other shoe, while I get my running gear on, but I'm setting the pace today."

They ran shoulder-to-shoulder along the surf line, past WaterColor to Grayton Beach. Both were caught up in their own thoughts and spoke very little. After approximately five miles, AJ held up her hand and signaled that she needed a rest.

"Stop, I need to catch my breath. You are pushing the pace."

"Sorry, there was a lot on my mind and I was in the zone."

"Let's walk back towards WaterColor. We need to talk." They walked in silence for a few hundred yards. Quinn spoke first. "I wanted to talk to you last night about the lawsuit that was filed while you were away."

"What lawsuit?"

"The International Natural Resource Council filed a suit against St. Joe on behalf of a dozen or so environmental advocacy groups. The suit asked for the revocation of the Army Corps permit for WaterColor, removal of all infrastructure from listed species habitat and $200 million in damages. We have a pretrial hearing in a week and a half."

"Two hundred million, wow, these guys play for keeps!"

"That's why I was scrambling to rescue my files last night. We need all the supporting documentation available to develop our case."

"Well, there is the money trail we were looking for. Two hundred million is enough to kill for. It may not be sex, but the passion is definitely there and they don't want obstacles in their way. You know that was not an accident last night, don't you?"

"I suspected as much, but it's confusing. Why would anyone want me dead?"

"It proves what we have been saying all along. You are a person of interest in this case. You know the history and understand the issues and passions. Whoever is behind this felt they would be better off if you were out of the picture and you need to know they could try again. Therefore, we will be providing you protection at least until that pretrial hearing and maybe longer.

"If it is about the lawsuit, we know who the suspects are, don't we?"

"Yes, but there will likely be a dozen environmental groups, regulatory agencies and angry citizen involved. You're not well liked and we have no evidence, only suspicions that any of them are involved."

"So, *you* are my protection?"

"Yes, you have a problem with that?"

"It just seems that a day or two ago, the tables were turned."

They started to run again almost in unison. "So, AJ, we have a murder investigation, an armed assault on a federal officer, an attempted murder, an environmental terrorist case and a major civil lawsuit going on at the same time. Some of the individuals involved, me included, have a role in all four cases. How do we keep them separated? You may find leads to the civil case while investigating the arson or George's murder. Can you just give us that information?"

"You need to have your attorney get a court order to access our investigation. All of these are spinning around one another. It's confusing. Oh, I wanted to tell you that we have located Virginia Stratford, the cat lady from Seaside. She is in Detroit. Mark and I will be flying up to question her on the first of next week. Also, we will be questioning Cal Summerford and Troy Pinkham in the next few days. Anything we need to be asking them?

"Yes, there is that overriding question of who is orchestrating these events. None of the environmental groups seem to know why they all showed up here at the same time. I would also be curious if Troy knows Cal Summerford and why Cal is targeting WaterColor. From where I stand, we have done everything right and the project should be held out as an example by environmental organizations. Instead, we are being sued for environmental destruction."

CHAPTER 38

TRIAL PREP

Back at the motor court, Quinn rummaged around for his suitcase and the rest of his clothes. The WaterColor Inn was not yet open, but some of the staff were currently undergoing training and a few rooms were ready for occupants. Quinn thought he would check with Brad and see if he and AJ could transfer over. He carried his beat-up suitcase along the sidewalk between Seaside and WaterColor as the sheriff's deputy trailed him in a patrol car. David and Brad were waiting on him in the conference room.

"There he is! I understand you were a popular guy last night," David said in a jocular mood.

"Apparently so! Here a little over a week ago, I was a murder suspect—now I'm almost a murder victim under FBI protection."

"So, the FBI thinks it was an attempted hit?"

"Hopefully, they are just being cautious. But, to answer your question, yes, they thought it was a professional hit. It's been a wild couple of weeks."

"Yes, and we are not done yet. This upcoming pretrial hearing looks like it is going to be a circus and you are going to be in the center ring."

"I'm sure you've had time to study the complaint; what do you think?"

"Yes, I have. Cal Summerford has done his homework very well. I suspect there has been someone behind the scenes feeding him information. The facts are too well presented for him to have done it by himself. Hell, I have been involved with the project from the start and I would have had trouble providing the level of detail he has in the complaint."

"So you are saying they are well-organized and a formidable threat," Brad said solemnly from across the conference table.

"Yes, it is a serious threat and we need to be well-prepared for the hearing. It is typical that the complaint makes it sound like we have done everything wrong and that our actions are suspected of being subversive. Quinn is the best hope we have of setting the records straight on our intent and management activities to protect the habitat for listed species. So Quinn, the first question for you relates to the quarterly trapping reports. They put a lot of stock in the documented fall in the beach mice population in these reports. What can you tell me about that?"

"We have recorded a fall in the projected beach mice population over the past three quarters. George and I both were very concerned. There have been no tropical storms or cold fronts that we can attribute the reduction. Also, a check with other resource managers show there has been no disease among the populations."

"Okay, no climatic event or diseases. What else?"

"We think the reduction can be attributed to the increase in predation, specifically from feral cats."

"Talk me through that will you. Housecats just don't seem to be that big of a threat."

"When they are around in numbers, they are a serious threat to wildlife."

Do you have any documentation regarding an increase in feral cats within the beach mice habitat?"

"Yes, we do! George had an aggressive trapping program going and was removing two to three cats a day from the dunes."

"Come on, two to three cats, be real here. A jury would laugh at us if we blamed a few cats."

"David, hear me out. George was removing two to three cats a day, but they kept coming back. There may have been half dozen or more feral cats on the dunes at any one time and they were all hunting mice. Under normal circumstances, we might capture one cat a year on the dunes. I'm talking about three per day."

"I know. I'm playing devil's advocate just to hear your argument. Are there any other reasons for the decline in population?"

"Other than the normal drop in trapping counts in the winter quarter, we have not been able to identify any other reason."

"Assuming it was the feral cats, what management practice did you implement to correct the problem?"

"George bought new traps and initiated an intense trapping program. He checked them twice a day and took captured cats to the SPCA."

"How many traps did he have in the field?"

"Uh…it's funny that you should ask that."

"Why?"

"I talked to George just a few days before his death and he had five traps deployed. But there were eight traps at the crime scene."

"How do you account for that?"

"The other three were purchased by the Fish and Wildlife Service office in Panama City."

"So, they were aware of the problem and attempting to help?"

"I don't think they were helping. Troy would not be that magnanimous. He clearly stated that the management responsibility was ours."

"If he wasn't helping with the other three traps, what was he doing?"

"That is a very interesting question, one that you need to bring up when he is on the witness stand. I, of course, have my twisted theory."

"And what is that?"

"Someone was bringing cats onto the site in those traps and releasing them."

"Oh, the jury is going to have a field day with that theory. Why would anyone be doing that?"

"To be blunt, if the mice population blinks out and the last remaining Choctawhatchee beach mouse dies while under our care, the award of $200 million in damages becomes *much* more likely."

"I cannot believe you are that jaded to think someone would be deliberately causing the extinction of a federally listed endangered species for money."

"That is exactly what I am saying," Quinn said as he turned to look at Brad across the table.

There was silence at the table for a few moments as they consider the possibility of a conspiracy. Quinn was the first to break the silence. "Before I forget, I talked to Agent Lindall this morning. She suggested we file a court order to gain access to the FBI's investigation."

"Why do we want to do that?"

"Because right now, there are investigations going on for murder, assaulting a federal officer, environmental terrorism, arson and as of this morning, an attempted murder—all occurring around this civil complaint. By filing for a court order, we can gain access to the investigation. Chances are that some, if not all, of these events are interrelated."

"I'm sure glad they didn't kill you off this morning. Having you around for this trial will be very helpful."

On the sidewalk below the conference room, a dark-haired man who looked out of place with a bandage across his nose and a kaki workman's shirt glanced into the building as he passed.

CHAPTER 39

THE INTERVIEWS

Agents Thompson and Lindall finally caught up with Cal Summerford at the Bay Pointe Marriott Hotel. He was sitting at the Lime's Bayside Bar at the end of a long boardwalk into Grand Lagoon. He was wearing a loose fitting Hawaiian shirt sipping a margarita.

"Mr. Summerford?" Agent Thompson asked as he and AJ showed their badges.

"Yes, I'm Cal Summerford. What is this about?"

"Mr. Summerford, we are investigating a series of crimes that have occurred in the last few weeks, including environmental terrorism and assault of a federal officer."

"I've followed the news. What does any of this have to do with me?"

"Maybe nothing, but since environmental issues are involved, we wanted to ask you a few questions."

"Let's get this straight, you have no legal authority to ask me any questions about the complaint I filed against St. Joe. That is a civil matter to be heard by the circuit courts. Are we clear on that?'

"We are not here about your complaint, Mr. Summerford."

"Good, so what do you want to know?"

"Are you acquainted with Officer Troy Pinkham?"

"Yes, I know Officer Pinkham."

"What is your relationship with him?"

"I'm not sure I have a relationship with Officer Pinkham. He is a U.S. Fish and Wildlife Service employee. He has public information that by federal law he is required to make available. As a member of the public, I have asked and received information from him under the Freedom of Information Act."

"What is the nature of the information you requested?"

"That is a part of the complaint and legally, I do not have to disclose that information to you, unless you have a warrant."

"We are asking for some cooperation here. You are not suspected of any wrongdoing. We are looking for leads in these cases. Now if you want, I can get a warrant and we can have this conversation again."

"Very well, the information I requested from Officer Pinkham was the WaterColor Habitat Conservation Plan and the quarterly reports on the beach mice monitoring. All were public documents."

"Was there anything else?"

"Let me think. I guess Officer Pinkham also supplied me with current copies of the Endangered Species Act and the Code of Federal Register for the implementation of the Endangered Species Act. Again they were all public records. What are you looking for? Maybe I can be more precise."

"Did you pay Officer Pinkham for the information he provided?"

"Pay him! Why would I do that, the information was free. Well, I take that back there was an outrageous fee for copying documents—something like a dollar per page."

So no money, services or goods changed hands with anyone at the U.S. Fish and Wildlife Service for the information you received?"

"Asked and answered, agent. Where are you going with this?"

"It just seems that with $200 million at stake, you would not mind paying for some insurance, that is all."

"Don't need it. These violations of the ESA are so egregious that they will speak for themselves. Now is that about all the questions you have? My drink is getting warm."

"Just a few more. What can you tell us about the environmental organizations that have congregated at the WaterColor?"

"I can tell you they are my clients and I cannot talk to you about them or their motives, because of client-attorney confidentiality."

"My question was why they all arrived around the same time—did you have anything to do with the orchestration of this gathering?"

"Ha, ha! These organizations belong to a pretty tight community. They all have their ear to the ground listening for environmental causes to champion. Hell, I heard about WaterColor from the Audubon Club and have tracked the project since then. We all heard the rumors that there were problems with the mice population. They decided to take action and here I am as their mouthpiece. Now let me ask you this—do you have any idea how serious this is? We are talking about the extinction of a species of animal here. When they are gone, they are gone forever. I'm talking about eternity! If St. Joe or anyone else is mismanaging a resource and causing a blink-out—that is a very, very serious situation. I cannot fault the environmental organizations for being concerned. That is why they exist in the first place."

AJ continued, "I noticed that the Soldiers for the Environment were not listed on the complaint. What can you tell us about them?"

"Oh, they are a young organization looking for a purpose. They remind me of the early days of the Green Peace, with that military bearing and uniform. They are long on zeal, but short on knowledge. Give them a few years and they will find their way."

"Can you tell us where you were the morning George Mott was killed?"

"Let me think. Oh, I guess I was here at the Marriott. I remember seeing the news on television during breakfast. That was a terrible thing and a great loss to the environmental community."

"Thank you for your time, Mr. Summerford. You have been very helpful."

"Glad to help. I'll be here at the Marriott through the pretrial hearing, if you have any other questions."

"Thank you for your help."

As Mark and AJ walked away, Cal chuckled to himself. "Stupid bastards, they bought that, hook, line, and sinker. F...ing beach mice—let them die!" Cal casually dialed a number on his cell phone and was happy to get a clean connection. "They're heading in your direction, so be ready. No, they were all softball questions. They do not have a clue as to what we are doing, so answer them straightforward and don't act nervous."

"He is pretty smooth and confident in himself. How did you read him?" AJ asked as they walked back along the boardwalk towards the car.

"I've got to take what he said at face value. He is an attorney doing his job. Other than the usual evasiveness we always get from attorneys, I think he was telling the truth. Is that the way you see it?"

"I'm not sure. Quinn makes a good case and, of course, the attempted hit makes everyone a suspect. Also, when you look at the money trail; Cal stands to make at least 30 percent or more of the award. I'm very sure he is taking that very seriously. There are some subversive activities going on and if Cal Summerford is not involved, I would be surprised. Let's go talk to Troy Pinkham. We can ask him a broader range of questions, since he does not have attorney-client confidentiality."

"First, let's stop by the front desk. I'd like to verify Cal's stay at the hotel and see if we can get a copy of his telephone calls."

The clerk at the front desk was very helpful. The record of Cal Summerford's stay at the hotel showed that he was in and out of the area for the past six months and that he lived very well while he was in town. His phone calls were extensive, in part, because the Marriott was located out of the way and had poor cell phone reception.

"AJ, we are going to have to study these calls. It seems that Cal has been a very busy guy while he was in town. Now let's go talk to Officer Pinkham."

Mark and AJ found Troy Pinkham in his office at the Panama City Fish and Wildlife Service office on Balboa Avenue. The small lobby was festooned with wildlife posters and photographs. A sign on an aquarium caught AJ's eye.

"Oh, look, they have a beach mouse in the fish tank. I want to see it. There he is! He is so tiny and cute with those big ears and eyes. He is just darling!"

Troy came up behind them and was smiling to himself over AJ's reaction to the mouse. Her response was exactly what they wanted from the environmental organizations. Cute was the ticket to big donations and Troy knew that the money was still coming in. Another $25,000 had recently been deposited in his off-shore account and he was quite pleased.

AJ turned and saw Troy standing in the doorway. "Oh, Officer Pinkham, tell me, is this a Choctawhatchee beach mouse? It is so cute."

"No, that is a St. Andrew beach mouse, but they are very similar in size to the Choctawhatchee mice. They differ only in coloring. The population of the Choctawhatchee beach mice are far too small for us to take even one individual out of the community, for fear of tipping the balance. I understand you want to talk to me. We can use the conference room."

The conference room contained a series of misaligned folding tables slid haphazardly together and dog-eared around the edges. There was the usual shuffle as the three moved the metal chairs to afford eye contact. Mark got right to the point.

"Officer Pinkham, we are investigating a series of crimes and related events that appear to be associated with environment issues of this area. Specifically, the FBI is investigating environmental terrorism associated with the arson of two houses in WaterColor and the assault on a federal officer at WaterSound. In addition, the sheriff has requested our assistance on the murder of George Mott. Your work on the environmental issues surrounding these crimes is one of the common threads in this investigation, so for starters, how well did you know George Mott?"

"I have worked with George for a number of years. He was a friend."

"That was not what we heard. I understand you had an adversarial relationship with Dr. Mott."

"We had our differences and butted heads on conservation management issues, but I always considered him a friend."

"Where were you the morning George was shot?"

"I was at the house getting ready for work and picked up the call on the sheriff's radio frequency. I drove to the site immediately to assist in the investigation."

"Do you commonly assist the sheriff in murder investigations?"

"No."

"So why was this different?"

"I knew George and he was on the WaterSound Preserve getting ready for the quarterly beach mice trapping. I thought I could help."

"How did you know he was preparing for the trapping event?"

"George does it every quarter on the new moon and that was two days after he was killed."

"Were you aware that George was trapping stray cats at the preserve?"

"No, I was not."

"Were you aware that three of the Fish and Wildlife Service traps were found at the crime scene?"

"Uh…no, I did not."

Blink-Out

"Who, other than yourself, has access to those traps?"

'Anyone here in the office would have access. We use them to catch rabid foxes and raccoons."

"So was there rabid wildlife on WaterSound?"

"Not that I am aware of."

"Who else in this office can I talk to about those traps?"

"I...I don't know who was using them."

"Do you have to check out inventory and sign for it when you are taking equipment to the field?"

"Usually we do."

"So it should be easy to find out who was using the traps, isn't that correct?"

Mark glanced sideways to AJ, "Can you step out and check with the other officers in the building and see who was using the traps?"

"Okay, I'll be right back."

"Officer Pinkham, I have copies of several letters you recently sent to a Mr. Brad Green regarding the WaterColor habitat management plan. Are you familiar with these letters?"

"Yes, yes, I am. I am required to monitor the activities of St. Joe in compliance with the plan and send enforcement letters when the conditions of FWS agreements have been violated."

"What conditions are you referring to?"

"The management objectives of the Habitat Conservation Plan St. Joe had agreed to perform to protect the Choctawhatchee beach mice."

"So you felt St. Joe was in violation of the Plan?"

"Yes, I do."

AJ returned to the conference room. "Officer Pinkham, I spoke to Jan and we checked the equipment sign-out sheet and those traps are signed out in your name."

"So, what were you using those traps for Officer Pinkham?" asked Agent Thompson.

"Oh, I forgot I checked them out. We keep poor records on the field equipment. They were probably in the back of one of the field trucks."

"How do you account for those traps being found at the crime scene where George was murdered?"

"No...no...I...don't know how they would have gotten there."

"So, just to clarify, you were not assisting George Mott in this effort to remove stray cats from the preserve?"

"No, I mean, yes!"

"Which is it, Officer Pinkham? Were you helping or not?"

"I...I...was going to offer those traps to assist in trapping the cats."

"You stated earlier that you were not aware of a cat problem at the preserve."

"Okay, now I remember that George had mentioned the cats."

Mark made some notes and finally looked at Troy. "Officer Pinkham, your responses to the questions on these traps are inconsistent. We are going to return to this later. But right now, AJ has some questions for you."

AJ leafed through some notes in her file and asked, "Officer Pinkham, are you familiar with the stray cat program at Seaside?"

"Uh, I'm vaguely familiar with their efforts."

"You allow this group to feed feral cats that close to the Grayton Beach dune habitat?"

"I have no authority over those people and their cat program."

"But you have enough authority to require St. Joe to spend hundreds of thousands of dollars to protect mice a few hundred yards away."

"They...freely entered into an Habitat Conservation Plan with the Service and I have the responsibility to ensure the conditions of the Plan are met."

"Do you know Virginia Strafford?'

Beads of sweat were beginning to appear on Troy's forehead.

"No, who is she?"

She is the leader of the stray cat program at Seaside." Troy notable stiffened with this line of questions and looked down at blank legal pad he had brought to the meeting, as Mark and AJ exchanged sideway glances.

"Oh, I may have met her at one of the presentations I made at Seaside."

"Officer Pinkham, do you know Cal Summerford and are you aware of his civil complaint against St. Joe?"

"Yes, I know Cal Summerford. He contacted me and filed a freedom of information request for data on our offices listed federal species work."

"Was the information you gave him targeting any one specific species or project?"

"He was specifically interested in beach mice, since that is one area this office specializes in protecting."

"Did Mr. Summerford pay you for the information you provided?"

"No…no, the information was all provided under the Freedom of Information Act. Here is a copy of his request."

AJ took the copy and reviewed the list of information, while Mark continued the interview.

"So other than the information listed on this request, did you coordinate further with Mr. Summerford?"

"No, I just gave him the information. That was all."

"There were no meetings, phone calls or correspondence between you two at any time in the last six months?"

"Well, I suppose he called the office a few times."

"A few calls? How often did he call you? Was it once a week or every day?"

"I don't know. We talked on occasion. I get calls from a lot of people in this job."

"Over the past few weeks, there have been a number of

environmental organizations congregating at the WaterColor project. Have you or anyone here at the Fish and Wildlife Service offices had anything to do with contacting these clubs and requesting they come to the project?"

"No…no, not at all."

"Why do you think they have come and why do you think they are all concerned with the beach mice?"

"I don't know anything about these organizations."

"As I understand, the Service has not published any public notices or provided any required statements in the *Federal Register*. Is that correct?"

"Yes, that is correct. We have not published any notices since the Habitat Conservation Plan was published three years ago."

"Then how did these organizations find out about the quarterly reports and the declining population?"

"I don't know. However, every report that comes through our door is public information."

"Have you received any requests under the Public Information Act from these groups?"

"I…I…can't remember."

"Have you given copies of the quarterly report to any of these groups? I'm asking this, because the declining population of beach mice is common knowledge. Where else would they have gotten the information, except from you?"

"You're confusing me now. I'm done answering questions until my lawyer is present."

"Okay, that is your right. Your lack of cooperation is duly noted. I don't have to tell you that lying to a federal officer is a crime and there are some notable discrepancies in your answers. I would get with your lawyer and have a talk with him before we meet again. AJ, are you ready to go?"

Back in the car, Mark and AJ evaluated Officer Pinkham's responses to their questions. "Well, that was interesting. There were more than a few cracks in his story."

"Yes, you had him on the ropes a couple of times. It sounds like these three traps are going to be a key issue in the case. He was really flustered when you brought those up."

"He was definitely uneasy at those questions. You know, he's a high-strung person who appears nervous all the time anyway. Are we over-reading his reactions to the questions?" AJ asked.

"Mmm, maybe—let's see how he does with his attorney present. In the meantime, let's get up to Detroit and talk with Virginia Stratford. I'm buying into Mr. Wilson's environmental conspiracy theory more and more all the time."

CHAPTER 40

THE STAIRS TO THE BEACH

It was Friday morning when AJ and Mark left for the Panama City Airport to make the trip up to Detroit, with the mandatory change of planes in Atlanta. Before she left, AJ and Quinn discussed the role Virginia Stratford might have played in the environmental activities revolving around the beach mice and WaterColor.

"AJ, she looks like a do-gooder who likes cats. Her role, if any, is probably minor. I'm afraid your trip up to Detroit will not be useful, but you never can tell. If we are correct and someone was releasing cats into the WaterSound Preserve, then she has to be a likely candidate for that. The big questions will be why she was doing it and whether she was doing it at the direction of someone. Before you go, we should contact the SPCA and Humane Society and see if they have been releasing cats to anyone, especially her. George was taking all the cats he caught up to the SPCA in DeFuniak Springs, which is probably a good place to start."

AJ called both societies and after questioning, she found that the SPCA had a standing order from the Seaside group to save any cats delivered and they would pick them up. "We are on the right track," she told Mark as they drove to the airport.

Quinn spent all day Friday going over testimony with David Pardue. They both agreed that they were about as prepared as you could get. "Go back to the hotel and take it easy this weekend. We have done everything we can. Get some rest and we'll reconvene on Monday morning. The pretrial hearing begins at 10:00 a.m. on Tuesday morning at the Panama City Hall near St. Andrews Bay."

"So, tell me, David, how do these pretrial hearings work?"

"It is a process to allow the judge to review the evidence to see if it is a valid complaint. By definition a pretrial hearing is a meeting in which the opposing attorneys confer, ordinarily with a judge, to work towards the disposition of a case. In such meetings, the discussion is related to the matters of evidence and narrowing of issues that will be tried. Cal Summerford will be arguing that his clients have standing to file the complaint to address their grievances. The judge may or may not want to hear evidence of wrong-doing on the part of the defendant. We are counting on his lack of knowledge about these environmental issues, which will mean he wants evidence, so the attorney filing the complaint will call a witness. We think it will be either you or Troy Pinkham. In either case we get to cross-examine the witness."

"What do you think the judge will rule?"

"They have filed a strong petition. I expect the judge will send it forward to trial and set a schedule for start of the proceedings. Of course, the best case for us will be for the judge to throw the case out. I will be asking for that at the start of the hearing. But I don't think he will rule immediately in our favor, but listen to the tenor in his voice. You may be able to tell if he is sympathetic to our side. If he is not, I ask for a jury trial. It's that simple."

"It does not sound too simple to me, but I'll follow your lead. Have a good weekend and I'll see you on Monday."

Quinn picked up a sandwich and a beer from the newly opened Fish Out of Water Restaurant and walked to the inn. The sheriff's deputy assigned for his protection was preoccupied and barely noticed him as he walked into the inn and went to his room. The inn had just opened to the public and a few new faces were walking the halls. After eating the sandwich, he called home. His wife, Nancy, had become more and more distracted during his calls. He was sure he had been away from home much too long.

"Hello, honey, how are you doing?"

"I'm okay."

"How did your doctor's appointment go today?"

"It was yesterday and I'm fine. Roberto is taking very good care of me."

"That is good to hear. Can you tell me more? Are you feeling okay? Is it hurting? Does he have you on painkillers?"

"I'm okay, so stop the third degree. You won't come home, so there is nothing you could do anyway."

"Yes, I'm sorry about that. This whole thing should be over soon and I'll be coming home. Is anything else going on there?"

"No, everything is normal except I do not have a husband here to help me when I need him."

And so the conversation went—strained like many others had been over the past months. He was a person of interest in the events swirling around him and restrained in place by legal responsibility, to the detriment of his personal life. So he said, "I love you," to the silence on the other end of the line and bid his wife good night.

After a few hours of boring television, he fell into a troubled sleep.

Morning came early—too early for the rest he needed. His agitated mind and troubled soul had kept him awake and out of balance for most of the night. He finally got out of bed at 5:30 a.m. to put on his running shorts and shoes. His plan was to run off the anguish that had settled over him after the phone call with his wife the night before—he was in a foot race to outrun his anxiety. He startled the clerk at the front desk when he rounded the corner and walked out into the brisk morning air. Quinn checked the early morning sky and followed the poorly lit beach-mouse-friendly pathway to the dune walkover. The red LED lights on the landside stairs over the dunes guided his way since he could not see his feet. The turtle lighting requirements allowed no direct lights on the beach side of the dunes, so he held on to the rail and felt each step with his feet as he began descending toward the beach. Halfway down the stairs, he heard a rustle behind him and sensed the movement of something large. The noise caused him to turn quickly to the right to see what was behind him. As he did, a heavy blow glanced off the side of his head above the ear sending him tumbling backwards down the long and rough stairway to the beach.

For the past week, Carlos had been patiently watching from afar and finally had the opportunity to strike. He had repeated his objective over and over until it was an obsession. If he did not complete his contract and kill this no-account bastard, he would be considered unreliable and no one in the underworld would give him a contract—his reputation was at stake. He knew these morning runs were his best opportunity and this morning, the skinny girl that his victim always ran with was not around.

Carlos jumped over the railing and ran down the stairs with a policeman's billy club in his hand to finish the job. *Everyone would think the bastard had died falling down the dimly lit stairs to the beach*, he thought, as he raced to finish the job. He could barely make out the form that lay in the white sand at the bottom of the stairs as he raised the club to strike again.

The glancing blow had stunned Quinn, so he lost his balance on the stairs, but had maintained enough consciousness to break his fall without serious injury. He lay on his back looking up the stairs toward the top of the dune. He could hear more than see someone coming rapidly in his direction.

Sensing danger, he lashed out with his leg and caught his assailant in the stomach, sending him somersaulting over his head and landing on his back with a groan. Quinn rose quickly to his knees, cupped his hands together and leveled a blow to the attacker's head. There was a sound of cartilage breaking followed by screams of agony. One blow was all that was needed.

Carlos had been confident in his street-savvy fighting ability, based mainly on overpowering surprise attacks on unsuspecting victims, but he didn't realize that he was going up against a former Marine. The kick to his stomach was a surprise and the fall knocked the wind out of him, leaving him gasping for air. Before he could gain control, a blow crushed his nose and blurred his eyes. The fight left him and he feared for his life. He had enough—now he just wanted to get away and forget he had ever heard of Quinn Wilson or WaterColor. He stumbled to his feet in pain and staggered away towards the beach, just as the sheriff's deputy, who had been summoned by the desk clerk, arrived with a flashlight to investigate the noise.

"Halt, don't move," he shouted at Quinn whose face was now covered in blood from his head wound. Quinn pointed down the beach and the deputy's flashlight followed his directions to see a figure staggering down the beach towards Seaside. He started to handcuff Quinn until he realized he was the person that he was supposed to protect, so he gave chase to the escaping perp and within minutes, Carlos was in custody and cursing Quinn for assaulting him.

"He attached me, man! I was minding my own business and he jumped me from behind," Carlos pleaded to deaf ears.

The deputy called in to request backup and the EMS for the injuries both men had sustained. Once again the parking lot was filled with flashing emergency lights as the sun began to rise. And again, the sheriff stood beside his patrol car adjusting this hat and surveying the scene in front of him. Quinn was sitting on the bench in front of the inn holding a towel to his head. Carlos, who had suffered a more serious injury, was receiving medical attention in the back of the EMS truck, with the deputies standing by with handcuffs.

The sheriff sat down beside Quinn without saying a word. After several minutes he spoke, "I guess I owe you an apology. You are a God damned pain in my ass, but not the scumbag I thought earlier. Trouble just follows you around. I have never seen anyone show up at so many crime scenes without being guilty of something. So tell me, do you think this is the guy that shot George Mott?"

"Your apology accepted. At this stage of the game, sheriff, I have no idea who this guy is, what he has done or who he is doing it for. This whole situation has too many moving parts to figure out. At a minimum, I would call him a suspect in George's murder."

"Where are your FBI friends? I'm sure they have an opinion."

"They are up in Detroit interviewing a witness. They left the county in your care, sheriff."

The sheriff apparently thought that was funny, since he responded with a single, "Umf!" The two men continued to watch the events in front of them in silence. Finally the sheriff walked over to the ambulance and stood looking at Carlos until the EMS technicians had finished bandaging his nose.

"You're in a heap of trouble, scumbag. You don't come into my county and commit murder and expect to get away with it."

"Murder? I didn't commit any murder. That man sitting over there attacked me. That is him sitting over there alive. I didn't murder anybody."

"I'm talking about the murder of George Mott three weeks ago. You're going to the chair for that one."

"I don't know what you are talking about."

He spoke to the deputy standing next to the prisoner, "Let's get him up to the station and we'll continue this discussion."

As the sheriff walked back to his patrol car, he glanced over at Quinn. He offered a touch to the brim of his hat and a slight almost indiscernible smile on his face. He was back in charge of the county.

CHAPTER 41

TEN STITCHES

Quinn was taken to the emergency room of a small 32-bed hospital that St. Joe had built through their foundation. While waiting for the doctor, he called AJ on his cell phone.

"This is AJ," the familiar voice said on the other end after only one ring.

"AJ, this is Quinn. Did I catch you at a bad time?"

"No, we're heading towards Virginia Stratford's house for the interview. What is up on your end?"

"Well, we caught the hit man this morning after a little tussle."

"What? Who was he? What happened? Was anyone…were you hurt?"

"Slow down now. I'm in the hospital now with…"

"You're in the hospital?"

"Let me talk, AJ. I'm okay. Well, nothing a few stitches won't take care of anyway."

"You're hurt!"

"Yes, he took a swing at me with a billy club. I'll need some stitches. I was heading out for a run this morning and he hit me from behind on the stairs going down to the beach. You remember how dark those stairs are with the beach mice lighting? He creased my skull, but I was able to fight him off and the sheriff's deputy arrested him. The sheriff has him up in my favorite interrogation room now. Who knows, he may even find out something."

"Oh, Lord, Quinn! Even though I'm up here in Detroit, I am still in charge of your protection. Where was the sheriff's deputy during the assault?"

"I believe he was asleep out in his patrol car. The desk clerk woke him up when he heard the all of the shouts of pain."

"Quinn, who was shouting in pain—you or him?"

"Let's just say he got the worst of the deal."

"I'm so sorry, Quinn…hold on a minute, Mark wants to talk to you."

"Quinn, I have been listening in. Don't need to remind you that this would not have happened if you had not been so cavalier about security. You should have awakened the deputy and had him with you while you were out of the building."

"Mark, you know those deputies do not run well in full uniform. However, he was very helpful catching the perp once he got to the beach."

"I want you to stay there in the inn this weekend. There may be other attempts on your life. With the pretrial hearing coming up on Tuesday, apparently they want you out of the way."

"Yes, I am quite confused about that. It's only a pretrial hearing. The process is to examine the evidence, standing of the complaints, and decide whether to take it to trial or not. There is no revelation that is going to take place, so what is the big deal?"

"Apparently, there are bigger issues at stake in someone's mind, so stay behind locked doors. I will be giving the sheriff a call to make sure you have protection. You got that?"

"Yes, mother. I got it."

The doctor finally got around to Quinn. The injury required ten stitches along the left side of his skull. The doctor indicated that he was lucky. If the blow had been two inches to the right, he might not have survived. A combination of the blunt force trauma and the fall down the stairs could have been fatal. After filling out all of the insurance information, Quinn called the sheriff's dispatch desk to see if he could get a ride back to WaterColor. Apparently, the request for security coverage had not made it down to the dispatcher.

"Sir, the sheriff's department is not accustomed to providing taxi service to citizens. We will not dispatch a patrol car to assist you. Have a nice day."

Quinn hitched a ride back to WaterColor with the EMS crew that was returning to their fire station. He sat in the back of the truck and tried to tune out the rock music that was playing too loud in the cab.

He called his wife during the drive back to tell her he was okay. No one answered her cell phone. He glanced at his watch and saw it was now 1:55 p.m., one hour ahead of his time in northwest Florida, and he wondered where she could be on a Saturday afternoon.

CHAPTER 42

THE CAT LADY

AJ and Mark arrived at the Stratford's house in the suburbs of Detroit at 10:00 a.m. Saturday morning. Virginia Stratford was alone and dressed as if she was preparing to leave on a shopping trip. She wore a purple sweater and bright-colored scarf around her neck. She looked the role of a well-off upper middle-class wife, who was secure in her social position.

"Mrs. Stratford, I'm Special Agent Thompson and this is Agent Lindall with the FBI. We are investigating several incidences that occurred in Florida. We understand that you were a winter resident at Seaside. Is that correct?"

"Yes, I just returned home just a few weeks ago. Won't you come in? Would you like a cup of coffee?"

Mark and AJ declined her offer and settled down on a rather ornate French colonial couch in front of the fireplace, as they each retrieved a small notebook and began to ask questions. Neither of them expected much from this interview and in light of the attack on Quinn that morning, they were both anxious to catch the 1:05 p.m. flight to Tallahassee. However, an investigation needs to be thorough and Mrs. Stratford might have some information that would help the investigation.

"Mrs. Stratford, when did you leave Seaside to return to Detroit?" Agent Thompson began.

"Well, it was about two weeks ago. That would be Saturday morning. I think that was April 28th."

"Did you fly back or drive?"

"I drove back. I spent Saturday night with my sister in Nashville. It is about halfway, so I visited with her for the day before coming home on Monday."

"We understand that you work with a group of ladies who take care of stray cats at Seaside?"

Yes, I do. We all love our cats and they would starve to death if we did not give them food and water."

"Are you the leader of that group?"

"I can't say that we are that organized as to have a leader. We all just agreed to take care of the cats and divided the work."

"Do you feed the cats anywhere else other than Seaside?" Both Mark and AJ noticed a sight stiffening of Virginia's posture with that last question and she became much more guarded in her responses.

"No, we take care of them just at Seaside."

"We understand that you catch new stray cats and take them to the SPCA—is that correct?"

"Yes, we catch the new kittens while they are young and take them in for vaccinations and to be spayed. Once they have recovered, we return them to Seaside and release them on the beach."

"We understand that the SPCA sometimes gives you new strays that are brought to their kennel, is that correct?"

"Yes, we sometimes get strays from them. If we did not, they would kill them and that would be just horrible."

"So you bring all these strays back to Seaside?"

There was another hesitation in Virginia's response and sensing that, Mark bore in on the issue. "Mrs. Stratford, we understand your concern for the cats. We are just trying to determine whether you have seen anything suspicious while you or the other ladies were taking care of the cats. Frankly, we were hoping that you were taking care of cats at other locations and may have seen something that would help this investigation. Can you help us?"

"Oh, I did not mean to lie to you but, yes, I put some food out at a wooded site east of Seaside on CR-30A."

"Does this site have a name?"

"It is near that sign that says WaterSound Preserve."

Now things are getting interesting, AJ thought as she asked the next question. "Mrs. Stratford, did you ever release any cats at the WaterSound Preserve?"

"He...he told me not to tell."

"Excuse me, who is he?"

"He said never to tell anyone. It was a secret, just between us."

"Who are we talking about Mrs. Stratford?"

"Officer Pinkham."

"Officer Pinkham asked you to release cats at the WaterSound Preserve?" AJ asked, almost in shock. While the nuance of this response was lost on Mark, she had talked with Quinn enough to realize what this meant. She tried to calm herself down to make sure her next questions did not sound surprised.

"How many cats do you remember releasing at the WaterSound Preserve?"

"I think it was about a dozen, maybe fifteen."

"Since some of them must have been wild, so how did you get them to the preserve?"

"I could bring some of them in cardboard boxes, but others needed a stronger trap."

"Where did you get these traps?"

"Oh, he really does not want me to talk about it. Please don't tell him that I told you."

"So Officer Pinkham gave you the traps to bring cats to the preserve—is that what you are saying?"

"Yes, but please don't tell him."

"Mrs. Stratford, who was going to take care of the cats in the preserve after you returned to Detroit?"

"I tried to train that young man before I left, but those people on the beach got in the way."

"What young man were you training?"

"I cannot remember his name, but he was with that environmental group that marched around WaterColor."

"The Soldiers for the Environment?"

"Yes, I think that was their name."

"So, you can't remember the name of the young man you were training?"

"No, I'm sorry."

"Did Officer Pinkham ask you to contact the Soldiers for help?"

"No, I just wanted to make sure the cats were taken care of while I was back home. I did not want to let Troy down."

"Troy—so you were on a first name basis with Officer Pinkham. How well did you know him?"

"We were friends. Both of us wanted to make sure the cats were taken care of."

"You mentioned the people on the beach. Who were they?"

"I don't know who they were. They came down the beach on their motorcycles and kicked at one of my cats. I'm sorry, but I have to be going. Have I answered all of your questions? And please don't tell Troy that we talked."

"I think that is about all of our questions," Mark said, "Do you agree, AJ?"

"We have just a few more, Mrs. Stratford, nothing major, but will you be back later this afternoon? Maybe we can stop by for a few minutes."

"I have a club meeting and luncheon and should be back around 2:30 this afternoon."

"Thank you for your time, Mrs. Stratford. We will drop by at 2:30 p.m."

They shook hands and walked back out to the car. Mark

noticed that AJ was tense and couldn't figure out why. "What's going on AJ? As far as I know, it is not against federal law to release cats into the wild."

"Mark, don't you see? We have just confirmed Quinn's theory. Officer Pinkham arranged to release cats on the WaterSound Preserve to put pressure on the beach mice population. He then accused St. Joe with dereliction of the Habitat Conservation Plan. Are you getting the drift?"

"So Quinn was right—big deal."

"Yes, it is a big deal. It's a 200-million-dollar extortion run by the International Resource Defense Council with the assistance of a U.S. Fish and Wildlife Service officer. And besides that, those people on the beach that Virginia mentioned—I think that was Clara, Quinn and me. I think Virginia is one of our shooters. We need to tail her to make sure she does not attempt to leave town before we can question her again."

"We have no proof, but we can ask the Detroit police to tail her and keep us informed," Mark said as he dialed the police dispatcher.

I'm no fool! Virginia said to herself as she threw some clothes into a suitcase. *They will figure out that I was the shooter. I've said too much and have to get out of here.*

It had taken 45 minutes to coordinate with the police and in that time, Virginia had disappeared. An all-point's notification to the patrol cops had not turned up any leads by 2:30 p.m. that afternoon when Mark and AJ sat in front of Stratford house waiting her return.

"It looks like we have been played, AJ. A couple more questions and we may have been able to arrest her on the spot for assaulting a federal officer and attempted murder. That would resolve two of the half dozen crimes that are logged on this case. So tell me again about Quinn's theory and how this woman plays a role."

"In a nutshell, Quinn thinks St. Joe, the developer of

WaterColor, is being shaken down. The way things look now it appears that the International Resource Defense Council is the prime suspect, with the help of the Fish and Wildlife Service, specifically, Troy Pinkham. It looks like Troy enlisted the assistance of Virginia Stratford to keep pressure on the beach mice by releasing and feeding cats. The environmental terrorism events were probably meant to do the same. I don't know how George Mott's murder is related, but I am willing to bet we know all the suspects. We need to talk to Virginia further. It's the first break we've had in this case."

CHAPTER 43

THE PERPETRATOR

The sheriff let Carlos sit in the interrogation room for a couple of hours to soften him up. They had him dead to rights on the assault charge, but he wanted more. *I can get a murder confession out of this guy and show those damn FBI agents that I know what I am doing,* he thought with confidence. Carlos was showing signs of being very nervous when the sheriff finally decided to do the interrogation. He entered the room and solemnly hung his hat on the rack as he postured to make sure this perp understood that he was the law and worthy of his respect.

"You're in a heap of trouble, scumbag, and I'm going to see you get the chair for this murder," he said as he started to set the stage for the interrogation.

"Why are you talking murder? I didn't kill anyone. He attacked me and I hit him in self-defense. I'm the victim here. He was alive and sitting on the bench when you put me in the patrol car. I did not kill anyone!"

"Don't give me this victim story. That dog don't hunt. We know you assaulted Mr. Wilson. That will get you eight years. I'm talking about the murder of George Mott three weeks ago. You are the prime suspect in that murder and if you don't start talking to me, I'm charging you with that crime. Now, to begin with, why did you assault Mr. Wilson?"

"I …I was going to knock him out and rob him."

"Rob him! Do I look stupid to you, son? He was wearing running shorts and a tee shirt. Did you think he was carrying any valuables with him? If you were going to rob someone, why were you hanging out in back of a nearly deserted hotel at 5:00 a.m. in the morning? I have to believe there are more lucrative places to stage a robbery."

"I was going to rob him, okay! I was hungry and had no place to go. He was the first person out of the hotel. I could not see well in the dark, so I took a chance."

"That's all? I'm not buying it, scumbag. I'm filing charges for murder," the sheriff said as he started to get up from the table."

"I was in Phoenix three weeks ago. I'm not guilty of murder."

"Phoenix? Okay, give me the dates and the name of someone I can talk to who can confirm you were there and I will call them."

"I…I…don't have anyone…nobody you can call." Carlos said, said since he was involved in a robbery in Phoenix and had left town in a hurry."

"No one, huh! That is a big city and no one can confirm you were there? So let's cut the crap. Was there a contract out on Mr. Wilson?"

"I'm not talking anymore."

"So, there was a contract out on him. Were you the yo-yo that drove the stolen truck through the room a week ago? That would explain why your nose is on crooked and that cut above your eye. I bet your boss was mad about that miss. Who put the contract out on him, Carlos?"

"That was a good hit—how was I supposed to know he left the room? He had been sitting there for hours. I'm not talking until I have a lawyer!"

"Oh, you are saying plenty, scumbag, just plenty. I'll get you a lawyer and we will talk again."

CHAPTER 44

THE ARREST

It was Monday morning before Mark and AJ caught up with a very subdued Virginia Stratford. She had left Detroit in a panic immediately after the interview and driven to her sister's place in Nashville. She saw them coming and mentally had given up on her criminal life before they rang the doorbell. Her imagination had run wild while she was on the lam. She would throw herself on their mercy. Surely they would understand that she was protecting her cats. They were her responsibility.

"Mrs. Stratford, unfortunately we missed connections in Detroit. You were telling us about some people who were driving motorcycles on the beach. But before you answer, I must inform you that your interstate flight to avoid questioning is highly suspicious. You have the right to have an attorney present during questioning. If you give up on that right, everything you say can and will be used against you in a court of law. Do you understand these rights?"

"Yes, I understand. I don't need a lawyer. I have done nothing wrong."

"So, you waive the rights to have an attorney present. Is there anything more you wanted to tell us about the events of that morning?"

"Those people," she said as she began to sob, "those people came down the beach on motorcycles and stopped right in front of me. One of them kicked at my cats and it made me so mad. I wanted them to quit, so I shot my gun in their direction and ran for my car. I heard other shots as I ran, but I don't know what was happening. I only wanted them to quit kicking my cats. Troy trusted me to take care of them and that was what I was doing."

"Did Officer Pinkham give you any directions regarding the protection of the cats in the preserve?"

"He only asked me to feed them every couple of days and they would be fine. I knew he wanted me to protect them."

"Did you ever encounter anyone else on site while you were taking care of the cats?"

"No, I was always there early and no one else was around."

"Did Officer Pinkham ever tell you about a biologist who worked on the site?"

"He told me not to bother him and sent me a message when he thought the biologist was going to be there, so I stayed away."

"So you were aware that George Mott worked to protect the beach mice?"

"Beach mice? No, Troy—oh, I mean, Officer Pinkham, never told me anything about beach mice."

AJ took a deep breath and glanced at Mark, who nodded his head slightly as he pulled a pair of handcuffs from under his jacket. He knew what she was about to say. "Mrs. Virginia Stratford, you are under arrest for an assault on a federal officer, attempted murder and interstate flight to avoid arrest. You have waived your rights to an attorney, so anything you have said can and will be used against you in a court of law. Now that you have been arrested for these crimes, we can again inform you that you have a right to an attorney to represent you on these charges. If you cannot afford an attorney, one will be appointed for you. Do you understand these rights?"

After a moment of hesitation, Virginia offered a weak and tearful response, "...yes."

"AJ, we need to book her and get her back to Walton County to face charges," Mark said as he dialed the local FBI field office.

After keeping Virginia in a holding cell at the local sheriff's office and confirming that she waived extradition to return to Florida, Mark and AJ were on the road heading back to Panama City with their prisoner in custody.

CHAPTER 45

THE PRETRIAL CASE MANAGEMENT CONFERENCE

At 10:00 a.m. Tuesday morning the pretrial case management conference for the civil complaint filed by the International Resource Defense Council against the St. Joe Company was underway at the Panama City Courthouse near St. Andrews Bay. The venue had been changed from the 14th Circuit Courthouse in DeFuniak Springs to Panama City because of the number of participants in the complaint and the public interest in the case.

The weather on the day of the pretrial conference was influenced by the counterclockwise flow around a low pressure area located over south central Georgia that was bringing high winds, squall lines with heavy rain and threats of tornadoes along the greater northwest coast of Florida. The surf line along the beach around Panama City was being hammered by high waves and St. Andrews Bay was fraught with white caps, as high winds with gusts of over 45 miles per hour swept off the Gulf. The view of the bay from the courthouse was one of turmoil, with waves breaking on the seawall, sending towering plums of spray into the parking lot. To the south of the courthouse, the city's municipal marina was only partially protected from the southwesterly wind and the boats strained at their moorings and rocked violently in their slips.

Participants in the management conference scurried in from the parking lot, shielded from the rain as best they could with raincoats and flimsy umbrellas. Inside the courthouse, small groups of people stood apart and talked quietly about different aspects of the trial. Each group watched with interest as participants in the trial entered and made their way into the courtroom. Cal Summerford seemed larger than life as he pushed through the door and out of the rain. He was blustering with indignation as he removed his trench coat and wiped the raindrops from his glasses as his large entourage of environmental organizations stood by in support. They were geared up for battle and he was their champion.

The courtroom was filled to capacity when Judge Archie Clements gaveled the court into session.

"This is a pretrial conference of a petition filed by the International Resource Defense Council on behalf of 12 nongovernmental environmental organizations against the St. Joe Company. The petition alleges blatant violations of the Federal Endangered Species Act. The ruling before this court is to confirm the validity of the complaint and rule on whether these charges should be brought to trial. I'll give both sides the opportunity to address the court before I make my ruling. Is that clear? If so, can we hear from the petitioner?"

"Your Honor, I'm Cal Summerford, counsel for the petitioners. We move that you acknowledge this complaint and the standings of the petitioners and send it forward for trial. The violations are so gross and evident that no further discussions are needed." This request was followed by a scattering of applause and a few catcalls from the audience. Cal played to the audience and in a show of confidence, he noisily dropped a large file on the desk, just to illustrate to the judge that he had done his homework.

The judge gaveled the audience, "I need to remind you that this is a court of law and not a carnival, so let's keep these outbursts for the final verdict. Bailiff, I want you to remove anyone from these proceedings who cannot follow my instructions.

Now, counselor, in regards to your motion, I would like to hear more about this position before I pass judgment. "Counselor for the defendant, do you have any opening remarks or motions at this time?"

"Your Honor, I'm David Pardue, counsel for the St. Joe Company. I move that this complaint be dismissed. My client has acted in good faith by entering into a Habitat Conservation Plan and following the provisions of that Plan to the letter. In doing so, the St. Joe Company is afforded certain rights and protection under Section 10 of the Endangered Species Act. Therefore, Your Honor, my client is protected from unfounded lawsuits such as the one filed by the complainants here today."

"So noted. Counselors, both sides have asked for motions. Therefore, I will defer action on either one until the court has heard further evidence."

Cal, who again was blustering and making grandstand gestures addressed the judge's comments. "Your Honor, I take exception to my esteemed colleague's reference to the St. Joe's Company being diligent in the administration of the Plan. Clearly, judge, they are developers with the objective of raping the land for profit. They cannot and should not be trusted with the protection of a precious environmental resource, such as these imperiled beach mice."

David rose to his feet in objection, "Your Honor, I object to the complainant's characterization of my client. These accusations are unfounded and presented without proof."

"Counselors, you both need to get your posturing out of the way so I can hear evidence in this case. Does the petitioner have a first witness?"

"We do, Your Honor, the petitioner calls Mr. Quinn Wilson to the stand and, Your Honor, I would like to note that Mr. Wilson is a hostile witness, so I would request the court's indulgence in my questioning."

"So granted. Mr. Wilson will you take the stand? Since this a pretrial hearing and I would like to conduct these proceedings informally, I will dispense with our swearing in of witnesses. Of course, you understand that you must tell the truth while on the stand? Mr. Wilson, do you agree?"

"I do, Your Honor."

"Mr. Wilson, please state your full name and title for the court."

"My name is Quinn Wilson. I am a vice president and senior environmental planner with the JSB&P consulting firm based in Tampa, Florida."

"Mr. Wilson, in your capacity of an environmental consultant, did you provide service to the St. Joe Company on the WaterColor project?"

'Yes, I did."

"Can you tell the court what services these entailed?"

"We provided environmental planning, land use entitlement, environmental permitting, civil engineering and construction management to St. Joe during the development of the WaterColor project."

"Was one of the tasks you performed the preparation of the Habitat Conservation Plan for the protection of listed federal species on the WaterColor project?"

"Yes, we prepared the Habitat Conservation Plan."

"'Is this a copy of the plan that you prepared?" Cal said as he handed Quinn's bound copy of the plan with a Fish and Wildlife Service stamp and initial on the cover.

"Yes, that is a copy of the Plan."

"Can you tell the court how many listed federal species occupy habitat within the WaterColor project and are addressed in this plan?"

"As I recall, there were eleven species addressed in the plan."

"Eleven species! Why that seems to be an unusually large

number of federally threatened and endangered species to occupy habitat on one project. Don't you agree, Mr. Wilson?"

"Yes, but..."

"Thank you, Mr. Wilson."

"Is the Choctawhatchee beach mouse one of the aforementioned eleven species?"

"Yes."

"Was this plan published in the *Code of Federal Register* in April 2006?"

"I'm not sure of the specific date, but yes it was published in the register around that time frame."

"Your Honor, I would like to have this Habitat Conservation Plan accepted as Exhibit A."

"Clerk, please note this plan as Exhibit A and enter it into the court's records."

"Mr. Wilson, can you tell the court the agreed upon provisions for the protection of the mice?"

"The St. Joe Company agreed to place a conservation easement on 1.5 miles of Gulf Coast beach, with sand dunes that provide excellent habitat for beach mice, relocate twelve breeding pair of mice to the preserve and monitor the mice population for the next twenty-five years."

"Thank you, Mr. Wilson. Can you tell me the purpose of the monitoring program?"

"The monitoring program is designed to keep a census on the beach mice population and to confirm the health of the colony."

"The Habitat Conservation Plan calls for the monitoring of beach mice habitat every quarter, is that correct?"

"Yes, every quarter."

"I call your attention to this quarterly report dated December 2007. Can you tell me about this report?"

Quinn, accepted the report and made a cursory review before responding, "Yes, this is a quarterly report prepared by

Dr. George Mott after the trapping event in December 2007. This was the fourth-quarter trapping conducted under the requirements of the Habitat Conservation Plan."

"Thank you. Can you tell us what the report says about the population of beach mice?"

"The report confirms a substantial increase in beach mice population after the relocation of 12 pair of mice to the WaterSound Preserve in July 2006. The modeled estimates indicate the population within the preserve had grown from 24 to over 125 specimens."

"Thank you. I would like to enter this quarterly report as Exhibit B."

"Now, Mr. Wilson, I would like to call your attention to the quarterly report dated December 2008. What can you tell me about the population of mice one year later?"

"The population has not grown and is exhibiting signs of stress. Population estimates have been reduced to less than 75 mice."

"If it pleases the court, I would request this quarterly report be entered into evidence as Exhibit C. So, Mr. Wilson, in your own words the Plan is failing, is that correct?"

No..there are..."

"Yes or no, Mr. Wilson. Is the Plan failing to grow the beach mice population as was stipulated in the Plan?"

This is not a yes or no..."

"Your Honor, please instruct this witness to answer the question."

"Mr. Wilson, please respond to the counselor's question."

"Your Honor, there are few definitive yes or no answers when dealing with habitat management issues."

"Your Honor, the witness is being evasive. The question again is whether the plan is failing to maintain the population of the mice as of this quarter report. The documentation is simple to read."

Blink-Out

"Answer the question, Mr. Wilson."

"Yes, but…"

"Thank you, I now call your attention to the December 2009 quarterly report. How many mice are now estimated to be in the preserve?"

"This plan estimates less than 40 mice, but…"

"Thank you. So, tell me Mr. Wilson, is the plan failing at this point?"

"The quarterly reports indicate…"

"Yes or no, Mr. Wilson? Is the plan succeeding or failing?"

"It is failing, but…"

"Thank you. Your Honor, I request this quarterly report also be entered into evidence as Exhibit D. I now call your attention to this photograph taken only three weeks ago. Tell me what you see?"

Quinn was surprised at the photograph and glanced over to David before responding.

It was a photograph of the sheriff's SUV mired down in the surf line and surrounded by deputy patrol cars and the wrecker.

"The photograph is of the sheriff's patrol vehicles on the WaterSound beach."

"Are vehicles allowed on the beach under the Habitat Conservation Plan, Mr. Wilson?"

"No, these vehicles…"

"Thank you, Mr. Wilson. Your Honor, I request this photograph be entered as Exhibit E. Now correct me if I am wrong, but isn't St. Joe responsible to keep vehicles off the beach under the provisions of this Plan."

"These are law enforcement…"

"Yes or no, Mr. Wilson, we have been through this before. Is St. Joe responsible to keep vehicles out of the preserve?"

"Yes, but…"

"Thank you, Mr. Wilson. I now call your attention to this

photograph taken on the same day at the WaterColor project. Can you tell the court what you see in this photograph?"

Again, Quinn glanced over at David and Brad before answering. "This is a fire on the north side of WaterColor near the Point Washington State Forest."

"Your Honor, I request this photograph be entered as Exhibit F.

Mr. Wilson, this fire is in flatwoods salamander habitat, isn't that correct?"

"That has not been determined."

"If it pleases the court, I would like to have the report from a Mr. John Palis stating the probability of habitat for the endangered Flatwoods salamander existing on WaterColor entered into evidence along with the photograph. Now Mr. Wilson, can you tell me the dates of the photograph and the report?"

"It appears that the photograph of the fire occurred one week after the report was submitted to the U.S. Fish and Wildlife Service."

"Don't you find this suspicious, Mr. Wilson? The probability of habitat for a newly listed species is burned one week after it was confirmed as occupying an area within the project. Do you think the environmental community is blind?"

David rose in objection. "Objection, Your Honor, the counselor's comments are speculative and unfounded."

"Noted, counselor, but I am going to let him continue. Mr. Wilson, please respond."

"Can you repeat the question?"

Cal again blustered and turned to the audience before asking the question again. "Your Honor, the witness is being difficult. The question was simply whether the timing between the report from John Palis and the fire in the salamander habitat was suspicious?"

"I don't think…"

'Thank you, Mr. Wilson. I believe the court understands

your reluctance to respond to this obvious question. I have no further questions for this witness. Judge, since we are operating informally, I would like to summarize that this evidence is indisputable, even gauged by these responses from St. Joe's own consultant. The Habitat Conservation Plan has failed through blatant disregard of best management practices or through criminal neglect. I move again that you find in favor of the petitioners, accept this complaint and place it on the docket for a speedy trial. Speed is critical on this case, Your Honor. If we delay, an entire species is in jeopardy of blinking out and disappearing forever."

"Based on the testimony provided by Mr. Wilson, I am prepared to rule on this complaint. However, in all fairness, I will allow the defendant counsel to cross examine the witness. Counselor?"

There was a flurry of activity in the rear of the courtroom as three individuals entered and sat on the defendant's side of the gallery. On seeing them enter, Troy Pinkham blanched white and began to sweat. He nervously got up and walked to the rail and motioned to Cal Summerford. The two whispered urgently for a few seconds and then Cal turned to address the judge.

"Your Honor, if it pleases the court, I would like to request an early lunch before my esteemed colleague cross-examines this witness."

"Very well, if neither counselor has any objections, this pre-trial hearing will break for lunch and reconvene at 2:00 p.m. this afternoon. Court adjourned."

The three people who entered the courtroom were FBI Agents Mark Thompson and AJ Lindall and in handcuffs between them was Virginia Stratford. Troy Pinkham raced from the courtroom as the judge gaveled the adjournment. Jan, Troy's supervisor, noted Troy's departure and followed him from the courtroom. A murmur of voice filled the courthouse as the audience spilled from the courtroom and again collected in small groups along the hallway and lobby. They all turned and watched Quinn pass as he walked out with David Pardue and Brad.

'You did good in there, Quinn," David offered with a conciliatory note.

"I would have done a lot better if he had let me answer the questions. These demands to answer complex questions with a yes or no just infuriate me. I don't think I've come across a clear yes or no answer on habitat issues during my entire career. There are always conditions, variables, and extenuating circumstances. David, are you going to give me more time to answer these questions on cross examination?"

"Yes, I will. But I think the judge has already made up his mind. We are going to trial and when that starts, you will think these questions were child's play. At this stage, I am happy that we are getting a closer look at their argument. It will help us prepare for the trial."

"AJ came out of the courtroom and scanned the hallway. She waved at Quinn when she saw them standing in the lobby and came over in a rush. "Hey, guys, I wanted to tell you that we arrested Virginia Stratford for the shooting on the beach. She has also told us that…"

Just them Jan ran up to AJ out of breath. "AJ, he is running!"
"What, who?"
"Troy is running. I followed him from the courtroom when we adjourned, so I could talk to him. He was very upset and talking crazy. I stopped him from getting in his car to talk further, but he ran toward the marina."

AJ turned back to Quinn as David and Brad both stepped closer to hear what she said. "Virginia told us that Troy was supervising the release of cats into the WaterSound Preserve."

In unison, the three responded, "What!"

"Yes, he is guilty of orchestrating the release of cats and that is probably just the tip of the iceberg. We need to arrest him!"

Agent Thompson, who had joined the discussion after placing Virginia in custody, overheard AJ's statement.

"Where is Troy now?"

"Jan saw him running toward the marina."

"Why would he be going there?"

Jan responded, "We keep the Services patrol boats there! When I blocked him from his car, he bolted in that direction. I think he's going to try and get away in one of the boats."

"AJ, you and Jan come with me." Then as an afterthought, "Quinn, you come too. You know these waters better than the rest of us."

"Wait a minute. You remember—I'm not law enforcement."

"Cut the crap, Quinn, and come on," Agent Thompson said as they headed across the lobby.

The four people discreetly left the courthouse by the back door and ran across the parking lot to the municipal marina. In the distance, they could see an open boat pounding through the white caps, heading north into St. Andrews Bay.

Fish and Wildlife Service maintained four boats at the municipal marina. One was missing. Two of the remaining boats were 18-foot open fishermen with central consoles and a utilitarian 115hp Yamaha outboard motors. The fourth boat was a 24-footer with a 225 Yamaha engine that was used for nearshore work in the Gulf. Quinn was quick to see the advantage of the larger boat and stopped the team from boarding the smaller one. "We will take this one," he said with authority.

Quinn started the engine and shouted orders to his landlubber crew to loosen the line on the boat. Troy was now ten minutes ahead of them, pounding hard across the waves in the center of the bay.

Quinn brought the boat out of the marina and felt the full force of the wind and waves for the first time. *This is no time for any small craft to be on the bay,* he thought as he pushed the throttle to half-speed and headed west.

"What are you doing?" Mark shouted over the whine of the engine and the howl of the wind. "He's going that way," he said, pointing north.

"I know. He has a head start on us and I'm trying to catch up. Trust me."

Quinn nursed the boat through the waves and into the lee of the western shoreline of the Bay. Once the waves subsided, he turned north and accelerated to full speed, and the boat flew through the calmer waters at over 45 miles an hour. Ahead they could see Troy's boat laboring in the center of the bay, pounding hard against six-foot seas. They *were* catching up.

They were about a mile and a half behind Troy's boat as they passed under the U.S. 98 Bridge and entered the broadest portion of the bay. Ten minutes later, they were neck and neck, separated by one mile, as Quinn turned north and left the sheltered waters along the western shoreline to intercept Troy in the center of the bay. Quinn pushed his boat to close on Troy as his crew held on to the back of his seat and were soaked by the wake crashing over the bow. The two boats pounded on through the gray brown waters of the bay.

"Where do you think he is going?" Mark shouted over the wind.

"Troy is heading for the mouth of the Intracoastal Waterway, where he knows there is calmer water," Quinn shouted back. "I should be able to head him off."

In the other boat, Troy was indeed focused on the Intracoastal Waterway as the only escape route open to him. Beyond the shelter stretch of the ICW were the Choctawhatchee Bay and the confluence of the Choctawhatchee River that extended all the way to the Alabama border and was surrounded by a variable wilderness. *Yes,* he thought, *the river would allow him to escape* the situation that was unfolding at the courthouse. When he saw Virginia looking at him with those sad eyes, he knew that the plot had been discovered and he had to get way from there as fast as he could. The water was so rough that he had not had a chance to look back. Now another boat appeared in his peripheral vision.

Oh, shit, they're after me and catching up! Shit, shit, I have to get away. They will catch up before I reach the Intracoastal Waterway.

In desperation he turned his boat sharply into Crooked Creek, a narrow tidal tributary of St. Andrews Bay. Quinn turned in pursuit as he saw Troy's boat careen over the shallow sandbar at the entrance of the creek. He slowed and steered towards the unmarked channel he knew existed closer to shore. Troy continued on at breakneck speed, narrowly missing the bridge pilings as he passed under CR 388. The creek narrowed as he sped north. An overhanging limb sheared the windshield off his boat and as he ducked for cover, the boat bounced off the shoreline, so he struggled to gain control.

Quinn navigated the channel at the entrance to Crooked Creek at a slower speed and proceeded at half throttle under CR 388. His crew was stirring as they checked their weapons and pulled off soaking-wet life preservers.

Troy was a half mile ahead as he neared the navigable end of the creek. He slammed the boat into the shoreline at full speed and the engine screamed as the prop spun out of the water. He jumped from the boat and ran north along an old firebreak.

Everyone on the pursuit boat heard the engine scream and knew the end of the chase was near. Mark moved to the bow of the boat in a crouched position with his weapon drawn. AJ braced herself near Quinn and leaned over until their shoulders touched. They could see Troy's boat ahead, as Mark barked out orders, "We don't know if he is armed, so be cautious. We need to get him back for questioning and see how deep this conspiracy goes and who else is involved! Quinn, you stay with the boat. Jan, you and AJ follow me and stay together."

Quinn decelerated the boat and brought it up to shore. Mark jumped ashore as soon as the boat touched the shore and started running up the firebreak. Quinn grabbed AJ's arm as she started forward. "AJ, there is nothing in front of us but ten miles of pine plantation. There is an old saw mill about a half mile to the left with a road over to the highway. Troy will likely head in that direction, but the fastest way out of here is by one of these boats. He may double back, so go!"

Quinn turned off the engine and silence settled over the creek as AJ and Jan disappeared into the pines. Overhead a blue heron, who had been disturbed by these intruders, squawked noisily as he strained to gain altitude. Another squall line came through, darkening the sky and lashing the leaves on the trees with more wind and rain. Quinn tied the boat to a stump and stood on the lee side of a large live oak tree to gain some protection from the wind. Quiet settled over the creek as he waited.

He was standing there when Troy stepped out of the pines and walked nervously towards the boats, his service revolver grasped in both hands as he approached. Quinn knew that he could not let Troy take the boat, so he called out his name to let him know that he was not alone.

Troy jerked around towards the sound of the voice, took two steps back and stumbled over a tree limb. Scrambling to his feet in panic, he said, "You! What are you doing here?"

"Take it easy, Troy—you are only making matters worse."

"This is your fault you know, you and that Dr. Mott. You are trying to ruin my life."

Quinn raised his hands in an attempt to appear less threatening. "What are you talking about, Troy?"

"You beat me. I wanted the project to fail and you went over my head."

'Troy, calm down—you are not making any sense."

"I'll show you who is boss, just like I showed George."

Quinn dropped his hands and walked slowly towards Troy, "What are you talking about, Troy?"

Troy stepped back again and nervously waved his gun towards Quinn. "Stay back…you…don't come any closer or I'll shoot you, just like I shot him."

"What did you say?"

"I shot him! I shot him! That is what I said. He caught me releasing cats and was so mad I had to shoot him. It was self-defense. He was going to strangle me. I saw it in his eyes, just like I see it in your eyes now. You want me dead, but I have the gun and I will use it again," and he began edging towards the boat.

Quinn became increasingly aware of the nervous twitching of Troy's hands. *That gun is going to go off, even if he doesn't intend to shoot me, so I need to be ready to make a move*, he thought to himself as he began to move closer to Troy. It was his only chance.

"Troy, calm down now and give me the gun. You are only making it worse. Give me the gun!" he demanded as he took two more steps in Troy's direction with his eyes trained steadily on those trembling hands.

"No….No, I won't, you stay back…you can't…" BANG!

Quinn twisted sideways as he saw Troy's hands tighten on the trigger from six feet away. The muzzle blast caught him in the face as he spun backward and fell into the creek face-first. His mind went blank.

"Troy! Troy! This is Agent Lindall with the FBI. Drop the weapon and drop it now!"

Troy spun towards the voice in disbelief, "No…no, you can't stop me."

He fired two more shots in AJ's direction as she charged down the path towards him ignoring the poorly aimed shots she could see kicking up a plume of red clay in front of her.

In a final act of desperation, Troy fell to his knees sobbing and put the barrel of his gun in his mouth and pulled the trigger. His body went limp as he fell near the bow of the patrol boat.

AJ ran past him as she shouted, "Oh, my God! No…no, Quinn! Quinn, are you all right?"

Quinn lay face down in the shallow water of Crooked Creek, blood covering the side of his face and staining the water next to his head. AJ hesitated for a second upon reaching him for fear of what she would find. Mark and Jan raced to her side, as she struggled to turn him over. The blood and debris from the creek obscured his face and AJ cried as she wiped the mud away.

Quinn opened his eyes and jerked in surprise to see AJ so close. After a few seconds of looking into her face, he regained his composure and gently pushed her back and sat up. Mark and Jan took a step back in surprise. Quinn rubbed his hand across his cheek and looked at the blood with curiosity.

"I think he missed," he said in a matter-of-fact tone of voice. "Troy was so nervous and his hands were shaking so much that I knew he was going to pull the trigger. When I saw his hands tighten, I twisted to the right. Apparently my timing was good. I caught the muzzle blast and felt a sting on the side of my face, so I didn't know if I had been shot or not."

"AJ punched him on the arm. You scared the crap out of me. We thought you were dead!"

More blood was running down Quinn's face, so he retrieved a soaking-wet handkerchief from his pocket to wipe it off. In doing so, he found that the blood was coming from a nick in his right ear, as well as from a rupture in the stitches on his head.

Mark was bent over Troy's body shaking his head. "Quinn, we all heard the confession and were planning on taking him by surprise when he pulled the trigger. From our location, we thought you were dead. This is not the outcome I was expecting when we left the courtroom. We only knew he was running and needed to question him. We have not had time to fill you in, but Virginia confessed to bringing cats to the WaterSound Preserve and shooting at your trio that morning. She was following Troy's lead on the protecting the cats."

"I am shocked to hear you say that! Troy has been so adamant about the protection of the beach mice. It just blows my mind that he would even think of releasing cats into the preserve."

"Virginia confirmed that she was feeding the cats on WaterSound at Troy's request. Troy also arranged for her to release cats into the preserve. We think the shooting may have been her overreaction to the protection of her cats, but we wanted to question Troy about that and see how far this conspiracy went. That option doesn't appear to be available to us right now," Mark said as he looked at Troy. "What do you suggest we do now?"

"That depends on how much crime scene investigation you need to do. We should call 911 and take the boat over to the boat ramp near the Boondock Restaurant. Do you want to take Troy's body with us?"

"Yes, we have eye witnesses to the confession and suicide, so no further investigation is needed. Let's load up and get out of this rain. I'll call the sheriff and have him waiting for us. We need to get you to the hospital as well, as you are still bleeding pretty badly."

It was a somber procession that idled back down Crooked Creek to St. Andrews Bay. The wind and waves on the bay gave way to the sheltered waters of the Intracoastal Waterway as they motored west. A few short miles later, they passed under the State Road 77 bridge and turned into the boat ramp on the southern shoreline, where a fleet of law enforcement and emergency vehicles waited with their lights flashing. The sheriff stood on the dock as Quinn maneuvered the boat up to the ramp. While his face was stern, in his usual effort to convey authority, his eyes were saddened on seeing Troy's body. He was a trusted friend of over 15 years and fellow law enforcement officer. His usual belligerent attitude was gone when he spoke, "Tell me what happened here."

Mark responded in his usual direct manner, "In short, sheriff, Troy confessed to murdering George, then took a point blank shot at Mr. Wilson and committed suicide before we could subdue him. He was in a very agitated state."

"I find that almost impossible to believe. Why would he have murdered George Mott?"

"We all heard his confession. George caught him releasing cats into the WaterSound Preserve to put stress on the beach mice population. They argued and Troy shot George to cover up the conspiracy to shake down St. Joe for violations of the Endangered Species Act."

"So...it was about the mice?"

"Apparently so, but now we have to figure out who else is involved."

The EMS technicians labored over Quinn to stop the bleeding. In addition to the stress on his scalp wound, there was a nick in his ear from the near miss and wounds on the right side of his face, either from the near point-blank muzzle blast or from the fall he took into the creek. AJ sat silently next to him, wrapped in a silver emergency blanket, watching the EMS technicians patch him up, while Mark supervised the removal of Troy's body from the boat.

"Are you going to be okay?" she asked with sincere concern in her voice.

He knew she was referring more to his emotional state, rather than the superficial wounds the EMS techs were patching up. He also knew that she was really asking about her own emotions and was looking for assurance that everything was going to be all right; after all shots had been fired in anger and a man lay dead on a stretcher just thirty feet away.

"Sure, I'm going to be okay. It takes more than a point-blank pistol shot to the face to put me down. The real question is how are you doing?"

"This was supposed to be a simple investigation into a house fire. It was my rookie assignment that was to take an afternoon. I wasn't even going to spend the night. And here we are. We've been shot at twice and you have survived two attempts on your life. I've had senior agents tell me they have gone their entire career without drawing their weapon. Now we have solved a murder and arrested a woman for assault on a federal officer. I told you, I am just an accountant, not an action hero!"

"Don't be so hard on yourself. From what I understand from Mark, you held your own under fire. I have seen strong men wilt when they are in combat for the first time. It is never easy, but you passed the test."

"I wanted to kill the son of a bitch when I saw him shoot you. From that close range, I was sure you were dead. I wanted to get close enough to put a bullet between his eyes. Nothing was going to stop me. I have never been that angry before."

Mark walked towards them, talking on his cell phone. "Yes sir. I understand, yes, sir" was a phase that he repeated several times. He looked stressed when he disconnected the call and surveyed the conditions of the two bedraggled people sitting on the tailgate of the EMS vehicle. "That was the judge. He was angry that the chief witness in this pretrial hearing did not return to the stand for cross-examination at 2:00 p.m., as he had instructed. I tried to explain to him what had transpired this afternoon, but he was more concerned with the dishonor shown to his court. He was ready to throw you in jail for contempt of court."

"Oh, that's just wonderful!" Quinn said as the EMS Tech applied a gauze bandage to his ear. "It seems like everyone is hell bent on putting me in jail. I hope you were able to talk him down."

"Court is to continue tomorrow morning at 10:00 a.m. The judge wants to deal with your contempt of court and get to the bottom of what is going on. This has become more than a pretrial hearing."

"Excuse me, sir, we need to transport this patient to the hospital. He is going to need stitches in his ear to stem the blood flow," the EMS tech said as he packed up his medical kit.

"I'm going with you," AJ said, as she shed her emergency blanket.

The wind had diminished and a ray of sunlight broke through the clouds for the first time that day as the EMS truck prepared to depart the boat ramp. Those remaining at the site seemed to be moving in slow motion as Troy's body was loaded into the coroner's van and groups of sheriff's deputies and Fish and Wildlife Service officers milled around as they attended to the last details of the event. The sheriff stood alone on the dock watching the boat being pulled from the water, the mud and blood attesting to the drama that had occurred at an isolated section of Crooked Creek. A few yards away, three deputies awkwardly launched the sheriff's patrol boat and prepared to return to the creek to survey the scene and gather what evidence remained at the site.

As daylight faded into night and the wind diminished to a light onshore breeze, a beach mouse in the WaterSound Preserve pushed the windblown sand from his burrow and sniffed the night air. The stench of predators who had stalked the dunes was gone and in its place the enticing aroma of sea oats that had been blown from their stalks by the high wind and lie in abundance on the dunes. Cautiously at first and then with more abandonment, he rushed to a windrow and nibbled greedily on the bounty of oats. Other beach mice joined in the forage. With their stomachs full, they joined in brief courtship encounters—short wrestling matches that fulfilled the prerequisite for the perpetuation of the species.

A few short weeks later, a new generation of beach mice would be born in the sandy dens dug into the dunes. They were destined to become sexually mature within six weeks. They were born during a period of plenty with minimal fear from the predators that had plagued their parents.

CHAPTER 46

RETURN TO COURT

"The 14th Circuit Court is now called into session. The Honorable Judge Archie Clements residing," the bailiff recited with a notable lack of passion or interest.

"You may all be seated, Judge Clements said with a scowl on his face. "Before we begin these proceedings, I want to admonish the counselor for the defendant on their lack of preparation. You were to have your witness available for cross-examination at 2:00 p.m. yesterday afternoon."

"Your Honor, I would note some extenuating circumstances."

"I am not finished, counselor! I expect that each of the parties of this suit and their clients to be fully prepared to present testimony and not waste this court's time. Do I make myself perfectly clear?"

Clay Summerford rose with great gravity from his chair to address the court. "Your Honor, if it pleases the court, I respectfully withdraw this complaint from consideration."

"Not so fast, counselor. A lot has taken place since our session yesterday and I want to find out what is going on before I consider your motion. Mr. Pardue, would you like to continue cross-examination of Mr. Wilson?

"Your Honor, Mr. Wilson spent the night in the hospital due to injuries he sustained in pursuing evidence for this trial. He is on the way to court now. Until he arrives, I would like to call Special Agent Mark Thompson to the stand."

"Your Honor, I object! Once again my esteemed opponent has

come to court unprepared. He has no right to call a witness and Agent Thompson is not on the list of witnesses for this petition."

"This is a pretrial, counselor. There is no list of witnesses. Besides, a few minutes ago, you offered to graciously withdraw your complaint from consideration. I'm trying to get to the bottom of this, so your objection is denied. Mr. Pardue, you may question the witness."

"I call Special Agent Mark Thompson to the stand."

As Mark made his way to the stand, the judge reminded him, "Agent Thompson, need I remind you that you are under oath to tell the truth even though this is a pretrial hearing? If you prefer, I can have the clerk administer the oath."

"I understand, judge. There is no need to administer the oath."

Mr. Pardue approached the stand, "Agent Thompson please give us your full name and occupation."

"I am Special Agent Mark Thompson, and I am chief of the Pensacola, Florida FBI field office."

"Agent Thompson, what brings you to Walton County?"

"Agent Lindall of our field office was sent to investigate a possible case of environmental terrorism at the WaterColor project."

"Can you describe that incident for us?"

"Yes, it was a suspicious fire at a home under construction at the project."

"Was this the only incident that required the attention of the FBI?"

"No, shortly after Agent Lindall was dispatched to investigate the fire, she was fired upon while conducting her investigation. Subsequently, Sheriff Pritchard asked for our assistance in the murder of George Mott."

"Agent Thompson, are all of these events interrelated?"

"I object, Your Honor. That question calls for an opinion of the witness."

"Sustained."

A hush fell over the courtroom as Quinn and Agent Lindall entered from the rear. Quinn had a gauze bandage on the side of his head covering his right ear and temple. Those attending made room for them in back of the defense attorney's table. After acknowledging their presence, Counselor Pardue continued.

"I withdraw the question. Agent Thompson, can you tell me what transpired yesterday while the court was in recess?"

"Yes, Agent Lindall and I returned from Detroit with Virginia Stratford in custody for assault on a federal officer. She confessed to firing shots at Agent Lindall the morning of April 4th. Upon seeing Ms. Stratford in custody, Officer Pinkham began acting erratically and sought to flee in a Fish and Wildlife Service vessel. Ms. Stratford had raised questions of Officer Pinkham's actions and he was wanted for questioning, so Agent Lindall and I gave pursuit with the assistance of Officer Jan Adler and Quinn Wilson."

"Please continue."

"Officer Pinkham beached his boat in Crooked Creek and hid in the woods during our search. While Agent Lindall and I were searching for him, he returned to the boat and held Mr. Wilson at gunpoint. At that time, he confessed to the murder of George Mott to cover up his activities on the WaterSound beach mice preserve. Agent Lindall, Officer Adler and me were close enough to hear his confession. He then fired a single round from a point-blank distance at Mr. Wilson. Next he fired two rounds at Agent Lindall and me. While we sought to arrest him, he turned the gun on himself and committed suicide."

"You say he murdered Mr. Mott to cover up his activities on the preserve? What activities was he involved with?"

"He was releasing feral cats into the preserve to prey on the beach mice."

A murmur sweep through the courtroom, as Counselor Summerford objected strongly. The representatives of the environmental organizations left the court room, not wishing to be associated with activities clearly in violation of the Endangered Species Act. It was becoming obvious that a scam against the St. Joe Company was unfolding. The judge gaveled repeatedly and called for order in the court.

"Your Honor, I strongly object! This is the opinion of the witness and there is no proof that Officer Pinkham was involved with these activities. Your Honor, I would also respectfully request again that this complaint be removed from the court's docket."

"Noted, counselor. Now, since this is a pretrial hearing, let me ask the question. What evidence do you have of Officer Pinkham's actions?"

Agent Thompson hesitated for a second before responding. "We have the signed confession of Virginia Stratford that states Officer Pinkham had requested she release cats that he brought to her into the preserve and that she feed cats in a secluded area to avoid detection. Officer Pinkham's confession before he committed suicide also referenced the release of feral cats into the preserve."

"Why would he be doing that?" the judge asked with interest.

"I am told that these feral cats are predators that place stress on the population of beach mice."

"And why would an officer of the U.S. Fish and Wildlife Service, who is to protect endangered species under the provisions of the Endangered Species Act, seek to stress this population of mice?" Counselor Pardue asked, with a glance at the judge to acknowledge his previous question.

Again Agent Thompson hesitated before answering, "Officer Pinkham held a grudge against St. Joe and wanted to see the Habitat Conservation Plan fail. As the population of mice decreased, he placed more regulatory pressure on St. Joe to comply with the provisions of the Plan. The letters Counselor Summerford placed into evidence attest to the regulatory pressures Agent Pinkham was placing on the St. Joe Company."

"Your Honor, I must object again. You are soliciting testimony on a complaint that has been withdrawn from consideration by the plaintiff."

The judge ignored Counselor Summerford's objection and turned back to Agent Thompson. "One more question, did Ms. Stratford or Officer Pinkham implicate anyone else in this conspiracy? Were any one of the complainants or their attorneys involved?"

"No, sir. Our investigation to date indicates no other person was involved."

The judge responded to this last answer with a long look at Counselor Summerford. "This court acknowledges the plaintiff's request. This petition is withdrawn from consideration. Agent Thompson and Sheriff Pritchard, this civil case has reached an unusual ending. I would request that both of your agencies proceed with a criminal investigation into these activities to find and prosecute those individuals involved. Case dismissed!"

Again the murmur spread through the courtroom. Clay Summerford placed his voluminous complaint and files into his briefcase in a huff and stormed out of the courtroom, pushing the reporters aside as he passed, until he could not proceed beyond the wall of television cameras and microphones.

"Mr. Summerford, would you care to make a statement?" they asked.

"I am utterly appalled at the actions of this trusted public servant. Agent Troy Pinkham apparently had a private vendetta against St. Joe and used the good name of the environmental organizations and my services to pursue revenge against that company. He obviously acted alone. None of my clients or me had anything to do with this. We are as much a victim of his action as the St. Joe Company. We simply trusted the information that was provided to us, under a public information request, by a trusted member of the U.S. Fish and Wildlife Service. I fault the Service's administration for not overseeing his actions. If anyone could see his intent, it would be his supervisor or the regional administrator. I also fault this community for allowing the WaterColor project to go forward. You have placed the lives of these endangered species into the hands of a greedy developer. It is intolerable. I think all of you are at fault and my clients and I have been defamed by the Services' lack of attention. It is a disgrace to the Service and this community. I have nothing more to say."

Upon making this statement, Cal Summerford departed for the Panama City Bay County International Airport where his private jet awaited him. Other groups milled around the corridors of the courthouse and slowly drifted away, leaving only AJ and Quinn setting on a bench outside of the courtroom. Sheriff Pritchard was one of the last to leave. He pointed a finger at Quinn in passing, "I would just as soon that you did not ever come back to my county, but if you do, check in with my office and I will make sure my deputies are prepared to work overtime." With that he touched the brim of his hat and trudged wearily towards the door.

"Well, AJ, I guess this is it. I need to be getting home. It has been....interesting to say the least. Now, just to check my status, I am no longer a murder suspect, a person of interest, or a consultant to the FBI—is that correct?"

"Yes, you have been cleared and are free to go...but can I call you if I have any questions while I'm doing the reports and follow-up investigations?"

"Of course, call me anytime."

"Quinn?"

"Yes?"

"I...I, oh, nothing...just thanks for the help and I hope we meet again." They shared a brief embrace and each headed for a separate door.

CHAPTER 47

THE AFTERMATH

Subsequent quarterly trapping reports showed a continuing increase in the number of beach mice within the WaterSound Preserve. Without the pressures from the feral cats, the colony's population continued to rise under the management program instituted by St. Joe. When the population of mice reached one hundred and twenty five individuals, the St. Joe Company biologist relocated 12 mated pairs of mice to the Grayton Beach State Park, where they again repopulated an area that had been devoid of mice for many years.

One peaceful evening while resting in front of a campfire outside of Portland, Oregon, Eugene Siedmann thought he was extremely fortunate when a tall and lanky female walked into his camp and knelt by his fire. She smiled at him as she retrieved her FBI badge and arrested him for assault on a federal law enforcement officer. The subsequent trial sentenced him to 15 years in prison.

Six months after the pretrial, Agent AJ Lindall was terminated from the FBI for her actions on that fateful morning in the WaterSound Preserve while on turtle patrol. The FBI could not condone an agent releasing custody of her weapon. She would cross paths with Quinn again in another role and on a different continent.

No connection between Troy Pinkham and Clay Summerford could ever be proven and Clay remained free to pursue his lucrative law practice within the environmental community. He continued to be loved by the environmental watchdog organizations and his success rate on civil trials remained very high.

Quinn Wilson returned home to find that his wife had left him without even leaving a note. Soon after, he resigned his vice president's position with JSB&P consulting firm and took a job with the National Geo-Spatial Intelligence Agency. He was assigned to the South Pacific.

THE END

CPSIA information can be obtained at www.ICGtesting.com
Printed in the USA
LVOW062340021212

309719LV00003B/115/P

9 781614 931362